CHURCH
OF THE
GOD
PARTICLE

A Novel

DAVID PIPER

ISBN-10: 1479120340
EAN-13: 9781479120345

Library of Congress Control Number: 2012915013
CreateSpace, North Charleston, SC

1

A HALF DOZEN air-conditioning units squatted head-high on a plain of hardened black roof tar. The curved silhouette of a parabolic dish at the center of the building, elegant in comparison, pointed to the sky. The dish was designed to broadcast, but it wasn't Sunday sermons it beamed into space.

An unseasonably cool wind chilled the preacher through his nylon jacket as he looked across the dark, flat roof. On nearby Lamar Boulevard cars queued at the stoplight, bathed in a luminescent mix of the nocturnal urban spectrum. Tempered glass framed their occupants' heads, some lit orange by glowing cigarettes or ghostly white by cell phones.

The preacher's son extended his right hand toward the first car and curled back three fingers, shaping his hand into the form of a pistol. The cars began moving through the intersection, and Drago snapped his thumb downward as each passed by. The reverend watched his son and shook his head. The boy could bring down the whole plan if he didn't control himself.

Masking his concern, Reverend Lucas Ruthlier began stretching a black neoprene cap over his head. A dozen insulated wires attached to electrodes embedded in the cap snaked outward and connected to an electronic bridge. From the bridge, a braided steel cable plugged into the side of a laptop. The preacher paused to look over the edge of the building. A homeless man on the street below pushed a shopping cart toward the shelter of a nearby greenbelt. If the next phase of the experiment failed, they might need just such a person to refine their methods. Best if it were someone who wouldn't be missed.

***

Alex twisted the bare end of a copper wire around the terminal lug of a palm-size radio transmitter. He looked two hundred feet down the ravine at the pile of paint cans stacked neatly on the ground in front of a limestone cliff. He and Charlie had meticulously arranged the cans after filling each of them with a different-colored organic dye. His favorite colors were the primaries: fire-engine red, cadmium yellow, and cobalt blue. They would mix with so much more panache than the earth tones.

A half pound of C-4 explosive was taped to a receiver, a battery, and a detonator nestled among the paint cans.

"You want to be Picasso today?" Alex asked Charlie.

"I prefer Rembrandt."

"Whatever." Alex handed him the transmitter. "But this ain't exactly realism."

Charlie pushed the big round button. With a *whoomph*, paint cans full of dye smashed against the white limestone. Laughing, the men ran to the smoking ground in front of the cliff and beheld their newest creation.

"That's better than shit-throwin' monkeys!" Charlie said.

"Certainly more colorful."

The rock face was a kaleidoscope of hurled paint. But after a few rains the organic dye would wash away, and the limestone would be ready for another artistic assault.

"That was one fine explosion," Charlie said. "How much C-4 does that leave?"

"There's a couple of more pounds in the shed."

"We need to use it up. I still can't believe Jasper brought that stuff home with him when he mustered out of the Guard."

"Yeah, I know. And legal problems won't be my only worry if I get caught. Trina will explode worse than the C-4 if she finds out I have it." Alex looked at his watch. "It's getting late. We'd better get going."

They walked to Charlie's pickup, parked next to a stand of cedar trees. Charlie drove them out through the pasture, its rich brown winter grass anchored by live oaks. At the county road he turned toward Alex's ranch. After a minute on the blacktop Alex saw the fence line that separated his land from Charlie's. His cousin steered off the pavement and turned onto a narrow service road that wound its way to the top of the south ridge.

Charlie shut off the truck and they got out. Below, the

canyon opened before them, and Alex gazed at his and Trina's ranch house at the bottom. A few hundred feet away from it lay the creek bed, with its perpetually gurgling spring. From the house, the driveway followed the creek out to the county road nearly a mile away. In the other direction was Charlie's house and his shop. Alex pulled his eyes away from the serene view and focused on the stainless-steel cable that stretched across the canyon in front of him.

He and Charlie had suspended the zip line to have a speedy route from the top of the south ridge to the canyon floor. Otherwise, the foot trail down the craggy side, with all its switchbacks, was a twenty-minute trek. They could drive down the back side of the ridge the way they had come, but that was a fifteen-minute pickup ride out to the county road, and then back along the gravel driveway into the ranch.

It was no secret, though, that the cousins also relished the heart-stopping entertainment.

Behind the north ridge were a dozen new homes on land Alex had once owned. When the county had installed a main water line along the paved road, families that had been living in the area for generations, including Alex's, had been forced to sell land to pay the higher taxes on its appreciated value. Alex had negotiated a deal with a developer, who promptly slapped up the new houses on five-acre plots behind the ridge. At least he couldn't see them.

Charlie kicked a stone over the cliff's edge. "What's Trina got to say about selling more land? I know money's tight, but that's a pretty radical solution."

"She's against it, so that's a showstopper," Alex said. "I just need to sell more paintings instead. Or sell them for more money." He ran his hand through his sandy, wind-blown hair. "I wouldn't try to make any land sale without Trina's okay," he said. "Otherwise, I'd be sleeping with Mangy."

Charlie laughed. "Even in a mood, Trina wouldn't make you sleep with that pathetic coyote."

Alex stepped into the shade of a massive live oak tree whose thick, stubby trunk was twisted a half turn from five hundred years of Texas wind. Its dark gray bark spiraled upward to muscular limbs supporting a dense canopy. It guarded the canyon that divided the Twisted Tree Ranch, and it was the defining landmark for miles around.

"Help me get this harness rigged up," Alex said. "I'm ready to fly."

Charlie handed Alex a climbing harness with nylon straps sewn to steel buckles. Alex stepped into it and cinched the apparatus around his waist and thighs. He stepped closer to the base of the big, twisted oak and looked out along the descending length of cable stretched across the canyon.

Charlie rubbed his chin and looked toward the horizon with a vacant look in his eyes, as if he couldn't focus.

"Are you okay?" Alex asked.

Charlie rubbed his chin again. "I'm okay. But I just had a weird vision—a cedar tree on fire."

Alex gave Charlie a hard look. He'd learned to pay attention to the strange visions that popped into his cousin's head. They had started when he and Charlie were children, and came infrequently, but some of them were prescient. Aside from Alex, Charlie was reluctant to share them. Too many people had ridiculed him with the accusation that he had an overactive imagination.

Alex pulled on cowhide gauntlet gloves. Charlie stepped onto an exposed tree root to raise himself, and he grasped the line above his head. He hung on it like a side of beef with a Stetson and a mustache, trying to pull the line lower so Alex could reach it. Charlie's two hundred pounds lowered the taut cable just a couple of inches, but it was enough for Alex to reach the roller assembly and snap the lanyard onto it.

Attached at the waist of his harness, Alex half hung from the line and half stood, trying to balance himself. He faced the edge of the limestone cliff. Satisfied that he hadn't forgotten anything, he focused on the impending thousand-foot ride across the canyon. The end of the trip was the scariest. The cable was tied around another oak tree near the bottom of the far ridge. A few yards before it, a bungee-cord braking system would save Alex from a disastrous impact with the tree.

High above the creek in front of him, three black vultures soared in lazy circles, looking for a meal. *What are they waiting for? Why don't they just land and eat, or else move on?* He was agitated, but didn't know why.

Alex knew without asking that Charlie had also scrutinized the harness attachments. Charlie was the most reliable person Alex had ever known. Whether it was a routine chore at the ranch or a calamitous personal crisis, Charlie was there.

"What are you and Trina doing for your anniversary?" Charlie asked as Alex prepared to launch.

"Oh, crap! I completely forgot." Alex's shoulders drooped. "Now I'm in deep shit. I forgot last year, too. Trina will be steaming. Man, as much as I'd like to, I can't seem to get it together when it comes to her."

"Well, at least you won't have completely forgotten. You've still got a little time to plan something. Maybe you could cook dinner and then watch for another meteor shower tonight."

"Yeah, maybe. Things have been rough with Trina and me lately. Actually, more than lately. We had hoped Seven would pull us together, but I think there's even more friction since she was born."

"Yeah, I can kinda sense it sometimes."

Alex bobbed up and down like a dangling marionette as the tension of the zip line lifted him in the harness. He sighed and said, "I'm outta here. See you later, Charlie." He clasped his gloved hands over the top of the roller assembly, found purchase on a jutting rock with his right foot, and launched himself into the realm of vultures.

The zip line was steep and fast. He hurtled forward, already fifty feet above the rocks that had broken away from the limestone cliff over eons and settled into a craggy slope. The line sang with a tearing buzz, like a tent ripping apart in a Texas hurricane. As Alex picked up speed, the pitch of the line's banshee scream rose.

He looked down at the fast-approaching L-shaped house his parents had built in the sixties to shelter the inhabitants of the Twisted Tree Ranch. The wind whipped his hair across his forehead as he gained speed down the zip line. Irritated that he had forgotten his anniversary, he felt nauseous.

A soaring vulture flapped in panic to escape from the human creature on the screaming contraption invading its tranquil airspace. Alex was close enough to see where its neck feathers stopped, and the gray, wrinkled skin of the bird's head started. Damned ugly bird, he thought. He removed his right hand from the top of the roller housing, reached around his rib cage, and withdrew Sweet Pea—his dearest weapon: a Taurus 9mm semiautomatic pistol camouflaged with olive green handle grips—from its holster. He flipped off the safety and fired repeatedly, but the unharmed bird kept flapping.

The front door of the ranch house exploded open as the last shot echoed away. Trina stepped onto the porch. Alex waved at her, pistol in hand, as he whizzed by high overhead. She didn't wave back.

The downward slope of the zip line flattened as he flew at the anchoring oak tree. Alex braced himself. Twenty feet from the tree the screaming roller assembly slammed into a hard plastic block that slid along the line. A thick bungee cord attached to the block stretched to its limit, decelerating Alex with stomach-turning quickness. He lowered his legs to the ground and dug his heels into the dirt as the stretched bungee then dragged him backward. Spent, the bungee cord relaxed to its normal state, and Alex stood, wobbly, on solid earth.

He waved at Charlie on top of the far ridge on the other side of the canyon. Charlie waved back and then climbed into his pickup truck.

Alex unhooked the lanyard from the roller assembly, loosened the buckles and straps, and stepped out of the harness. He slung it over his shoulder—the Texas equivalent of a cardigan sweater draped around the neck of an Ivy League preppie. As he walked toward their house with his gear, he could see that Trina, her arms crossed, waited on the porch. Her brown hair hung straight to her shoulders on one side, but curled down the other side, as if she had been interrupted using the hair dryer.

"I heard shots," she said as he neared.

"Yeah, I took a few shots at a buzzard as I went by it on the zip."

"Why would you do that?"

"Because they're flying vermin?" He phrased it as a question, because he knew that he didn't have a sensible answer. "And it just kept circling."

"That's what vultures do." Trina pointed skyward. A half dozen vultures, black against the dusk sky, glided with motionless wings, surveying potential roosts for the night. "They're everywhere. They belong here. I know you know that, so why shoot at them? You're on a wildlife refuge— *our* wildlife refuge. What were you thinking? You can't shoot straight on solid ground, let alone that contraption."

She pointed overhead.

Alex sensed anger at more than his gunplay.

"I aimed where I wasn't." Alex knew his reply didn't help his cause even before Trina exploded.

"Sure, you aimed elsewhere—like maybe toward our house, with Seven and me in it?" she shouted. "Or over the ridge, where there is a whole subdivision of houses and people? Are you crazy? You can't control that kind of shooting."

Trina placed the palm of her hand on her forehead and then slid it back over the top of her head. "This is a pointless conversation, Alex. There's no way you can convince me or anyone else that shooting a pistol from a zip line is not unsafe. Please don't do it again."

"You're right. It could be dangerous."

"Could be?"

"Okay, it's dangerous."

"Like pulling teeth," she said wearily.

Alex figured it was better to bluff his way through a bad situation than admit that he forgot their anniversary. "Look, what do you say we go into town and have a nice dinner to celebrate our anniversary?"

Trina's expression hardened further, and she gritted her teeth.

Wrong choice.

"Please don't insult my intelligence by pretending that you didn't forget again, Alex. It's almost six o'clock, for God's sake!" Trina's ears were crimson. "Is it too much to ask that you remember something so important? At least, important to me."

"It's important to me, too, Trina." *I'm an idiot....* "I'm sorry I forgot. You and Seven are the most important parts of my life." Alex shook his head.

"I'm not sure what to say to you, Alex," Trina said as he followed her into the house. "You're considerate when you remember to be, but you don't remember often enough. I know you love life. I just want you to bring some other people along for the ride. Me, especially. Take some responsibility."

Trina's spontaneity was the trait that had drawn Alex to her when they first met. That and her beauty. She was quick to laugh and quick to anger, and she never lied. Her volatility never ceased to attract him.

"Let me try to make it up to you tonight," he said. "I'll grill a couple of steaks and make a salad. We can have a nice dinner and talk."

"I can't. Jennifer called a little while ago. Steve has the kids tonight, and she's really bummed out. Since we didn't have any plans I told her I'd stop by and hang out for awhile." Trina's eyes said the rest: *What do you expect when you don't think about me until the last minute?*

Alex sighed and said, "Will you hang out with me later, when you get back from your sister's?" He tried to put his arm around her, but she pulled away.

"'Hang out'?" she said, frowning. "'Hang out' is what Jennifer and I do. What you and I do is something else. Don't wait up for me."

***

Reverend Ruthlier settled into a reclining lawn chair and clasped his hands over his stomach. Drago lit a nearby propane heater and settled into the other recliner, facing the opposite direction. Together they could view the entire night sky, as they had for weeks, impatient for results. The city's light pollution was insignificant; they were looking for something bright. Across a background of stars, the dot of a communications satellite crept eastward.

Drago pointed it out and said, "What if we snag it?"

"Impossible. Too much mass."

"You look like Medusa with all those wires coming out of your head."

"What I look like doesn't matter." Drago blinked at the snub. "It's time for the dish," said his father.

The reverend rubbed a small plastic figurine with his thumb and then stuffed it back into his pocket. Drago typed a command into the laptop, and the parabolic dish whirred into motion. When it stopped it was pointing directly overhead.

"Energize it."

"Yes, Father." Drago tapped the enter key on his laptop. The shopping center's parking lot lights dimmed, then recovered as Austin Energy's utility grid compensated for the surge of current. The reverend quieted his mind and concentrated, staring into the edge of the Milky Way. A shooting star streaked toward the horizon, and both men jerked upright in their loungers. Another meteor flashed a trail, brighter than the first.

"This feels promising!" said the elder Ruthlier. "Look for a lavender tail."

Drago began to drum his fingers on the arm of his recliner, catching his father's excitement. They stared upward, eyes straining into obscurity. Reverend Ruthlier relaxed again and focused his thoughts.

The night sky flared with the incendiary brightness of a dozen full moons. Streetlights shut off as pinkish purple light flooded the cityscape. Out of the sky glow emerged a fireball, its lavender tail sizzling from the stratosphere. Descending in the west, it punctured a few sparse clouds and blazed out of sight below the horizon.

The preacher bolted out of the recliner, ripped off the neoprene cap, and rushed to the roof hatch. Drago followed his father to the steel-caged ladder that led down into the guts of the immense building.

"You first," Ruthlier commanded, and Drago scrambled down. The preacher started after him, then reached back to pull the heavy roof hatch closed as if it were weightless. He continued down, grasping the rungs of the ladder like an excited bear descending through the branches of a tree.

The men ran across an elevated second-story platform inside the cavernous building. The polished concrete expanse of main floor extended below them. The church's congregation would be down there in a few weeks, riveted by the reverend's sermons.

"Don't forget the radio!" Ruthlier shouted. The two men rumbled down a metal stairway from the elevated platform and piled into the reverend's Lexus parked on the concrete. Drago tossed the radio in the backseat and slid behind the wheel. He activated the building's articulating steel door to the outside loading ramp and gunned the car out of the building. As they pulled away, Ruthlier looked with fondness at his new church that was taking shape in the shopping center.

Sheets of plain brown paper taped to giant windows thwarted scrutiny from the curious, and the building appeared as just another real estate relic in transition. But each day as the stores in the shopping center disgorged sated customers, the church's interior was forming. And each night the experiment progressed on the roof.

Drago headed towards the hill country west of Austin. Reverend Ruthlier flipped the switch on the police-band radio. There was nothing but the usual chatter about speeders and other Austinites behaving badly. It was too soon for reports.

"The tools are still in the trunk?" Ruthlier said.

"They are."

"If there's a crowd when we arrive at the fall zone I'll distract them with the word of God."

"And if there are only a few people at the site?"

The reverend opened the glove box and removed a Smith and Wesson .357 revolver. Its dark metal glinted in the dashboard light. "Then we improvise." He released the cylinder and rotated it to make sure it was fully loaded, then snapped it back into place.

Ruthlier turned the pistol over in his right hand and

looked at his little finger. He thought about the silver ring with the lavender crystal that he had worn there for so many years. The crystal was now wired into the circuitry of the electronic bridge that controlled the parabolic dish. Working through the array of sensors in the neoprene cap, it had just delivered the greatest achievement of Ruthlier's life. Men had died for that crystal. Ruthlier suspected that still more would follow. Perhaps even himself and his son. But the deaths were inconsequential compared to the importance of the crystal, he mused. Its technology had finally been proven.

Ruthlier glanced at Drago. He could see the tattoo on his son's throat even in the dim light of the car. It never ceased to irritate him. "I've worked too many years not to come back with that meteorite, Drago. We cannot leave without it—no matter what it takes to recover it. It's essential for the next phase."

"I understand, Father. Stay on Highway 71 west?"

"Yes. As spectacular as that fireball was, people will report it. We will figure out where to go when the news comes across the radio."

2

BRILLIANT LAVENDER LIGHT poured through the windows; jagged shadows twitched on the walls. Alex shot a perplexed look at Charlie, sitting at the other end of the couch.

"Fire?" Alex rolled off the couch and raced to a window.

At the peak of brightness, a shock wave slapped the ranch with a rude bang, cracking a crooked line down the pane in front of him. Then silent darkness returned.

Trina! exploded into Alex's thoughts. His wife had left for Austin in the Toyota an hour earlier.

Charlie's daughter, Samantha, had been playing video games in a bedroom, and she ran out in a teenage panic. "What happened?" she said. Alex's five-month-old daughter wailed from the nursery. Samantha looked at her father with frightened, questioning eyes.

"We don't know what happened, Sam," Charlie said in an even tone, trying to steady the girl. "Maybe a plane crashed nearby. Can you try to calm down Seven while we figure this out?" Samantha nodded and hurried back to the bedroom to tend the baby.

Alex's initial, sickening fear was that a nuclear device had detonated in the city. But the television was still on, he reasoned. He snatched the remote off the coffee table and cycled through the channels.

"All the network stations are still broadcasting," he said to Charlie. He went through the channels once again, but more slowly. None of the stations had interrupted their programs, another sign that the Lone Star capital was intact.

"A plane crash?" Charlie speculated. "If it was, it's close."

Alex imagined burning wreckage, strewn baggage, and mangled corpses. He grabbed a flashlight from the kitchen and looked out the window, and he and Charlie threw on their jackets.

"There's a tree on fire where the driveway splits," Alex said.

"We should call nine-one-one," Charlie said. "If there's been a plane crash they can get help rolling this way."

Alex picked up the phone and, grateful to hear a dial tone, made the call. Charlie waited as Alex and the dispatcher proceeded through the list of standard questions.

Alex swung the mouthpiece upward and said to Charlie, "She says they're getting a lot of reports." Then to the 911 dispatcher he said, "We're going outside to look around.

One of us will call you back. Send a fire truck."

Alex imagined a chaotic 911 center struggling to answer ringing phones, teasing out clues in order to assemble a framework of what had happened. He wondered whether, when he called again, his report would be lost in the pandemonium. As the men hurried toward the front door, the TV basketball game was interrupted by a man in a suit with luxurious hair and gleaming, straight teeth.

"This is Chad Mason at the KWIB Weather Center. We've received dozens of calls about a bright light in the sky west of Austin a few minutes ago. It appears that a meteorite entered the atmosphere and fell west of town. There is no reason to worry. It's not uncommon; hundreds of meteors burn up every day as they enter the Earth's atmosphere. Most are no larger than a grain of sand, although this one was almost certainly bigger than that."

"Almost certainly?" Alex said.

The weatherman touched his earphone and paused. "I'm being told that we may have a video of this meteorite from our twenty-four/seven tower cam that overlooks Lake Travis. We'll show you that video as soon as we can."

"Why is a weatherman telling us this?" asked Alex.

"Strangest weather I've ever seen," said Charlie.

Alex's disposition buoyed upon hearing the nature of the breaking news. Instead of steeling himself for a search of burning plane wreckage, he now anticipated the adventure of searching for an otherworldly object literally in their backyard.

Samantha reemerged from the back bedroom holding

Seven. Charlie explained what had happened. "We're going to check it out. Stay here with the baby."

"Okay, Dad. Be careful, though!"

He and Charlie left the house and walked toward the blazing cedar tree. "How in the hell do you do that?" Alex asked. "That vision you had this afternoon was right on the money. Look at that thing burn."

"I have no idea. Too bad they aren't about the stock market. We'd all be rich." Alex thought about the land he wanted to sell and the cash it would bring.

"How do we find a meteorite? Where do we start?" Charlie asked.

"The meteorite that wiped out the dinosaurs sixty million years ago was as big as a city, they say. I guess we're looking for something smaller than that."

"Yep, I reckon so," said Charlie in the light of the burning tree. "There must be something of it left."

There were broken branches lying on the ground, but nothing indicated the meteor's direction of travel. The tree was at the base of the north slope as it rose above the creek.

"That slope is undisturbed, so it couldn't have come out of the south. The house is west of the tree, and we weren't incinerated, so it couldn't have come from the east," Charlie said.

The gravel driveway ran past a natural spring and onto Charlie's property to the west. Alex walked with Charlie down the driveway toward the county road, shining the flashlight from side to side.

The backlight from the burning tree cast Charlie's shadow a foot farther than Alex's. Charlie was three inches taller and thirty pounds heavier than his cousin, and his shadow was magnified by his wide-brimmed cowboy hat. He strode with an easy gait, seemingly without purpose, but Alex had to hustle to keep up. Charlie only appeared slow; Alex had seen him dodge a rattlesnake strike the summer before.

Charlie had once been an extra in a Western that was filmed a few miles from the ranch. He didn't have a speaking part; his role was to authenticate a street scene by ambling across it in the background. They had to shoot the scene four times because Charlie was more noticeable than the lead actor, and the director had to keep moving him farther away from the camera.

A cold front was moving through the hill country, and the night was predicted to turn frosty. Alex had forgotten his gloves in his haste to investigate the fire. He kept one hand inside his denim jacket pocket and alternated the flashlight so he could warm the other, pulling his wool stocking cap over his ears.

Two hundred yards from the burning cedar tree, a long gouge down the center of the driveway revealed the meteorite's path.

"Whoa! Look how it plowed this driveway!" Alex said. He sighted down the foot-wide gouge, and it lined up with the burning tree and the dark pool of springwater directly behind it. "It looks like it came out of the east, ricocheted off the gravel drive, and then nailed the tree."

"It just might be cooling its jets in the spring," Charlie said. The cousins retraced their steps past the cedar tree, which by now had fizzled down to sputtering and smoking branches.

The most precious feature of the Twisted Tree Ranch was the natural spring, which gurgled clear water from the base of a low limestone shelf. The water emerged pure and cool, filtered through miles of porous limestone upstream. It flowed into a pool eroded in the rock below it, and from there it overflowed down into the creek. The creek wound its way through the pristine woods of the ranch, its waters converging with other creeks and rivers until it flowed into the Gulf of Mexico, two hundred miles downstream.

The cousins approached the flagstone apron Alex's grandfather had laid around the clear pool decades earlier. Before setting the last stone, he had buried a galvanized steel pipe underground from the low end of the pool and brought it up fifty feet downstream into a brass spigot with a red handle. Whenever a Colvin wanted a cool drink of fresh springwater, the red-handled spigot beckoned.

Charlie kicked a stone and said, "Let's see what's in that spring."

The men stepped onto the wet rocks at the edge of the pool, and Alex shone his flashlight into the water. They stared down at a dark-colored, stony object the size of a large brick. They whooped with excitement.

"Check *that* out!" Alex yelled.

The beam from the moving flashlight shone through

21

the swirling water, animating smooth and shiny metallic edges. Between the edges, dark cavities swallowed the light in a final stand at obscurity after eons in deep space. "Now what? What do we do with it?" Charlie asked.

"It doesn't look hot," Alex observed.

"It can't be hot. It's like plunging a red-hot horseshoe into a barrel of water. It cools immediately," Charlie said. "I wonder if it's safe to touch. Maybe we shouldn't even be standing close to it." They both took a step back. "Let's look around where it first hit."

They walked through the cool night air, past the smoldering cedar tree and the gouge in the driveway, shining the flashlight ahead of them along the meteor's path.

"There's going to be a lot of interest in this, Alex. It's not every day that a meteorite lights up a major city and is recovered."

"We should charge admission." Both men laughed.

"I suppose it's gotta be worth something," Charlie said.

They reached the section of the gravel drive where Alex and Charlie's great-grandfather had hired a road crew to dynamite an elevated roadway from the side of the limestone hill above the creek. The old driveway had followed the edge of the creek, and then crossed it several times in order to avoid massive boulders that had tumbled from the hillside. Any heavy rain would wash out the gravel, deteriorating the drive into a sloppy, rutted mess. The new section of driveway had changed the ranch. Supplies could enter and products could get out according to a dependable schedule. An exposed coffee-colored vein of chert in the soft limestone, fractured and eroded from eons of water and weather, shone in Alex's flashlight beam.

"Shit, look at the size of that impact crater!" Alex exclaimed. "There's no way a vehicle is going to get through here. That hole's as big as my pickup!" The shoulder of the driveway was gone, its rubble piled in the creek bed twenty feet below.

"I'd say the meteorite struck here first, causing that nasty shock wave we felt in the house," Charlie said. "Then it must have gone airborne, maybe guided by the side of the hill, until it came down where the gouge is. It took a big skip, fried that cedar tree, and finally splashed down into the spring. Like a hole in one for God."

"Oh, man." Alex surveyed the damage to the driveway. "This is going to cost me."

"Going to cost *us*."

"The fire truck is going to have to stop here. I guess they'll have to hoof it the rest of the way to the tree." Alex shone the light once more at the crater in the driveway. "I need to let Trina know what's going on. She'll have to leave the car out there and walk to the house when she drives back tomorrow."

He punched in her cell number, heard one ring in his ear, and then heard a phone ringing nearby. Confused, he looked at Charlie, both trying to pinpoint the source of the ring. Then Alex felt the blood drain from his face as he recognized the ring tone of Trina's phone emanating from the creek below them.

He shone the light downward over the destroyed edge

of the driveway. Rocks and fresh dirt filled the creek bed—and jutting out from under the rubble was the front end of Trina's silver Toyota.

"Oh, God, no. No!" Alex screamed. He and Charlie scrambled down to the wreckage.

Alex pounded on the exposed hood as he rounded the front end of the buried car.

"Trina! Trina! Hang on, Trina! We're here! We'll get you out of there!"

With their bare hands they attacked the dirt covering the driver's side of the car. From the direction of the county road at their backs, the flashing lights of the fire truck and a string of other vehicle headlights approached.

"Trina!" Alex yelled over and over, panicking more with every silence afterward.

The fire truck's air brakes snorted on the driveway above the buried Toyota, a line of police and sheriff's vehicles skidding to a stop behind it. More vehicles, including television broadcasting trucks, followed; the meteorite must have been a big draw on the police radio band. Charlie jumped up and down, waving, and yelled at the firefighters as they rolled out of the truck.

Alex screamed at them as he continued frantically scraping dirt off the car, "My wife's inside; I think my wife's inside!"

Firefighters in black suits with white reflective armbands slid down the embankment in their helmets, carrying shovels and axes, while one remained above, talking into his shoulder-mounted radio.

One of the firefighters—a woman—touched Alex's arm as he shoveled away dirt as fast as he could move. He shook her off, but she grasped his arm again and said firmly, "Sir—let us handle this. We'll get her out." Alex looked at her, almost unable to process her words, but she finally hooked his elbow and pulled him away from the car while her partners exposed the driver's side of the Toyota.

The car had rolled and come to rest upright, but the windshield was shattered inward, and the driver's window was shattered outward. A firefighter flung the remaining glass out of the driver's window with a gloved hand. He jammed his flashlight through the window, and then his head.

He jerked back, and Alex staggered a step toward the car.

The firefighter held up a hand. "Don't."

The woman firefighter put her arm around Alex's shoulder, and he let her and Charlie guide him to a small boulder and sit him down. She sat next to him.

"It's my fault," Alex said, shoulders slumped forward, tears falling into his lap. "Oh, Jesus, what have I done?"

"It's not your fault, Alex," Charlie said. "It's not anyone's fault."

"I pushed her away," Alex moaned. "She should have been here at the ranch with me tonight. She must have decided to come home early." He stood and clutched at his stomach.

"Alex," Charlie said, "let's go back to the house." He put his arm around his cousin's shoulders.

The words failed to register with Alex. The realization of Trina's death slammed into him as if it were the meteorite itself. Alex's knees buckled, and the woman firefighter caught him. He tried to get to the car again. If he could only see her ... maybe she would come back. She had to—for Seven.

The woman—her nametag read "Flores"—gently pulled Alex back to the rock. "My partners will take good care of Trina," she said. "It's best to give them space so they can do that. C'mon, I'll go with you to the house."

"No. I want to stay here. I'm not going inside to sit on my ass."

"Then stay by me," the firefighter said. "We can talk. Tell me about Trina."

Lost in shock, Alex had nothing to say.

"What's your first name, Ms. Flores?" Charlie asked.

"Flora."

Flora Flores. *"Flower flowers"* in Spanish, Alex thought inanely. Memories of Trina began to pinwheel in his mind. Images of her whirled faster and faster until they blurred into an apparition of a woman whose intricacies were impossible to capture. The spinning inside his head merged into his vision and the ground beneath him began to slide.

"Hang on, Alex," Charlie said. He put his hand on Alex's shoulder, Flora steadied him from the other side.

"Let's get you back to the house, she said."

"No! I don't want to go back!" he snapped. He looked at the crowd that had invaded his property *Who in the hell are all these people? They shouldn't be here.* Trina's words from that afternoon rang in his head. *Take responsibility for something.*

A surge of resentment passed through Alex at the ever-larger crowd of gawkers. "Who's in charge here?" he asked Flora. "Besides me."

"The police," said Flora.

"They need to get rid of these people. Who's calling the shots?"

The assault of headlights from the snaking line of arriving vehicles glared at Alex as he, Charlie, and Flora walked away from the smashed car. Clouds of dust illuminated by headlights hung in the air like a dirty fog. An ambulance had been able to negotiate the creek bed up to the wreck, and paramedics were extricating Trina from the Toyota.

Peering through the dust into the harsh lights, Alex could make out dozens of silhouetted figures moving around or standing. Some wore uniforms, but most appeared to be with the news media or just sightseers. Two large TV vans, one with KWIB emblazoned across its side, had extended their antennas upward, as if hailing the meteorite's arrival.

Alex felt his adrenaline surge along with his anger; he welcomed the change of focus.

He strode over to a tall young man wearing a law enforcement uniform and a crisp, tanned leather cowboy hat and asked him, "Who's in charge here?"

"That would be Captain Steiner, sir." The tall policeman pointed at a stocky, similarly dressed man a hundred feet away.

Before the policeman could ask him any questions Alex began walking toward the other officer. The stocky man in charge watched as the trio approached. Alex made sure the wary policeman could see that the only thing in his hands was a flashlight, even if he did want to crack someone's head with it.

When he was close to the stocky policeman Alex said, "I live here. The woman killed in the car is—was—my wife. I live in that house." He shone his light toward the ranch house.

"Are you Alex Colvin?" Captain Steiner asked. Alex nodded. "I'm sorry for your family's loss, Mr. Colvin." Then to Flora Flores he said, "Hello, Flora. Ms. Flores and I have worked together before."

They know death, Alex thought. "Who are all these people?" he asked with a sweeping hand. The crowd pushed up to the yellow plastic Do Not Cross tape that had been strung from any available rock, bush, or tree.

Captain Steiner said, "Aside from law enforcement and EMS, they're mostly members of the press, lawyers, and onlookers. Unfortunately, a lot of folks made it in before we had a chance to restrict access, but I've posted an officer at the end of your driveway where it meets the county road. No one else is getting in here unless they have a damned good reason."

"Good." His simple reply reassured Alex that he was still lucid and had a modicum of responsibility to exercise in this horrific tragedy. Trina would want that.

Were you two the first people on the accident scene?"

asked the trooper.

Alex clenched his jaw. "Yes," he said in a hiss.

Steiner withdrew a small pad of paper from his breast pocket. He scribbled notes as Alex and Charlie forced out the story of the previous hour. As they talked, Alex watched the ambulance with Trina's body retrace its route along the bank of the creek and then down the gravel drive once it cleared the jam of cars. He couldn't shake the image of Trina's car reappearing on the driveway with his wife at the wheel— until an odd motion in his peripheral vision caught his eye.

"Who is that guy?" Alex pointed to a wiry man walking slowly on the opposite side of the creek. He carried a box in the crook of his right arm with a steel tube projecting from the bottom of the box attached to a disk for sweeping the ground and moved it from side to side. Even though the light was dim, Alex could see the man staring at a glowing meter on the box. He was dressed in tight black work pants and wore a dark jacket over a white T-shirt. The man stopped and calibrated the meter with a small screwdriver.

"He's searching for the meteorite!" Alex exclaimed in disbelief. "Is he one of yours?" he asked Captain Steiner.

"Not in that outfit," Steiner said. "Nor is he anyone else's that I know of."

Alex thought of the tow truck hauling his wife's destroyed car to town. *Why couldn't this jerk have been in it instead?* He walked toward the man, picking up his pace. Charlie, Steiner, and Flores hustled to catch up.

"Hey, asshole, what are you doing?" Alex yelled.

The man continued to search. When Alex got close, the man shifted his grip on the metal detector so he could swing it head high.

"Who is asking, asshole?"

Steiner stepped between the men before Alex could throw a punch.

"What's your business here?" the Ranger asked the wiry man.

"I am just looking for souvenirs. This is a famous place now." His English was formal and perfect, but he had a slight accent. Alex guessed it was Eastern European.

A tattoo of a curved dagger, its blade appearing to slice into the flesh under his larynx, wrapped around the man's throat. The handle extended to beneath his right ear. Red ink drops of blood completed the riveting skinscape.

"You will have to leave, sir," Steiner said.

"What about all of them?" the man asked with a sweep of his free arm to encompass the crowd behind the tape. "I wish to be afforded the same privileges as they have to be here."

"They have no privileges and will be leaving also. This is private property, and you are trespassing. Go home. If you don't, I'll arrest you. Do you understand?"

"Oh, yes, I understand your system very well," the man said. He stared at Alex for a long second and then turned and walked away into the darkness behind the plastic tape. He was light on his feet as he glided over obscured rocks in the grass as easily as a night creature. As he passed a live oak he jammed the screwdriver in the trunk and then yanked it sideways, leaving it stuck in the tree, bent. He looked back at Alex with a sneer.

"Man, that guy is creepy," Charlie said. The others nodded. "We should probably go get that meteorite. Alex, there's no reason you have to be involved with this."

"No, I'll go. I want to see this through." The thought of quietly sitting somewhere fighting off waves of grief terrified him. "But after we get that goddamned rock, I want it taken away from here," he said in a quavering voice.

"Flora," Charlie asked the firefighter, "what does your crew have to handle toxic material?"

Dependable Charlie, Alex thought. *Always there for me.*

"We had to check out an unidentified chemical spill a couple of days ago and the hazmat equipment is still on the truck," Flora said. I'll round up everything we need and meet you back here."

Captain Steiner said, "One of my men said there was a professor here from UT who wants to be involved in the recovery of the meteor." He pointed at the crowd of people segregated by the plastic barrier.

As Steiner, Alex, and Charlie approached the crowd, one voice carried above the general din. A man in a dark greatcoat stood atop a boulder, leaning toward the throng below like a sailing ship's figurehead plying a sea of people.

"It is written in Earth's great religions," he railed between deep breaths, "that there will be a transformation of thought—a transformation of thought that changes how mankind sees the universe and himself in it!"

31

"This guy looks wacky," Charlie said. "Check out that hair." The broad-shouldered man's silver locks swept backward and shone in the moonlight.

"Are you ready for the coming change?" the man on the rock bellowed. "Almost a century ago the prophet Einstein revealed the skin of the cosmic onion. Our scientists have peeled back layers, penetrating deeper and deeper into the quantum universe. But what about you, my fellow universal beings? How many layers have you peeled away of your own cosmic onion? How many layers remain before you will transition to the next phase, the phase into which the fated owner of that automobile has just passed?" The preacher extended both hands toward the accident site, as if to embrace the convergence of the meteorite with the occupant of the towed-away automobile.

Anger shot through Alex. He turned to Captain Steiner and said, "That nut job with his fucking cosmic onion is the next guy I want out of here. And the sooner, the better."

Steiner nodded and said something to one of his men. The other officer made his way through the attentive throng toward the preacher.

"I am the Reverend Lucas Ruthlier of the Church of the God Particle. I am here to tell you the Elemental One is coming! The Lavender Fireball brings the Word! Are you prepared for the Elemental One? Is your mind open? He will be revealed soon! Gravity brought down this holy omen, but gravity is not what it seems. Gravity can be manipulated. The key is the God particle!"

The trooper reached the preacher and ordered him off

the boulder, gesturing toward Alex. The reverend huffed away with a look of indignation and then a hot glance at Alex. Ruthlier walked to a Lexus sedan and got in on the passenger's side. A few seconds later, the wiry man with the metal detector appeared from behind a tree and got in on the driver's side. The preacher appeared to be shouting at the other man as they drove out.

Alex and Charlie watched as Steiner addressed the crowd. "Is there a Professor Sorensen here?" he shouted. Television camera lights illuminated, and reporters yelled questions.

A high-pitched but strong voice projected from the crowd: "That's me!"

Belying the voice, a small, sixtyish woman in a red windbreaker emerged and then ducked under the plastic tape. Her blue jeans were faded and worn, and her leather hiking boots were speckled with patches of dried mud. The sides of her graying hair fell just over her collar, and a short ponytail protruded out of the back of her UT baseball cap. A compact camera hung from a strap around her neck.

As the professor emerged, she stopped short in front of a reporter.

"Don't throw your cigarette butt on the ground, sir! It takes five years for one of those things to decompose. You are a guest here. Act like one." The flustered reporter picked up the butt, but then didn't know what to do with it.

"Ma'am, come with me, please," Steiner said. He led her to where Alex and Charlie waited and then introduced them. "These gentlemen are the landowners. They think they know where the meteor is."

Overhearing Steiner, the gaggle of reporters yelled questions once again toward anyone who might answer: "Have you located the meteorite?" "What will be done with the meteor?" "Mr. Colvin, can you tell us how you feel about this tragic accident?"

The reporters reminded Alex of that afternoon's circling vultures, and they disgusted him as much. Like the birds, he had the perfect answer for them, but Sweet Pea was in its holster at the ranch house. To Captain Steiner he said, "Get those sick bastards out of here, too."

"Not a problem." Steiner moved toward the reporters. As he passed Sorensen he said to her, "One of the fire crew is waiting down the way for us with hazmat gear in case we need it to handle the meteor."

"Meteorite," she said. "It's a meteorite if it actually impacts the Earth."

"Yes, ma'am."

A sheriff's deputy worked to unravel the traffic jam on the driveway, directing cars that had arrived before the roadblock was in place. He turned them around and sent them back toward the county road. As he dispersed the reporters and the sightseers, Alex's mind drifted to the meteorite lying in the spring. Such a little rock could wreak such personal havoc. What were the odds? The true definition of astronomical.

"What are you doing?" an angry voice rang out from the area where the reporters had been assembled. "Let these people have some privacy," ordered a woman who was pulling the cover over a collapsible camping chair. A man in a dark sweatshirt with a camera slung around his neck stepped out from behind a tree.

"I thought I saw something back there," the man said.

"Don't bullshit me," said the woman. Her dark hair swirled up and away from her head like a tiny Texas tornado. "You were hiding. Waiting for some grief pics."

Alex started toward the photographer, and the man began walking in the other direction toward his evicted brethren. Alex changed course and approached the woman. She was wearing a black shirt and vest with the word "PRESS" displayed across the front. An LED array attached to an elastic headband shone in whatever direction she turned her head. A pad of paper protruded from a vest pocket.

"Thanks for calling that guy out," Alex said.

The woman flicked off her headlamp so it wouldn't shine into Alex's eyes. "Not a problem, Mr. Colvin," she said. "I'm Quizzy Shatterling with the *Austin Chronicle*." She extended her hand.

As Alex shook hands. The Chronicle was a weekly Austin publication. He occasionally picked one up at the Sac and Pac on Highway 71. "I've read a few of your stories."

Captain Steiner approached. "Ma'am, you need to move along, too."

"Of course, Officer." Quizzy Shatterling was tall and thin, able to look Steiner in the eye through the small circular lenses of her wire-rimmed glasses. She pulled off her headlamp and dropped it into a canvas backpack on the ground. She inserted one arm through the strap on the backpack, but when she picked up the camping chair the backpack slid down her right arm to the crook of her elbow, causing her to drop the chair.

Alex watched her struggle with the equipment. She raised her arms above her head to insert them through the backpack's straps, pulling back the sleeves of her shirt. Tattoos covered her right arm, but the left was unmarked.

Captain Steiner waited while the woman rearranged her load so she could carry it.

She may not be coordinated, but at least she's prepared, Alex thought. He welcomed the distraction of her efforts, and he remembered how she had run off the other reporter. *She's odd—and she might actually have some principles.*

He turned to Quizzy. "Come on. But don't burn me with a bad story."

"I'll write an accurate story." Then she added, "With sensitivity."

"She can stay, Captain," Alex said to Steiner.

"Your call," Steiner said.

Led by Alex and Charlie, the group walked up the gravel driveway.

"There's a spring behind that smoking tree, or at least what's left of that tree," Charlie explained. "There's a strange rock in the water, kinda burnt-up-lookin'. We figured it must be the meteorite."

"How big is it?" asked Quizzy.

"It's about as big as a brick," Charlie said. He formed the approximate size with his hands.

They continued down the driveway, where Flora Flores was waiting with another firefighter and an assortment of hazmat gear. Laid out on the ground were a one-piece white bodysuit, a hood, gloves, boots, face mask, and an oxygen tank. A Geiger counter sat next to a metal container the size of one of Charlie's beer coolers. The container had airtight seals, heavy-duty hinges, and an oversize latch that could be secured with a padlock. Sorensen assessed the equipment, and the group proceeded toward the spring, each carrying something.

"The odds of any extraterrestrial biological substances on a meteorite are infinitesimal," Professor Sorensen said. "But since we have the hazmat suit and container, we'll go ahead and use them."

"If you put the meteorite in a sealed container to prevent its contamination, how do you go about examining it?" Quizzy asked.

Sorensen replied, "We'll do a series of tests and analyses on small samples in a 'clean room' at UT, and the rest of the pristine meteorite will be quarantined. But I'm more interested in its trajectory as it fell. It curved away from the vertical. That is impossible without an aerodynamic or other outside influence. It's like it was being pulled by something. I saw the replay on the weather report. It was very strange."

"You think?" Alex said.

"I'm sorry, Alex. I know this is distasteful. But since it

came down on your property, you are the legal owner of the meteorite. Barring unforeseen biological, chemical, or radiological hazards, it'll be returned to you."

"Keep it. I don't want the damned thing," Alex said.

"There are dozens of tests I'd like to run, and the whole process will take months. But you should know that this meteorite could be worth quite a bit of money."

Alex said nothing, and Charlie asked the question: "How much is 'quite a bit'?"

"It's hard to say. It's not unheard-of for a sizable meteorite whose fall is widely viewed to fetch thousands of dollars."

Maybe it will pay for Trina's funeral, Alex thought as he ground his heel into the dirt.

Despite the cool night air, Flora appeared to be wilting—although not to the extent of the smoldering tree. *She looks like she's going to puke,* Alex thought. As they walked past the tree, Charlie took the Geiger counter from her.

The troop reached the spring and stood on the flagstones encircling the pool of clear water. They turned their flashlights on the submerged object in it. No one spoke; the interloper beneath the water commanded reverence as it shimmered in the lights like a thing alive.

"Oh, my," the professor finally said in a soft voice. "That *is* unusual. It's a rare beauty. Extraordinary. It isn't your typical meteorite."

Alex clenched his jaw.

While the professor talked, Flora Flores wriggled her compact frame into the hazmat suit, assisted by the other firefighter. Sorensen continued, animated like a birthday girl with a long-awaited present.

"Just look at those iridescent blues and greens. If I didn't know better, I would say they are traces of copper. That would be a first."

Flora shuffled to the edge of the pool in the cumbersome hazmat suit, carrying the airtight container, struggling to keep her balance. She stepped into the water, opened the container, and laid it on its side in the water next to the meteorite. With a gloved hand she scooped the space rock into the opening.

"Fill up the container with water, too," the professor instructed. "Since it cooled off in the spring isolated from the air, we should replicate its environment as best we can."

Flora closed the container's lid and latched it; then, breathing hard, she struggled to lift it by its handles.

"Let me give you a hand with that," Charlie said as he stepped into the water, oblivious as it covered his leather boots. He grabbed a handle on one end of the container, and he and Flora carried out their dripping prize and deposited it on the flagstones at the pool's edge.

Captain Steiner stepped up to the container and tapped its side with one of his black boots as if he were nudging a sleeping drunk. Flora removed her face mask and respirator, then sat down on a rock to pull off her gloves and rubber boots. She stood up, and with the help of her coworker climbed out of the suit. She walked in front of Quizzy, and Alex could see the contrast in the women. Flora was six inches shorter and muscled like a fighter, and she was sweat-soaked, as if she'd just spent the whole day in the gym. She sat down on a rock to rest while the night air evaporated perspiration from her clothes and body.

One on each end, Charlie and Captain Steiner hauled the container back toward the bustling, floodlit staging area of the accident site. Most of the onlookers had disappeared into the night, but a few of them still waited at the county road for the last word from Steiner. Quizzy trailed the bearers of the meteorite, once again jotting notes under the glow of her elastic-banded headlamp.

Alex leaned against a live oak and watched as the group dispersed. The weight of the night's events seemed to press him into the tree. He and Charlie would soon gather their children in the ranch house. Five-month-old Seven would know only that her mother was missing. He and Trina had settled on the baby's name because she was the seventh generation in a direct line of Colvins, and they had thought the name might bring her luck. What a cruel joke.

Thoughts of a radically changed future distracted Alex, and he barely noticed Flora gathering hazmat gear into a pile in front of her. She reached for the plastic water bottle in the leg pouch of her pants and swallowed what was left of the contents in a single gulp. Lugging the gear, she started the walk to the fire truck. Her flashlight beam found the galvanized pipe with the red-handled spigot rising from the ground.

Flora unscrewed the cap of her water bottle and turned the red handle. She held the bottle under the gushing stream until it overflowed. Deeply she drank, replenishing her energy like uncountable other creatures had done at the perpetually flowing spring of the Twisted Tree Ranch. Only when she had finished drinking did the source of the water register with Alex.

1961

THE WALK FROM the orphanage began on the cobble-stones of Franklin Avenue and ended three blocks away in the dusty alcove of the Blessed Sacrament Elementary School. The dust accumulated despite Sister Ruth's dutiful sweeping every evening. The ubiquitous stuff powdered furniture and obscured vision across the flat western Kansas landscape.

Dust on a windy day was a part of life on the high plains for all the peoples who had ever lived there. It was impossible to eliminate, so Sister Ruth satisfied herself with a modicum of control. However, when the wind blew thirty miles an hour for days in a row, the dust infiltrated the deepest and most obscure recesses.

Each morning during the dry summer of 1961, thirty-six children filed through the front doors into the school's alcove. No one thought much about the dust. No one, that was, except Fred Zimmerman. When the young student pushed open the doors he lingered and studied the accumulations in the corners. The dust itself wasn't that interesting, but the contrast to the other surfaces he passed on his short walk to school fascinated him.

First Fred had to cross the rounded red cobblestones in the section of Sixth Street that hadn't yet been paved. When he reached the school's playground, he liked to shuffle through the gravel, rolling little pebbles under his shoes. All the other kids walked around the tractor-tire sandbox in the playground, but Fred stepped into it, bent over, and scooped a handful of sand. He marveled at the texture of the grains as they fell through his fingers, their tiny, shiny faces reflecting the sun. His walk ended in the alcove. The individual grains of dust were almost too small to see in a pinch between his fingers. Cobblestones, gravel, sand, then dust. Fred liked the orderly transition from large to small. *It must go further,* he thought.

Every morning when Fred arrived at the Catholic school, Sister Ruth sent him to the boys' room and made him wash his hands. She had learned long ago about Fred's peculiar habit of examining small things. Some of the other kids in the school called him Sandy, but never to his face.

Fred was a year behind his other classmates, but not because he was a poor student. In fact, Sister Ruth thought he was the brightest student she had ever taught in her twenty-seven years at the school. He had been held back a grade three years earlier because a car wreck at Nine Mile Corner had claimed his parents and little sister. The horrific accident jolted him into a state of mind where he

43

couldn't sit through one class, let alone a whole day.

In the truest spirit of service, Father Lucas, who oversaw both the orphanage and the church, devoted himself to the shattered boy's recovery. It took all his personal skills, faith, and considerable prayer in the aftermath of the wreck to console and guide Fred through that disastrous period. During the boy's depressed state, Father Lucas and Sister Ruth watched over him as if he were a disoriented hatchling in the nest. Fred would be silent for days, then spin out of control and fight anyone. Once he climbed onto the roof of the church and sat dangerously close to the edge until Father Lucas coaxed him down the fire department's ladder.

Sister Ruth and Father Lucas rejoiced when Fred's depression gave way to frustration. At least it was a change. They prayed he would be less of a danger to himself. He still fought, but the incidents lessened as he expended his anger. Their consistent message to the boy was that God had plans for him, but they were unknowable at such a young age. They reinforced the idea that Fred's purpose on earth was to do great things someday. The Lord Jesus watched over him and would return to reward the true believers.

After two years of their loving supervision, Fred emerged from his darkness. That year was to be his final in the Blessed Sacrament School. He would enter the public school system as a seventh grader next year.

"What's smaller than dust?" asked Fred one morning after he passed through the alcove.

"Lots of things, Fred," said Sister Ruth. "Go wash your hands and look at the water. Then come tell me what you see."

When Fred returned, he said, "It was just brown water with some soap suds."

"What do you think made the water brown?" asked Sister Ruth.

"The dust from my hands."

"Yes. The dust was dissolved by the water and suspended in it. The water broke down the dust particles into even smaller particles. So that's something that is smaller than dust. Do you know what 'suspended' means?"

"Yes."

"Do you remember the pieces of leaves we looked at under the microscope last year?"

"Yes. They were made up of cells."

"Very good. Cells are smaller than dust particles, too. And also all of those tiny living creatures in your saliva you looked at."

Fred nodded and said, "What's the smallest thing in the world?"

"An atom is the smallest thing there is. But it has several different parts in it. So those are the smallest things, I suppose."

"Do the parts of an atom have parts?"

"I don't know," said Sister Ruth. "I don't think so. Now go take your seat. It's time for math class."

Fred hurried with anticipation to his desk.

***

Fred attended church every Sunday. After all, he was living in a Catholic orphanage, and his surrogate parents were a priest and a nun. Everyone he knew, no matter their religion, believed in predictions about the imminent return and unearthly power of a savior. These extraordinary powers contained in the frail body of a man fascinated him. Fred also dwelled on the prophets who foretold miraculous and monumental events and sometimes even precipitated them. How could they have known? he wondered. How could seas part, stone walls collapse from the sound of trumpets, and great pyramids rise without machinery? He contemplated how the laws of nature could be defied.

The walk to Colby Junior High School was seven blocks farther than the one to the Catholic elementary school. Nevertheless, Fred enjoyed it, unless the sidewalks were frozen in sheets of ice. The new route passed more attractions and oddities. On the way to school each day, Fred walked past the home of the Olsen family. The Olsens had been the beneficiaries of a holy miracle three years earlier. At least, that was what the *Colby Free Press* had called it.

The Olsens' German shepherd–collie mix, Barney, had saved baby Jackie's life. On that day, the wind had ceased— a miracle in itself. The unusual spring day of calmness and warm sunshine drew the family into the backyard, where they set up Jackie's playpen. Mrs. Olsen tossed a rubber ball in, and Jackie attempted to throw it out, while Mr. Olsen barbecued hot dogs.

The entertainment peaked when Barney chomped down on the corner of the playpen and began dragging it across the lawn. He strained and growled, pushing himself backward and uprooting grass. Baby Jackie especially enjoyed the ride, and her parents, weary of the ball-toss, watched with amusement. As Barney lay resting after his herculean pull, a large limb snapped off a Chinese elm and thudded into the ground where the playpen had been moments before.

Mr. Olsen switched the lifesaving dog to canned food after the miracle, but Barney was old, and he died the year Fred started walking to the public school. On this particular day Fred stopped to admire Barney's grave, paying special attention to the little yellow plastic dog on a stick that marked the animal's resting place in the corner of the yard.

Even animals can predict the future, he marveled.

On his way to school one day, Fred stopped at the Olsens' and looked around to see that no one was watching. He reached over the fence, pulled the plastic dog off the stick, and stuffed it into his jacket pocket, and then fled. Exercising his compulsion had instilled a sense of power in Fred. Afterward, with the grave marker in his possession, a feeling of serenity settled over him.

The county fair was in town that week. On the way home from school Fred detoured into the fairgrounds, where he spent the rest of the afternoon on groaning, clanking rides. His favorite attraction, though, was Madam Frieda, the fortune-teller. Frieda Wheeler cut hair in a shop in Wichita when she wasn't traveling with the carnival. After collecting Fred's thirty-five cents, she told him, "You will discover great things in your life, and people will seek your knowledge. Stay in school." For Fred, it was money well spent. There was no doubt he would stay in school, but it also inspired him to know that people would someday seek his knowledge.

After the fair, as he lay in his bed with science books spread over the mattress, Fred withdrew the plastic dog from under his pillow. He examined it and let his mind wander. How did Barney know the limb would fall? His adolescent logic concluded that if a dog's brain and nervous system could open a window into the future, then man, with his bigger brain, could surely find a door to higher powers. The answer to the puzzle would be found with the smallest particles in the mind of God, he surmised. Keep dividing them into smaller pieces and examine them— soon time itself would break down. The structure of the universe would be revealed. The connection between man's mind and the solid objects surrounding him would become clear.

Fred imagined a vibrant swarm of particles rushing through the nervous systems of all living creatures. Each particle contained a faint glimmer of a greater power, and all of them together would unveil the power of the cosmos. He assumed that man, like animals, had the latent ability to perceive and manipulate these particles if he quieted his chattering mind. The great prophets and miracle workers of ancient science and religion must have discovered this ability, he concluded.

Lying among schoolbooks on his bed, Fred electrified himself with his vision of swarming particles carrying the secret energy behind the curtain of the physical world. He caressed the plastic dog in his hand. He wished he could be nearer to Barney, but that wasn't possible unless he wanted to dig up the dog. Too risky, he thought. But the urge stayed with him. He would have to settle for the plastic representation. He held it to his breast, and a warm calmness enveloped him.

***

Fred was a geek before the term was coined, but he was big enough and tough enough that none of the other boys bothered him. However strange they thought Fred, they kept it to themselves. He could have played fullback on the football team, but he had no interest. His passion was science and math, and he excelled.

He also traveled to other schools with the debate team and improved his speaking skills. But he was too intense, too forceful with his opinions. Debate honed his ability to speak in public.

By his sophomore year Fred was taking calculus courses at the local junior college. His teachers were using the word "genius" more often in their conversations about him. He breezed through the curriculum and graduated early from high school.

Foreseeing that Fred had the talent to be a superior research scientist, prestigious universities across the country offered him scholarships. The door was open; he could go wherever he wished. He chose Stanford for its physics program, and to be near a large city, with the anonymity it provided. He loved Father Lucas and Sister Ruth, but his time in Kansas was ending.

One task remained unfulfilled. It had crept into his thoughts like a teenager's sexual urge captured the body. A plaster shrine of the Virgin Mary beckoned him like a siren. In a remote corner of the Catholic cemetery, she stood in her blue shawl under a shroud that kept the rain off her sacred head. Long before, Fred had realized that disappearing religious cemetery icons in a small town would be sensational. He had suppressed his desire to steal, fearful of discovery, and fearing that once he started, he wouldn't be able to stop. But he would soon be away from Colby, and the police could never establish a pattern. And this was Mary! Fred assumed that she must have known about her future role in history. The statue attracted Fred like the gravity he would soon be studying at Stanford.

It would have been a simple matter to purchase his own Virgin, but an icon from a cemetery, he believed, would be imbued with holy energy by those who had prayed to it for so many years.

A few weeks before his departure to California, Fred parked two blocks away and walked the alley to the cemetery. He had been watching the place like a common burglar and knew when the police made their rounds through that part of town. He crawled out from the bushes after midnight and prayed to God that there wasn't a steel rein-forcing rod in the pedestal of the statue. With one sharp chisel blow it popped upward off its base like a holy jack-in-the-box. After a quick caress he laid the Virgin in his knapsack, and the serenity and calm he had known after stealing the plastic dog returned. For the first time, Fred felt ready to leave his hometown.

3

QUIZZY JOTTED MORE notes and then looked at the professor, who was sitting behind a pile of computer printouts on her desk. "Is that data from the meteorite tests?"

"Yes."

"You got all that since last night?"

"She who snoozes, loses. This was an unusual meteorite. I didn't want to lose any transitive data." Quizzy looked at her with a puzzled expression. "That's data that doesn't stick around. The first series of tests we ran was for life detection. We're looking for anything that's not a contaminant from the Earth or our atmosphere. In the small chance that unearthly life is found and we make history, events would take on a life of their own, no pun intended. No one could predict what would happen. Last year, scientists put microbes scraped from cliffs in England on the exterior of the International Space Station. When they analyzed them months later, most were still viable. In the infinitesimal chance that unearthly life is found, it would be earthshaking news, as someone in your business most certainly knows."

"The Colvin Meteorite..." Quizzy said. "That sounds so strange, considering it killed its namesake. I think I like "Lavender Fireball" better, even if it was coined by a nutty preacher."

"The tradition is to name them after where they fall. But I think I'll start calling this one something else." Sorensen continued. "This meteorite is metal. Metal meteorites are usually formed when asteroids collide with one another and produce fragments that drift into Earth's orbit. Then they're pulled down by its gravitational field. The astrophysics people are eager to study the elemental constituents and structure of this one. Its trajectory was strange—like something other than gravity was acting upon it."

Quizzy stopped taking notes and asked, "What's a 'clean room?'"

"A clean room is actually a room within a room within a room," said Professor Sorensen. "Each room is sealed and has added layers of protection. The innermost room contains the specimen, viewable behind glass and accessible via rubber gloves. I'm sure you've seen the setup in the movies. Ours is downstairs."

"How do you determine whether there's life on the meteorite samples when they're in the clean room?" Quizzy asked. "Do you look at them under a microscope?"

"Yes, that's one way. That happens to be the first step, because it's the least invasive method. Subsequent stages look more deeply, so to speak, but are more disruptive to the very life we seek. The process is a careful progression. Eventually we get around to using a spectral analyzer. Last but not least, there's good old-fashioned culture testing in a petri dish."

"It sounds like you test for any indication of life as we know it. But what about life as we don't know it?

"We don't know what we don't know. If there is a form of life or an energy pattern radically different from what we have ever observed on Earth, we might not recognize it." The professor shrugged her shoulders. "We don't have all the answers."

"Thanks, Professor. That's all the questions I have." Quizzy's mood darkened. "I heard some bad news this morning," she said. "I called Flora Flores, the firefighter, with a couple of questions about last night. She's very ill. She has a brain tumor." Sorensen rocked back in her chair. Quizzy continued. "Flora had just gotten off the phone with her doctor when I called. She'd been having headaches, so she went in for tests yesterday before the meteorite hit. Her biggest worry seems to be her nine-year-old son. She's divorced. It sounds bad."

"Oh, no! I'm just sick to hear that. Flora was such a pro last night. She was so good with Alex and Charlie. She took charge—just what that family needed. I'll call and tell her she's in my thoughts. I wish there was something I could do. But like I said, science doesn't have all the answers."

4

CHURCH OF THE GOD PARTICLE
Reverend Lucas Ruthlier, Pastor
4000 South Lamar Blvd. Suite 400
Austin Texas 78704
(512) 555-1234
www.ParticleOfGod.com

May 2, 2013
Alexander Colvin
17607 County Road 1440
Bee Cave, TX 78733

Dear Mr. Colvin:
First and foremost, let me express my sympathy for the recent tragic loss of your wife, Trina. I hope that you continue to heal through this difficult period, and that each week is a little better for you. If there is anything I can do

to help you with your journey, please call or write me.

One of the guiding principles of the Church of the God Particle is that there are no random acts. Everything happens for a reason. Often these reasons are obscure and buried under successive layers of meaning. Only after one peels back all the layers is the true meaning of an event revealed. I believe that the events on the night of your wife's death have a deeper meaning, also. I hope you will find comfort in the thought that Trina's passing is a thread in the larger tapestry of a new reality. I have an unwavering belief that the fall of the meteorite on that fateful night was an omen for great changes in mankind. Believers within the Church of the God Particle will be at the forefront of that change.

Our congregation believes that the Night of the Fireball is sacred, and we consider Trina to be a saint. Her physical passing attracted the attention of the world to the coming of the prophet, the Elemental One.

A tenet of our belief is to be physically close to the sacred symbols that reveal God's wisdom to us. It brings us comfort and enlightenment when we bathe the atoms of our corporeal structures in the atomic waves emanating from those symbols. In fact, we believe the Elemental One will be revealed when he is united with that most sacred object, the meteorite known as the Lavender Fireball.

It is in this spirit that I ask you to consider donating the holy Lavender Fireball to our church. I believe at this time Professor Sorensen at the University of Texas is still studying the meteorite, and I trust she will soon deliver it unharmed to you. I also know that there is a monetary value placed on the meteorite by the commercial marketplace. Nevertheless, I am appealing to your sense of higher moral values to designate the Church of the God Particle to be the sanctuary of the holy fireball. We are a growing congregation that convenes in a unique place of worship. We don't have the funds to compete in the open marketplace for the meteorite; therefore I pray you will consider my request. I look forward to hearing from you.

Yours in quantum,
Reverend Lucas Ruthlier

***

Alexander Colvin
17607 County Road 1440
Bee Cave, TX 78733

May 4, 2013
CHURCH OF THE GOD PARTICLE
Lucas Ruthlier, Pastor
4000 South Lamar Blvd. Suite 400
Austin Texas 78704

Attn Mr. Ruthlier:
You are correct about the meteorite being at the University of Texas. It will be necessary to saw the space junk into

small pieces to analyze it thoroughly. Those pieces will then be immersed in acid, incinerated to a crispy residue, bombarded with toxic energy waves, and in the end, crushed into oblivion. If there is anything left of the Holy Lavender Fireball I will most likely flush it down some shit hole befitting its hellish nature.

Sincerely,
Alexander Colvin

5

"PHYSICAL LABOR FOCUSES the mind," Alex's father had told him many times. Head low, he shuffled toward Charlie, who was sitting atop a rented backhoe. The crew Charlie had hired to rebuild the driveway was lashing rebar together on the ground in front of him. Trina's family and much of Alex's family, including his mother, were staying at the ranch during the days before the funeral. Those who had arrived in pickups or SUVs were able to four-wheel all the way to the house by driving through the creek bed, avoiding the damaged section of driveway. Those who drove cars had to park before the crater and walk to the house or hitch a ride in another vehicle.

They had been telling anecdotes about Trina in the house. The stories warmed Alex, but he needed a break from the emotional swings. Mindful of his father's advice, he had excused himself and slipped out of the house to lend a hand.

Charlie operated the backhoe, digging footings in the creek bed to support a retaining wall he was going to build with landscaping bricks. It would support the dirt he had already pushed and dumped into the collapsed side of the crater.

As Charlie dug the driveway, Alex imagined another chrome-toothed backhoe bucket dipping in and out of an expanding future grave for Trina Colvin at the Bee Cave Memorial Cemetery.

Charlie had hired two energetic Mexican brothers at a day-labor center in Austin, and they were talking to each other in Spanish, wiring rebar together. They were the only laborers still willing to work after they were told the location of the job. Already word had spread that the Twisted Tree Ranch was touched by the hand of God.

Like any reputable religious experience, the Lavender Fireball was acquiring a dichotomy of good and evil. There was the evil driveway crater, scene of deathly mayhem. Its antithesis was the good spring, the place where the fiery instrument of death was neutralized by the enveloping clear water like a cosmic baptism. The day-laboring brothers, men of faith, had agreed to work to repair the sinister crater only if Charlie agreed to let them visit the redeeming spring when they finished for the day.

"Good to see you out and about," Charlie yelled to Alex from the windowless cab of the backhoe. He tapped down the throttle lever of the diesel engine so they wouldn't have to shout.

"I needed a break from the funeral arrangements," Alex said. "I just want everything to be over with. Seven is sick, too. Mom is going to take her to the doctor."

"I read your obituary. I mean Trina's obituary that you wrote for the newspaper. It was a little edgy, I thought, with the 'arbitrary God' part," Charlie said.

"Yeah, well, that's how I feel now. Trina's folks didn't care for it, either. They didn't say anything, but I watched them as they read it in the paper, and they winced a little. They're God-fearing people. I suppose I'd do it differently if I had another chance."

"Hopefully you'll never have another chance," Charlie said. "Also, I didn't say that I didn't like what you wrote."

"I called our insurance guy this morning," Alex said. "The driveway isn't covered, but he offered his condolences. I told him I'd rather have the money.

"The agent said it was considered 'an act of God.' What kind of God would do this to us? Even if it had hit the house, it wouldn't have been covered, he said. And then he had the gall to try to sell me a rider that would cover any future meteorite damage. I asked him what he thought my chances of collecting on that would be. He pissed me off, and I yelled something about throwing good money after bad for worthless insurance and hung up on him."

Charlie hesitated, then asked, "Did he say anything about the Toyota?"

"No, I hung up too soon. Probably the same deal, though."

"Maybe not. Cars pay out different." Charlie paused. He

lapsed into an expression of worry, but then offered a feeble smile. "Flora Flores called me this morning."

"I liked her," Alex said. "She seemed like a straight talker."

Charlie nodded. "Yeah, and I just got a big dose of it. She called to see how we were doing. We talked awhile and I asked her if she'd like to go to dinner sometime. Then she dropped a bomb on me. She just found out she has a brain tumor. Glioblastoma, she called it. Shit, can you believe that?" He grew pale. "She got the lab results the morning after the meteorite. She's going to start chemo next week." Charlie shook his head in disbelief.

"Oh, man, Alex said. "I'm really sorry to hear that. Maybe they caught it early enough."

Charlie shrugged. "Who knows? She said at least her headache disappeared after she drank from the spigot at the spring. The magical meteorite, she called it."

Charlie pursed his lips and pumped the backhoe clutch several times. Turning back to Alex, he said, "If you're looking for something to do, you can help those guys with the rebar. Make sure they're not skimpin' on the lashing wire. I'll be done digging this out pretty soon. The concrete truck should be showing up anytime. We need to get that steel laid in this trench."

Thankful for the work, Alex joined the two brothers. They wrapped and tied wire around the steel joints while Charlie scraped dirt out of the footing trench with the backhoe.

When Charlie finished the trench, he shut off the engine, but a low growling sound continued, emanating from the other side of the creek in the trees. Alex moved closer to the laborers, who had a better vantage point. Mangy, the pathetic-looking outcast of the coyote pack that roamed the hills above the ranch, was up on his hind legs, eyeballing a fat green katydid on the side of a cedar tree. He lived somewhere in the canyon, but never hunted with his brethren. His tail was missing, and his ears were mere nubs on the top of his head. His fur sprouted in knotted clumps on parts of his body and didn't grow at all on other parts. He was a survivor, though, and had earned the respect of the men, even if he was an opportunistic chicken eater.

Since Charlie had fortified the coop, Mangy changed his eating habits. He was the only coyote Alex had ever seen that ate insects off the bark of trees. He stood upright on his hind legs with his front paws braced on the tree and snatched bugs off the bark like a colossal, hairy lizard. When he ate an insect he growled in a low, throaty rumble.

He cocked his earless head from side to side, studying the insect. Saliva drooled from his mouth in viscous strings.

"Chupacabra! Chupacabra!" one of the brothers shouted as he jumped up and down, unable to control himself.

"Chupacabra!" Now the other brother was animated and shouting.

"No chupacabra!" Charlie yelled back. "*Es* Mangy!" That name had no meaning to the brothers.

Charlie shouted, "*¡Es un coyote! ¡Él vive aquí en el ran-*

cho!" He tried to explain that the animal lived in the canyon and high hills above, sweeping the surrounding countryside with his arm, but his Spanish was inadequate.

Mangy crunched his buggy prey with crooked teeth, jaws opening and closing as if he were eating taffy. He swallowed the insect and loped into the trees.

"Chupacabra!" the brothers shouted.

"Coyote!" Charlie shouted back.

"Chupacabra!"

For the first time in three days Alex laughed.

The concrete truck arrived and poured its load into the trench where the men had placed the steel reinforcement. After they smoothed it down the brothers visited the spring. They prayed and then splashed water on their faces and drank from the red-handled spigot until they were full.

The next day when Charlie went to the day-labor center to find two more men to help lay the brick for the retaining wall, a hundred workers strained forward, shouting and waving their arms to be chosen. They were all eager for the opportunity to work at the magical Twisted Tree Ranch.

6

REVEREND LUCAS RUTHLIER sat in a rear pew at Trina Colvin's memorial service. Undaunted by his ejection from Trina's accident scene, he was back, enraptured with the fireball and all things associated with it. The reverend silently watched Alex and his family in the front of the church. The woman firefighter who had been at the meteorite scene approached Charlie Colvin, and they exchanged a few words. The warmth between them was apparent.

Ever since he had arrived in America as a preacher, Ruthlier's message had never wavered: *There will be an omen from the heavens heralding the arrival of a new prophet—a prophet with unique powers that will change the world.*

Reverend Ruthlier himself intended to be that prophet.

The memorial service unfolded. Skipping the finger-food reception in the church's basement, Ruthlier slipped out and stopped for pie and coffee at a local shop. Then he drove across town to the Bee Cave Cemetery and found an inconspicuous spot with a view of the freshly dug grave.

Oppressive clouds sagged motionless in the overcast sky as the car carrying Alex Colvin and his mother entered the cemetery. Colvin's child was strapped into the car seat behind them. The rest of the procession followed the lead cars into the cemetery, and the mourners gathered around the open grave. Funeral drizzle wet the grass and gravestones, but the rain wasn't hard enough to soak through clothes yet. No one had thought to bring an umbrella; rain hadn't been in the forecast.

The cemetery caretaker appeared holding an armful of black umbrellas. Dressed in his work clothes, he passed them around without a word and then disappeared. This simple gesture appeared to overcome Alex, and he began to weep.

Reverend Ruthlier shrugged. Sometimes people got hurt in the course of great historical events. As the minister at the grave site started another prayer, Ruthlier ducked into his Lexus and drove out the back exit.

7

THE BARE DIRT covering Trina's grave had turned to sticky brown clay overnight, and it was easy to see where the cleated tires of the backhoe had deposited it. Livid, Alex followed the muddy tire tracks in his pickup. He drove slowly along the maintenance road with mowed-down weeds in the center that led to the Colvin section of Bee Cave Cemetery, and then curved down the hill to the caretaker's ramshackle office.

The office was a one-room cinder-block building. A black plastic sign with white letters read, "Marvin Moley." Alex guessed that the sturdy utility building next to the office contained tools, grass seed, and fertilizer. A yellow Case backhoe that was too tall to fit in the utility building rested under the slanted metal roof of an adjacent pole barn.

Alex parked his pickup, got out, and slammed the door. He marched to the cemetery office and banged on the metal door, shaking the small building. Marvin Moley answered, looking surprised at such an energized visitor so early in the morning. Behind Moley, Alex could see a beat-up oak desk piled with papers and magazines sitting on a worn-out linoleum floor.

"Good morning, Mr. Colvin!" Moley said uncertainly.

"What the hell is going on around here?" Alex yelled with enough force that Moley took a step back. Alex tried to calm himself, remembering how grateful he had been when the caretaker had handed out umbrellas the day before.

"I'm not sure what you mean."

"My wife's grave. It's torn to hell."

"What do you mean, torn to hell?"

"It's a disaster. The headstone is down, and there's dirt everywhere."

"What? That doesn't make any sense. I finished up around six yesterday, and everything was fine."

Alex visualized Moley dumping the last bucket of dirt on Trina's grave. "I came out to put some flowers from the funeral on the grave, and I found it like I said. I followed the muddy tracks down this road to here. Hell, just look at that backhoe." The backhoe, parked in its usual place under the pole barn, was splattered with globs of drying mud.

"Well, I'll be switched!" Moley exclaimed. "I need to go up to the grave and have a look."

"Jump in," Alex said, working to keep his temper in check. He drove Moley up the maintenance road to Trina's grave. Tire tracks crisscrossed the Colvin section; grass was mashed down and chunks ripped out. Trina's headstone had been knocked off its base and lay on its side. Alex's anger surfaced again as he surveyed the damage.

"I don't understand why anyone would want to do this," said Moley. "I mean, you read about this kind of thing, but here in Bee Cave? This ain't Austin! It must've been kids out raisin' hell. I gotta report this."

Without speaking, Alex handed him his cell phone.

Captain Steiner arrived in his patrol car twenty minutes after Marvin Moley called 911. "Is there a key to that backhoe?" he asked the caretaker.

"Yes, sir, we keep it on that pegboard." Moley pointed at the wall. "But the office was locked."

Steiner scribbled on his pad. When he finished, he tipped back his gray felt cowboy hat and scowled.

"Alex," he said, "I need to speak with Mr. Moley alone and wrap things up here. Why don't you go home, and I'll get in touch with you this afternoon." It wasn't a request.

***

Steiner watched quietly as Alex drove out of the cemetery; then he turned to Moley. "Okay, Marvin, what do you think the chances are of someone coming out here on a rainy night, hot-wiring your backhoe, and taking it for a joyride to a section of the cemetery where there was a burial that day?"

"I just don't understand, Captain," Marvin said.

"Can you tell if that grave was dug up?"

Marvin's mouth moved, but nothing came out except "um" and "uh." Finally, he said, "Well, I don't really know if I could tell or not. I mean, that's already a fresh grave and everything. There would be no way to know if the ground had been disturbed, since it was disturbed to start with."

"So, to really know if the body has been disturbed we'd have to go into the casket, right?"

"Yeah, I guess so. But I couldn't do that without a permit. Even if I did just bury Mrs. Colvin yesterday."

"And a permit requires a court order and family notification, which is exactly what Alex Colvin doesn't need right now," Steiner said. "Okay, let's just keep this between you and me. Most likely it was some bored teenagers who had too much to drink, blowing off steam." Steiner scowled and shook his head, hoping Moley would buy into his version of the event. "I want to look around some more. It's okay to clean up the mess and fix that headstone. If you find anything else out of place, give me a call."

Sitting in his patrol car before he left the cemetery, Steiner opened his pocket notepad and began doodling as he tried to make sense of what had happened. Slowly, the random lines he drew coalesced into a long horizontal rectangle. Inside the rectangle Steiner drew a stick figure lying on its back, feet pointing upward. Above the rectangle he placed a large question mark.

1971

A T STANFORD, FRED Zimmerman became an acid head. In 1971 that wasn't unusual, even in the department of physics. Nearby San Francisco's raucous social norms spilled onto the campus. Fred discovered the unpredictable results of uninhibited drug experimentation while dodging the disastrous consequences of brain damage.

He watched the televised Vietnam War juxtaposed with a president's assurances that all was well, and he developed a creeping cynicism and disdain for authority. His politics drifted farther to the left, but only for the time being.

Regardless of the chemical distractions, Fred sailed through his undergraduate work with honors. He was recognized in the physics department as someone to watch. To celebrate his acceptance into the physics doctoral program, he stole an exquisite ceramic head of John the Baptist, one of his long-admired prophets.

Facing turmoil in the streets, the San Francisco Police Department ignored what seemed to them to be random cemetery thefts of religious icons. The families whose grave sites were being desecrated turned in reports, but their outrage was insufficient to marshal stretched police resources into a serious investigation. With no apparent pattern, the incidents were dismissed as common vandalism.

"Horsepower upstairs" was a phrase Fred's colleagues sometimes used to describe his phenomenal mathematical ability. "Zealot" was a word the same people used to describe him when he mingled theoretical physics with religion.

Fred failed to understand their misgivings. To them, religion was the practice of cultural philosophies, telling stories of God, and charity to those less fortunate. Fred judged himself to be a religious man, and he had no qualms with that label. However, some of what his colleagues considered to be religion, Fred also perceived as the fundamental physics of the universe. He was unable to separate the two. If the laws of physics acted as an intelligence, then so be it. God's nature was what it was, and discoveries about it didn't alter it. Fred's ability to focus allowed him to manipulate complex equations in his head, but his inability to soften that focus was increasingly causing him problems.

Unlike his colleagues, it made no difference to Fred whether his discipline of study was referred to as physics or as God. He further exasperated the dean of the Stanford physics department when he quoted Shakespeare: "A rose by any other name would smell as sweet."

The dean said that Fred was a sanctimonious bastard, even if he did have an extraordinary mind.

8

THE MAROON PAINT on Alex's four-wheel-drive truck may have been faded, but the vehicle still had the guts to negotiate the rocky hills of the Twisted Tree Ranch. The drone of its deep ribbed tires on the newly repaired driveway had put Seven to sleep in her car seat. Jessie sat on her haunches in the backseat next to Seven, sniffing the air through an open window. Bags of groceries occupied the other front seat. Alex pulled under the carport and walked to the house carrying a bag with one hand and holding Seven on his hip with the other, and then stopped dead.

The door to the house was ajar a few inches, and the wood around the latch was splintered. Jessie stopped short of the door and began sniffing the porch, then barged through the front door. Alex quickly surveyed the grounds around the house. No vehicles—no sign of anyone. What kind of sick person would burglarize this place after what happened to him last week? Seven, now awake, squirmed in Alex's arms. He ran his fingers through the baby's hair and kissed her cheek. "Apparently they're gone, or Jessie would be eating them by now," he said to Seven. The baby smiled.

Carrying his daughter, Alex went through the open front door. The living room floor was strewn with cushions, books, and curios off the shelves. Jessie stood in the center, agitated, her eyes roaming over familiar objects in unfamiliar places. Every room had been ransacked. "It's okay, Seven." He set the girl in her crib. "C'mon, Jessie." Accompanied by the bull terrier, Alex methodically went through the house. Nothing missing. TVs, computer, stereo, digital camera.... Even Trina's jewelry was still in the dresser.

He gritted his teeth. Trina was gone. Only her jewelry remained. A wave of anger swept through him. The image of the freakish lavender light coming through the windows riled him. The meteorite. Could the intruder have been after that? Professor Sorensen had taken it with her, but not many people knew that. And that crazy preacher had already asked for it.

For the second time in a week Alex called 911, and he reported the burglary. He scooped up Seven out of her crib and went outside with Jessie. He breathed deeply, trying to calm himself. Tire tracks of a dozen vehicles from the previous week still crisscrossed the area in front of the house. There would be no way to get any meaningful impressions. Alex walked around the house and through the backyard. A metal shed on a reinforced concrete slab sheltered dirt bikes, a bush hog, welders, a red plastic kayak, a flatbed utility trailer, and a collection of tools accumulated over decades by generations of Colvins. The shed's door, too, had been kicked in.

He paid a cursory glance at the machinery and tools, but it was the wooden storage cabinet in the corner that attracted him. His father's old pocketknife, normally in the cabinet, was stuck in the white-painted door, bent oddly to one side. Alex studied the knife. *Bent like the screwdriver in the tree.* He opened the door and moaned when he saw the empty shelf. His C-4 was gone.

Alex worked the point of the blade out of the wood and set the ruined knife back on the shelf, where it had been since his father's death. He wondered about the penalty for possession of illegal explosives. If the thief were caught, he could point the police toward Alex. Panic crept up his backbone. He looked at his daughter. *I can't go to prison. Not with her....* "I need to get that C-4 back, Seven."

By the time Alex walked back around the house, two Travis County sheriff's deputies were pulling up in a Chevrolet Tahoe. Alex showed them inside, then took them into the shed.

"And you say there's nothing missing at all?" one of the deputies said.

"As far as I can tell, nothing was taken," Alex said. "I'll change numbers on my credit cards and go through all the precautions with the banks and credit reporting agencies, of course. I think whoever did this was after the meteorite that fell here last week. I'm told it could be valuable."

After the officers dusted for prints and left, the image of his father's pocketknife gnawed at Alex's stomach. It was a calling card. A taunting, in-your-face calling card. He went to the back room, turned on the computer, and Googled "Church of the God Particle."

The Web site was done simply in a lavender backwash, and contained little information about the church's philosophy, except for saying that everyone created his or her own reality. The site also said that the congregation awaited the arrival of someone or something called the Elemental One. The home page contained a glamour shot of the church's leader, Reverend Lucas Ruthlier, framed in the luxurious folds of a lavender robe. It was the same man—the one who'd blathered from the rock until the cops shut him up. His radiant silver hair flowed backward from a meaty jaw and hypnotic blue eyes. *Either he wears contacts, or that pic has been Photoshopped,* Alex thought. It rankled him that the prevailing color of the church's Web site was the same as the meteorite that had inflicted so much pain.

Another page was dedicated to the construction progress of the new church in a renovated Nations Home Hardware building. There were flattering architectural drawings spotted with smiling people of different races. *It's going to be such a happy place,* Alex thought sarcastically. But the image that riveted Alex was an action shot of a wiry man pounding a nail. The caption below it read: *Drago Ruthlier, son of Reverend Ruthlier, labors for the cause.* The picture was shot in profile, and the man wore a high collar, but Alex was sure the nail pounder on the screen was the man with the metal detector and the throat tattoo. Alex had an overwhelming feeling that he was the same prick who had kicked down his doors and stuck the knife in his cabinet.

Alex Googled *Drago Ruthlier, Austin, TX.* Nothing showed up except a plethora of reverse phone number services. He pulled the Austin White Pages out of a desk drawer and found the name and an address on South First Court. He Google Earthed the address and studied what appeared to be a duplex in a cul-de-sac.

Alex dialed Charlie's home number.

"Hi, Sam. Is Charlie around?"

"No, he's in Austin at a meeting. You could probably get him on his cell."

"No, I don't want to interrupt him. I'll call him later. But I need a big favor. Someone broke into our place, and I need to run into Austin for some stuff."

"What? Oh, no!"

"I know— it's hard to believe. The sheriff's men just left. I need to buy some door hardware. Could you possibly come over and watch Seven for an hour or two?"

When Samantha arrived, Alex left the house carrying a brown paper grocery bag and walked to his truck. When he was hidden from the house, he pulled Sweet Pea and his shoulder holster out of the bag and laid them on the seat. He drove the truck behind the shed to a pile of scrap metal and pulled on a pair of cowhide gloves. Picking through the pile of metal, he located a short section of four-inch pipe from an old clothesline support. He dug out a couple of steel end caps from the heap and duct-taped one of them onto an end of the pipe. He scooped the open end through the gravel piled on the shoulder of the driveway, filling the pipe. Then he sealed it with the other end cap and more tape. Finally, he tied two loops of rope around each end of the three-foot pipe and then taped the rope loops so they wouldn't slide. He hoisted the heavy assembly over the side of the truck bed and headed for Austin.

By the time Alex reached Drago Ruthlier's apartment building, he was seething. What kind of asshole burglarized a family that had just lost its mother? Alex pulled into the cul-de-sac and studied Drago Ruthlier's duplex. The sides of the building were gray-painted brick, and all of the curtains were pulled. The common driveway to both units was empty, and he couldn't see any neighbors outside.

Alex shut off the idling truck and pulled on a pair of buckskin gloves. He lifted the rock-filled pipe by its rope handles, walked to the front door, and rang the doorbell. Empty. He swung the heavy pipe into the door just above the knob. The jamb split, and the door flew inward. In one smooth motion Alex dropped the pipe and stepped into the duplex.

Alex glanced around the apartment. There was a glass case on the wall displaying more military knives. The apartment was small, and it took only a few moments to search the bedroom and then the bathroom. There was another knife on the toilet tank, but no C-4, at least not visible. He grabbed the knife and went into the kitchen. He threw open the cabinets and then looked in the refrigerator.

Alex looked at Drago's knife that he held in his hand. With a compact swing he embedded it in the front door of the refrigerator. *An eye for an eye,* he thought. He turned and walked briskly out the mangled front door. He picked up the steel battering pipe lying in the doorway, knowing that the gravel in it could be matched to his driveway. When he got to the truck, he drove out of the neighborhood until he found a quiet place to park and decompress. The C-4 worried him, but at least he felt a measure of satisfaction—even if it was revenge.

Alex drove to the nearest Home Depot and purchased the heaviest front door lock he could find and then headed home. Charlie phoned him as he drove, and they met under Alex's carport. They talked about the missing C-4 and Alex's attempt to recover it.

"Jesus, I can't believe you busted down his door!" Charlie said. "What if he'd been home?"

"He wasn't."

"Keep an eye over your shoulder for awhile. Don't worry about the C-4. If Ruthlier Junior gets caught with it and says he got it here, it's the word of a thief against yours. There's no way to prove it was here. I'd scrub down that cabinet, though."

Alex nodded. Always steady Charlie. What would Alex do without him? "Have you heard anything from Flora?" Alex knew that Charlie had been out with the firefighter several times, and things seemed to be going well.

"Yeah, and it's good news. Her headaches disappeared, and they did another PET scan. The tumor has shrunk twenty-five percent. The doctors are going to hold off on the chemo and check her again next week. It's a damned miracle!" Charlie was beaming.

1981

TWO YEARS AFTER his dissertation was accepted at Stanford, Fred Zimmerman sat in a coffee shop around the corner from his apartment in Chicago. Warmth seeped into the bones of his fingers from a hot cup, soothing the day's stress from the lab. His work lay spread across his table, and he tried to concentrate on a pair of graphs near his elbow. Instead of the graphs, however, Fred dwelled on the other scientists whose help he needed to advance his project.

It's their problem, not mine, he thought.

In less than a year at his first professional job he had managed to re-create the "Stanford situation." He was unable to separate his personal views from his work. He struggled with his provocative nature. He was ostracized by his colleagues. Fred was stuck in a vicious cycle: he disdained his coworkers, and they avoided him. He was on his own, without any cooperation or support for his projects.

It had been the same at Stanford his last year, and it almost derailed his PhD. Fred understood that he was going to have to stop proselytizing about an embedded force of nature in the nucleus of an atom that could be manipulated by the human brain.

He was too new in the field, despite his brilliance, to step out of the established dogma. Hostile colleagues could constrain his career, or even end it by crowding him out of precious lab time like a weak puppy pushed away from the milk.

"Excuse me, but would you mind terribly if I sat at the other side of your table? The rest of them are full, and I really need a break for a few minutes. I promise I won't disturb you."

Fred suppressed his occupational hassles and focused on the woman standing next to his table holding a cup of coffee. His first observation was that she was gorgeous. She was in her late twenties, brown haired, and as tall as he. She radiated an alluring softness as she regarded Fred ensconced at his table. But in her gray business suit, she presented herself as someone who was used to asking for what she wanted and then getting it.

"No, I wouldn't mind," he replied. "There's enough room. Let me get some of these papers out of the way for you."

"Forgive me, but I can't help noticing that your papers look very complicated. Nothing but graphs and equations. Are you a rocket scientist?"

Fred smiled. He couldn't tell whether she was serious.

"You're warm," he said.

She waited, but he didn't elaborate. "Okay, I'll play," the woman said. She reached down to the table, and with her left index finger rotated a paper so she could read it. Fred watched as the pressure on her fingertip forced blood into the cuticles on both sides of her manicured nail. On the little finger of her hand was a small agate set in a silver ring—her only ring.

"Physics," she said.

Fred pulled his eyes away from the woman's hand and looked up at her. "Very good. Did you guess or do you know?"

"Some of both. I know what it isn't. It's not chemistry and it's not engineering."

Fred gestured to the newly cleared space at his table. "I believe your table is ready," he said, and she sat down. "I'm Fred Zimmerman." He extended his hand. She had a firm, warm grip, and they locked eyes.

"Irena Davidoff. Thanks for sharing."

"I'm happy to do it. How do you know what the equations are not?"

"I have a degree in industrial design. My work touches on architecture, engineering, and hazardous materials, so I'm somewhat familiar with the look of those formulas and equations. These are different."

"What have you designed in industry lately?"

"I don't design things, at least not machinery. I went into process and quality control instead. I do operational measurements and statistical analysis—that sort of thing.

I'm a consultant. Most of my jobs last about six months or so. I travel a lot. But I'm thinking I may have made a mistake getting into a field with so much travel. It's hard to sink roots with a job like mine."

"I suppose that's one good thing about my work," Fred said. "Other than an occasional conference, I stay here in Chicago."

"And what kind of work would that be?" asked Irena Davidoff.

"I work at Fermilab. Ever heard of it?" Fred asked, because most people hadn't.

"Of course. It's the home of pure theoretical physics research. A world-class institution."

A twinge of pride went through Fred despite his personal problems at the place.

"What is your goal there?" Irena asked.

What an odd question, he thought. Most people would ask what he was working on. "My personal goal is to biologically harness the energy of God at the nuclear level."

"Are you sure he exists there?"

"I will prove it."

"Have you proved His existence at the nonnuclear level?"

"To myself I have."

"Are you enlightened?" she asked.

Another odd question. "I have my ups and downs."

They sipped coffee, regarding each other.

"Do you live here in Chicago?" he asked.

"Yes. Now I do. I'm originally from New York. My parents live there. They own a restaurant. It's called Davidoff's, believe it or not."

"Davidoff. Is that Russian?"

"Yes, the name is Russian. My father's family was from there a long time ago. We, however, are Hungarian. I was born in Hungary. That is to say, we were Hungarian before we came to the United States. Now we are American."

"Your English is perfect. You must have come here at a young age."

"Yes, when I was two. My father was something of a rebel and spoke his mind. When the Soviets cracked down in '56 and sent in the tanks to crush our little revolution, we had to flee with just the clothes on our backs, as they say. We were given asylum in New York, as were many others. We are part of the Hungarian diaspora."

"And what is *your* goal?" he asked.

"I have many."

"Tell me one."

"I just made a new one. I want to be the first to know when you prove the existence of God."

"Well, you can be the third—after God and myself."

"I suspect it won't be news to God that He exists." She sipped her coffee. "So, what's your current project, if I may ask?"

"I'm trying to verify a theory by a British physicist named Peter Higgs. Higgs posits that there is a field of subatomic particles called bosons that confers mass to all matter in the universe. The particles are called Higgs bosons, not surprisingly, but they've been nicknamed God particles because of their overarching and fundamental effect. I know Higgs is on the right track, but I think he's just scratched the surface. There is much more to these God particles than he realizes! I'm convinced they are the gateway into the mind of God Himself. If a properly tuned human brain were linked into the energy of God particles, a person could manipulate matter—an object—with his mind."

Fred found a blank piece of paper and drew a simple diagram on it. Irena stared at the paper as if it were a map to buried treasure. Fred warmed at the woman's attentiveness.

"All these other papers describe an experiment. It involves electrons, but the principle applies to God particles." He pointed a pencil at his drawing. "You take a piece of cardboard and cut out two narrow slits parallel to each other. Then you shoot electrons through the slits so they strike a detector that's set up behind them. Sometimes you shoot electrons through one slit and sometimes through the other, and sometimes you shoot the electrons through both slits at the same time. The behavior of the electrons depends upon whether the electron detector is turned on or off." He paused for a second. "Do you understand what that means?"

"Tell me."

"That's not supposed to happen! Why should electron behavior depend on whether the detector is turned on or off? It's as if Isaac Newton dropped his apple out of the tree, and it would hit the ground only if he watched it fall.

Otherwise, it would hang in midair until he looked at it, and then it would fall."

Irena seemed perplexed. "I'm not sure I understand."

"That's precisely my point! No one understands. It's as if the electrons possessed intelligence, and they knew in advance whether the detector was on or off, and then they chose their paths."

"How can that be?" she asked.

"I don't know, but I intend to find out. The behavior of those experimental electrons seems influenced by the experimenter's behavior—whether or not he activated the detector. The experimenter's behavior was determined by his brain. Ergo, the behavior of the electrons was influenced by the experimenter's brain. The experiment clearly demonstrates a mind/matter connection! My theory is that matter can be manipulated at the nuclear level by complex biological organisms like ourselves—if we are in a conducive state of mind."

"I've never been called a complex biological organism before," Irena said with a smile. "That's fascinating."

"It is to me—in the extreme," he said. Fred frowned, and his mood darkened. "But my colleagues do not agree. They ridicule me. None of them will cross the professional bright line that separates behavior, religion, and philosophy from the mathematical laws of physics. Those hypocrites go to church on Sunday and profess a blind belief in miracles spawned by a supernatural being. But on Monday they jump back over that line, never crossing it again until the next Sunday. Jekyll and Hyde theoretical physicists are what they are. They'll integrate differential equations, but not their own belief systems. And I am frustrated to no end. I can accept that they wish to stay in their own small sandbox, but for God's sake, allow me to visit the beach once in a while." His knuckles were white around his coffee cup.

"You are a passionate man, Fred Zimmerman. You'd make a good preacher."

Fred let go of his problems at work as the few minutes Irena had requested at his table turned into an hour. They talked of freedom to pursue dreams, God, and revolution. For the first time in his adult life he sensed that he had discovered someone who understood him. Even though they had just met, Fred already hoped that Irena had the qualities that would sustain them through a life together. And Irena seemed even more eager than Fred for a long-term relationship. Six months after their coffee shop meeting, Fred and Irena were married.

***

After a worse-than-usual day of enduring collegial snipping, Fred carved a cantaloupe as he helped Irena prepare supper.

"I can't bear to see you like this, Fred," Irena said to him. "Listen, I met someone interesting a few weeks ago. I think you should talk to her. She is from Romania. There is a Romanian consulate here in Chicago, and she works there as a business development specialist. Her name is

Miruna Lupei. After we eat, I'll give her a call and see if she's free."

"We need people of your caliber to help us grow our country," Miruna said to Fred that night. "Your wife would be accorded an equally high status with her industrial design expertise. Romania is a charming, growing country. Did you know Bucharest is sometimes called the Little Paris? It is true that our systems are different, and there would be an adjustment period. But we have built a world-class research center. You would have unrestricted access to the facility and be allowed to experiment on whatever you thought would advance the field of theoretical physics."

Over the next months they met many times. Miruna presented a socially diverse and uninhibited professional future in Romania. The couple would be living in one of the best parts of town and be paid more than most other state workers. The worst aspect for Fred was the identity change. The patient but focused Miruna explained that it would be best for everyone if Fred and Irena lived in Romania with a name other than Mr. and Mrs. Fred Zimmerman.

"Why draw unnecessary attention to yourselves as a couple who emigrated from America?"

***

Fred had always wanted to visit Texas. Like Kansas, its vast landscapes emanated quiet power until they erupted with lashing storms. Irena and he left Chicago and drove southwest to Big Bend National Park on the Rio Grande River. Hurricane Alicia was projected to make landfall in the eastern part of the state the next day, but Big Bend was dry and safe. The weather forecasters were accurate, and the hurricane pounded the coast while dumping a foot of rain on its way north. Fred and Irena packed their bags at the lodge that morning and prepared to drive east to where the storm had just passed.

"What's this little plastic dog, Fred?" Irene asked as she laid clothes into a suitcase.

"Oh, it's nothing. Just a good-luck charm I've carried for a long time." Barney's grave site marker was the only memento he would carry to his new life in Romania. The rest of his cemetery saints were in a storage locker in Chicago under an assumed name. When the rent payments stopped, the locker would be cleaned out. Fred pondered with sadness what would happen to the secret treasures he had so lovingly accumulated.

Driving to San Antonio on Highway 90, they watched as muddy water in the creeks and rivers flowed faster and higher the farther east they traveled. By the time they made it to Victoria, the waters were churning just beneath the bridges. Irena drove south toward the coast on a remote county road.

Like much of Texas, rarely traveled roads used low-water crossings at creeks instead of bridges. If there was any flowing water it normally trickled through galvanized culverts buried under the roadways. During normal rains the water rose enough to cover the crossings, but not high enough to interfere with vehicles. On exceptional days, the water flowed high enough to push cars off. This day, muddy water flowed like poured chocolate six feet over the crossing at Coatee Creek. Patches of frothy white foam, leaves, and branches glided over the crossing in deceptive tranquility until they dipped over the road's shoulder into a roiling brown liquid grinder.

Irena and Fred got out of their car and left open the front doors. She reached into the car and yanked the gearshift into neutral. The car rolled ahead into the water. In seconds it was pushed sideways and carried over the concrete edge of the crossing. It rolled over into the pool below, doors flopping like fins on a shiny carp. The water carried the vehicle into a boulder larger than the car itself. Metal screeched against stone, and the sunroof collapsed from hydraulic pressure. The windshield burst, and the car tumbled downstream.

Fred was realizing the full impact of his faked death. He watched his car disappear in the water like the history of his life. Father Lucas and Sister Ruth! *What have I done?* he thought. *They will be crushed like that car.*

"Let's go, Fred," Irena said. "We need to get out of here before someone comes along."

Fred got to his feet, and he and Irena walked back up the road several hundred yards to an abandoned farmhouse. Behind it, obscured from the road, a car was parked. Miruna Lupei was waiting for them inside the house. After inquiring whether they had had any problems with the

Impala, she said, "Your new identity papers are being created, and they will await your arrival in Bucharest."

"I want to choose my own name—our names," Fred said.

"It's too late for that. Everything has been arranged. Besides, it's just a name. Aren't you the one who likes to quote Shakespeare about that?"

"It's my name, and I wish to choose it. You are asking me to give up everything. It's a small concession in exchange."

Miruna looked at her watch. "Very well, who would you like to be?"

"I intend to be myself. However, the name I wish to use is Lucas Ruthlier."

"Ruthlier!" exclaimed Miruna. "It's not even a Romanian name! It's impossible."

"Fred, be reasonable," Irena said. "The groundwork has already been laid. You want a name that will blend in—not be questioned."

"We can think about it on the way," Miruna said. "Right now we need to get out of here."

"No. We decide now. I'm not leaving until you agree. It's not debatable. I'll walk out of here and claim my car was washed away, and I managed to escape with my life." He looked at Irena, questioning with his eyes whether or not she would go along.

Miruna squinted hard at them both. Fred wondered if she was armed. Maybe she would just shoot him and dump his body in the creek. But he knew that she had invested too much time, and he was too valuable to lose over a squabble.

"Very well, Fred. You can be Lucas Ruthlier. We will work it out. Now we must leave. You have a boat to catch."

They drove until nightfall and stayed in a Louisiana Holiday Inn. By the next evening, they had reached south Florida and another Holiday Inn. Before dawn, Fred and Irena booked a fishing cruise at the local docks on a boat owned by a Cuban. The boat left the bay and headed for the deep water of the gulf. It didn't stop until it tied up to a dock in Havana. No one had fished. The next day, Fred and Irena were on a Soviet plane to Bucharest, and into the hell that was Romania in the 1980s.

***

Lucas and Irena Ruthlier settled into a dismal Bucharest apartment building owned by the state. Miruna Lupei had neglected to mention that the nickname "Little Paris" was coined before the country's mercurial dictator bulldozed much of the capital's charming historical district to clear space for gray apartment buildings. He had visited North Korea and was somehow inspired by their dreary architecture.

Most of their neighbors were communist officials and unimaginative bureaucrats who dared not complain about living in identical homes. The accommodations were Spartan, yet comfortable enough for Fred. But Irena wanted more.

Lucas Ruthlier was a mathematics tutor, according to his freshly typed official papers. The man at the Securitate, Romania's totalitarian secret police, told them it would be suspicious for Ruthlier to be identified as a physicist. Someone might make the connection to his past endeavors in America. Brilliant physicists were rare and conspicuous. Displaying more than a little hostility, the man said he had already reworked Ruthlier's paperwork once.

The redone paperwork showed that Lucas Ruthlier was the only child of American parents who had immigrated to Romania from America and established citizenship. It had been a routine task for a Soviet agent to insert fake birth and marriage certificates in the archives of rural West Virginia courthouses, establishing the fictitious lives of the Ruthlier's.

According to Lucas Ruthlier's new documentation, his father had taught English at the university in Timisoara. Young Ruthlier's paperwork parents supposedly had been killed in an automobile accident in the countryside. Two very real graves were marked by a small, flat headstone chiseled with a simple "Ruthlier" above their individual names, birthdays, and identical dates of death. There were even two bodies in the graves—a man and a woman who had published a neighborhood newsletter that expressed unfavorable opinions about Timisoara's corrupt and bloated administration. Ruthlier was uneasy at first about having two sets of parents perish in car crashes, but then he rationalized that the second set somehow honored the first.

During the first year, Ruthlier concentrated on learning the new system and mastering the lab's facilities. He learned as much Romanian as he could in his spare time. He disliked cocktail and dinner parties thrown by the bureaucrats, so Irena often went alone. Ruthlier's few friends were the neighbors from their apartment building who also strolled through the park across the street.

The physics program, as promised, was supported with a river of Soviet cash, and the labs were well equipped. The Soviets wished to carry out research in an environment even more secretive than in Russia. Their top scientists rotated to Bucharest for a "sabbatical," where they engineered weapons even farther away from the West's spying eyes.

As the months dragged by, Irena became more and more disenchanted, yet she was unable to voice her complaints. When she discovered that she was pregnant, her disenchantment evolved into bitterness. By decree of the president's wife, contraception and abortion were illegal. "I'll be stuck in this goddamned place forever," she fumed.

On a rainy Monday evening after a day at the lab, Lucas Ruthlier poured himself a glass of Romanian merlot made from grapevines imported from France a century earlier. He poured a glass of grape juice for Irena and pushed it across the kitchen table to her.

"What's the occasion?" she said in a voice devoid of expression.

"They've set the launch date for the rendezvous with

Mir. It's three months out." Mir was the Earth-orbiting Soviet space station.

"That's nice." Irena went to the sink and dumped out the grape juice from her glass. She returned to the table and filled it from the wine bottle.

"Go easy on that."

"Don't worry yourself. Everything will be fine."

Ruthlier shot his wife an annoyed glance. "This will be the first attempt in zero gravity to move a stationary object with a subatomic particle beam controlled by a cosmonaut's brainwaves!" He paused for effect, but his wife's dull expression didn't change.

Undaunted, he went on. "The target will be a suspended lithium sphere the size of a baseball. Lithium is the metal with the least mass. The cosmonaut has been in biofeedback training for months with an EEG machine, learning to control his brainwaves. They must emanate in exactly the right pattern to sync up with the God particles in the lithium sphere. The cosmonaut's scalp will be covered with an electroencephalographic array embedded in a neoprene cap that will capture his brainwaves. Those brainwaves will be amplified through a peterphenyl crystal infiltrated by chains of neodymium molecules and then broadcast as a particle beam out of a mini parabolic dish. It's taken me three years to produce that crystal. It's the interface between the human nervous system and the parabolic dish."

Irena perked up. "That crystal must be very valuable."

"Priceless. It's about the size of a five-carat diamond, but infinitely rare—there is only one in existence. The neodymium gives it a shimmering lavender aurora."

"I think you should make me one, too."

"Would you be willing to die for it? The Securitate would have us both shot." The ruthless Securitate state police service operated hand in hand with Ruthlier's military research division. Squads of Securitate kept detailed records of how and with whom everyone functioned. "They wouldn't shoot us until we were used up, though."

"Used up how?"

"In experimentation."

"What kind of experimentation?"

"The unpleasant kind. The stakes are too high not to use every conceivable method to achieve success. The benefit to mankind could be incalculable. It could conceivably lead to a leap in human evolution."

Irena suddenly seemed interested, even if Fred thought she was angling toward making money somehow. "So, success is moving around a baseball in space with brainwaves?"

"Brainwaves control the particle beam. Essentially, a person envisions the object moving, and it would happen via the beam. However, it takes a tuned brain, neurologically speaking. The brain's various waveforms must be harmonized with the infiltrated crystal. The harmonized waveforms resonate with the God particles in both the crystal and the lithium sphere. My colleagues and I have been trying for the last couple of years to generate the combination of compatible waveforms from the brain that would resonate with these God particles. But none of us on the research team has yet been successful. Therefore, we implemented more aggressive experimentation using prisoners. But still, we've had no positive results. Not even with psychotropic drugs and lobotomies."

"Christ, that's too much detail for me. I think I'll pass on that crystal." Irena refilled her glass.

"It's true the experimentation can be detrimental to the subjects. It is important work, though, and somebody must do it."

"Getting a forced lobotomy doesn't fall under the definition of work, Lucas." Irena took a long sip of merlot. "Why send this experiment into space? I don't understand the logic of that."

"Because we haven't achieved success on Earth. It's far easier to influence the gravitational effect on an object in zero gravity. But most importantly, any object brought down to Earth would then act as an amplifier in future applications. It could then be possible to manipulate matter within Earth's gravity field using only brainwaves—without the crystal technology or the particle beam."

"Are you saying that someone could have telekinetic ability?"

"Yes, that is exactly what I am saying. And more! A person could conceivably turn his power inward upon himself and then defy gravity. Actually fly—at least in theory." Ruthlier was beaming.

"If you say so." Irena rubbed her extended belly. "What's for supper around here? I'm famished."

***

The launch date arrived. Ruthlier and a handful of other physicists watched a black-and-white closed-circuit monitor inside their physics laboratory in Bucharest. From the plains of Kazakhstan more than two thousand miles away, a television camera captured the image of a steaming Soyuz rocket on its launch pad at the Baikonur Cosmodrome.

At the end of the countdown the screen flashed white. When the picture rematerialized, it showed the twisted, burning girders of the destroyed launch tower. The rocket had exploded, consuming the cosmonauts and, more important to Ruthlier, the viability of his precious experiment.

Devastated, Ruthlier attempted to plow forward with his research. He refined the crystal infiltration process and built a replacement. But money to sustain the project waned, and the physicist despaired. The Alternative Weapons Research Committee refused to stage another expensive launch for the zero-gravity test.

9

PROFESSOR LILLIAN SORENSEN sat at her desk, distracted by a stain she had just discovered on her otherwise white lab coat. She was famished. Her light lunch had long ago dissipated, and she had at least another hour of office work.

The Lavender Fireball—what a sensational name for an inert rock, she thought. The meteorite sat on her desk; it was anything but a fireball now. She and her graduate assistant had drilled, scraped, and sawed away little pieces of the meteorite like academic miners, then analyzed them down to the molecular level. Sorensen never expected to discover anything alive or even organic. Despite a twinge of disappointment, the rock still fascinated her.

Sorensen speculated about the value of the meteorite. A collector of historical artifacts named Thomas Loya seemed very interested; he'd called several times. And then there was the pushy Reverend Lucas Ruthlier at the

Church of the God Particle. She had told him that she'd soon be returning the meteorite to Mr. Colvin, and yes, in the meantime, it was very secure in her office at UT. She had made an unfulfilled mental note to Google him and his church. Alex Colvin would soon have the pleasure of dealing with these people. She hoped to return the fireball to him by the end of the week. She had developed a pleasant rapport with Alex during their occasional phone conversations about the meteorite.

The meteorite had consumed the professor's energies, and she was eager to move on. There were new and exciting projects to pursue. The recent discovery of an Amazon bioluminescent fungus was particularly interesting, and its investigation was drawing her energies. She pushed the meteorite to the side of her desk and then slid a stereo microscope into the vacated space. Sorensen flicked on the lamp and peered into the eyepieces. Hundreds of yellowish, single-cell creatures glowed eerily in the light.

Sorensen opened the top drawer of her desk and retrieved a pocketknife. She halved an avocado that had been ripening on a shelf by the window and then inserted the blade under the seed and pried downward. The large, slippery seed remained in place, but the knife slipped and pricked her index finger.

"Shit!" she cried.

A drop of blood welled up from the wound and dripped onto the meteorite, followed by another. Sorensen wrapped her finger in a paper towel, washed her hand in a lab sink, and returned to clean the first blood drop off the meteorite, but didn't notice the second. Then she finished the carving job on the avocado. When she had consumed the last water cracker and avocado slice, she looked at the papers on her desk—fortunately not bloodstained—and then at the e-mails on her computer screen. Running her hand through her gray hair, she shook her head. Enough work for today, she thought. *I've even given blood!* There was nothing here that couldn't wait until tomorrow. Sorensen rolled her chair away from the desk, shed her lab coat, and hung it on its hook. She turned out the lights, locked the door, and walked briskly away from her UT office.

***

Woody Reeter's foot ached as if it had been crowbarred. He didn't know whether he could finish his rounds for the night. He had saved the best office for last, though. The janitor for the UT School of Biology limped down the hallway, shifting as much weight as he could onto his wheeled supply cart. His otherwise skinny right leg was red and swollen at the ankle from another gout attack.

The name "Professor Lillian Sorenson" was brushed in fine gold paint on the frosted glass of the varnished oak door. He unlocked it with his master key and was reassured to see the meteorite in its usual place on the professor's desk.

He and his wife had been drinking beer in their Austin backyard the night the fireball burned through the sky.

Reeter's wife was so alarmed that she began to sob.

He had held her and said, "It's okay, baby. It's okay. Shhh.... It's a sign. A good sign. From the Lord." The news of the next few weeks had strengthened Reeter's belief that the meteorite was a supernatural omen of better times to come.

He had learned that a mythical beast had been seen where the meteor touched the earth, and a young firefighter had been cured of cancer. To Reeter, this was proof that unknown forces were at work. For the past weeks when he cleaned Professor Sorensen's office, he had placed his hand on the meteorite and said a prayer.

He extended his hand toward the stone. But before he could touch it, Reeter noticed a dark red spot. He looked closer, touched the spot, and then fingernailed its edge.

Blood! It bleeds!

Charged with adrenaline, Reeter raced through the rest of his cleaning duties, the pain in his foot unnoticed. When he arrived home he gushed out the story to his incredulous wife. Then he phoned everyone he knew at his recently adopted place of worship: the Church of the God Particle.

10

ALEX WATCHED FROM a rocky perch halfway up the hillside as Flora stopped her car below him and filled her water jugs at the spring. She and her son had spent most of the afternoon at Charlie's, so they must have enjoyed themselves, he thought. Good for Charlie.

Alex's sweat-soaked Longhorn T-shirt clung to his back and chest. He was ten pounds lighter since the Trina's death a month earlier, and his hands were calloused from hours with the ax. His sandy locks stuck out over his ears from beneath his baseball cap.

He watched Flora's car recede down the driveway through the canyon. Live oaks and cedar elms overhung the grassy banks of the creek, shading rocks eroded round by ceaseless springwater. Scrubby persimmon, mesquite, and pungent juniper trees anchored the soil on the steep slopes. Limestone outcroppings the size of houses dominated the steep sides and offered dry purchase for prickly pear cacti.

Just before she entered the curve that would take her out of Alex's sight, Flora met a green car coming from the county blacktop. The two cars stopped, the drivers obviously talking. After a couple of minutes, the cars started moving again, and the green car soon stopped in front of Alex's house.

He recognized the gangly figure of Quizzy Shatterling as she rapped on the front door, her dark curls waving in the breeze. She had called him after the funeral to express her condolences and again a week later to see how he was holding up. Talking with her was effortless and left him feeling a little lighter.

Getting no answer at the door, Quizzy stepped off the porch and looked around. She bent over with her hands on her hips and explored the chunks of petrified wood along the edge of the driveway added over many years by Alex and his father. Quizzy picked up a fist-size piece, turned it over to examine all sides, and then tossed it up and down a few inches to know its weight. She spat on the stone and rubbed it with her finger to reveal hidden color. Even from far away Alex could see the tattooed sleeve of dark ink on her forearm as she reached down and set the rock precisely where she had found it. She looked up and down the driveway.

"She doesn't miss much, Jessie," he said to the English bull terrier at his side.

Quizzy walked with long strides to her car and reached for the door handle.

"Hello!" Alex yelled.

She straightened and gazed in the direction of the voice.

Alex waved full arcs with both arms. Quizzy waved back, and he started to descend the hill.

"I'll come up," Quizzy shouted. "What's the best way?"

"Walking!" he shouted back. "Walking is best." From afar he couldn't see if she was smiling. Regardless, he felt buoyed. He shouted again, pointing. "Around that big rock, then through those trees."

Quizzy picked her way up the rocky trail and its switchbacks. She made fair progress, taking advantage of her long legs. When she reached Alex she was breathing hard, and a spot of perspiration had soaked through her T-shirt below her neck.

Alex could now see the dark, swirling ink of her tattooed arm: a chameleon wearing wire-rimmed glasses balanced on leafy vines, holding a thick book in its lizard hand.

"Wow," Quizzy said, out of breath. "This is so nice up here. It's a strenuous walk, though."

"You get used to it."

She surveyed the landscape below her: the ranch house with its grassy backyard, the shed, Alex's painting studio, and the gravel driveway splitting west to Charlie's place and east to the county road. The meteorite repair was conspicuous, and the glistening spring with its rumored restorative powers shone in the sun.

"It's so green around here with all the cedar," she said. "Unlike my place."

"And where would that be?"

"I have a condo in one of the towers downtown."

Alex pondered a journalist's salary and the price of downtown real estate.

"A small condo," she added, as if she could read his mind. "In a way, though, it's green, if you're talking carbon footprint."

"Have a seat on that cedar stump," Alex said as he gestured to a fresh chain-saw cut. "Actually, it's ash juniper, but everyone calls it cedar. Don't ask me why." He eased himself onto a fallen trunk near his chain saw and ax. A dozen smaller trees lay felled nearby, sawdust piled around their stumps. He made a mental note to take more ibuprofen for his sore back when he returned to the house. "Charlie's daughter is babysitting my daughter over at her place. I saw you pass Flora on the way in."

"Yes! It was good to see her again. She says she's been feeling great."

"I know. I'm really happy for Charlie, too. They seem to be getting pretty friendly. *More* than friendly." Alex tipped his head toward the bull terrier. "This is Jessie." The dog sniffed Quizzy's outstretched hand.

"Hi, Jessie," she said, and scratched behind the dog's ears. She looked over the mangled cedar trees, then turned to Alex. "And how are you, Mr. Bunyan?"

"All right, considering...." He appreciated her humor. "I've been keeping busy with projects around this place. The more cedar I cut, the more water will drain into the creek. I cut so much I just leave an ax up here all the time under that rock ledge. Also, I sold several paintings since you were here ... before. They were all landscapes of the ranch. There's a lot of interest these days about this place."

Quizzy scooped up a handful of sawdust, squeezing a sappy pinch between her thumb and forefinger, inhaling its sharp aroma. "Mmm, that's strong. It smells like the inside of a cedar chest."

Her eyes glistened, and Alex sensed it was from something more than the cedar.

"Are you okay?" he asked.

"Yes," she said, recovered. "It's just that my father gave me a cedar chest just before he died." She let the sawdust trickle through her fingers.

"When was that?"

"A long time ago. I was a teenager. It's too long a story for here," she said with finality. "Alex, I came out to thank you for ... the night when the meteorite came down. I feel very privileged that you allowed me to stick around, as you said, on the worst night of your life."

Alex nodded. "You wrote a good article. Thanks for not sensationalizing a lot of painful details."

"Not a problem. You know there is more to this story, don't you? I'm going to do a much longer follow-up piece. This thing has taken on a life of its own with the so-called miracles. People believe your spring cures cancer, that you have a chupacabra as a pet—no offense, Jessie—and I just heard that the janitor at Professor Sorensen's building says he saw the meteorite bleeding one night. People are all

109

spun up about this. And not just in Austin. It's all over the Internet."

"Yeah, I know. Did you notice the 'no trespassing' sign when you turned in from the county road?"

"Yes, but I figured since you knew me it was okay."

"No, no, that's not what I meant. You're welcome here. I had to put up a sign to keep other people out. Every wandering sightseer and truth seeker wants to come out to this place and take a piece of it home with them. Hell, they sneak in from over the ridgetops. I ran one guy off who was taking a bubble bath in the spring with his girlfriend. They were having a lot of sudsy fun, if you get my drift. It took a whole day for the soap to drain."

"Can I quote you on that?"

"Yeah, I suppose. If it'll help keep people out of here. Say that I've got Cerberus, the hound from hell, living with my chupacabra. It loves the taste of human flesh. Sit, Cerberus, sit!"

Jessie squatted on her haunches.

Alex smiled. "No, maybe you'd better not print any of that last part. It'd just attract more nut jobs to this place. Print whatever you think will keep people away. Spin it with Texas property rights. A man's home is his castle, et cetera."

"I'll tell the truth about strangers not being welcome out here. As I said, this story has taken on a life of its own. The other angle I'm working on is the Church of the God Particle, led by Reverend Lucas Ruthlier."

"He sent me a letter."

Quizzy raised her eyebrows. "And?"

"He wants me to donate the meteorite to his church. Says it's holy or something like that."

"That's rich! May I see the letter?"

"I threw it away already."

Quizzy flashed him a disappointed look. "Do you think it might still be in your trash?"

Alex considered lying, just to see someone dig through his garbage. *I need to get out more*, he thought. "No, it's gone."

"Damn! What else did the good reverend say?"

"That's about it. He's sorry for my loss and to call him if I need consolation."

"So, are you going to call?"

"Not a chance. But I did write back to him."

"And?"

"Basically, I told him to screw off."

Quizzy chuckled. "Well, if you do happen to talk to him and feel like sharing, I'd be all ears. I haven't found out much about the guy yet. Ruthlier appeared in Austin in the early nineties, but until recently he's been secretive. He had been leading a small sect of devout followers, but the meteorite seems to have changed his nature. After it fell he placed classified ads for his church everywhere. He's even stapled flyers on street corners and telephone poles. Membership has swelled. He has a Web site, but there's nothing more informative than church hours, location, and a welcoming message to everyone. There is precious little about doctrine or philosophy. I've got more feelers out, though.

Something will turn up on him."

"Yeah, I Googled the bastard. His church is on South Lamar Boulevard," Alex said.

Quizzy added, "He and his son, Drago, are renovating the old Nations Home Hardware building in the Southside Shopping Center. There's a Pilates place on one side and a psychologist's office on the other."

"Mind, body, and spirit all in one trip," Alex said. "For the unbalanced individual who seeks total realignment."

"You make it sound like a tire shop," Quizzy said. "One thing's for sure, though—he's pulling in a lot of people these days. They filed a building permit to remodel the old office area upstairs into two apartments. Apparently, they'll both live there."

"Nearer my God to thee," Alex said.

They relaxed in the shade, enjoying the view of the land and the cloudless sky above the canyon. Below, a stand of live oaks shaded the ranch house. Cut limestone blocks on the bottom half of the house supported clapboard, painted white. The extended overhang of the eaves blocked any sun that made it through the oaks.

"When a hard rain hits that galvanized steel roof it sounds like hail," he said. "Actual hail sounds like a family of raccoons dropped from the trees to bang rocks on the metal." Up the driveway, a dust devil danced across the fence onto Charlie's land.

"What's that cable for?" Quizzy asked.

"Cheap thrills. It's a zip line. Charlie and I put it up."

"It looks terrifying."

"It's not for the meek. I haven't been on it for a while. I had a bad day the last time I rode it. It was the day of the fireball. Jeez, now even *I'm* referring to the damn thing as the fireball. It's gotten way too famous," Alex said, frowning. "Maybe it will make me some money when I get it back from Professor Sorensen. She says she's about finished with it. What a sick consolation prize."

"So, you're going to sell it?"

"Hell, yes. I don't want it around here, and I need the money. I suppose I'll put it on eBay."

"You could always donate it to your favorite religious organization."

"That ain't happenin.'"

"You know, for me to do a proper story about the fireball and Ruthlier's church, I need to go to one of their services. There's one every Sunday." She let the moment linger but got no response. "Care to go with me?"

"That ain't happenin', either. I heard enough of that gasbag preacher the night he was out here."

"Let me know if you change your mind."

"I'll be sure to do that." He noticed Quizzy studying the cable stretched across the canyon. "So are you interested in a ride on the zip line?"

"The chances of me riding that zip line are about the same as you going to the Church of the God Particle. I hate heights."

Alex tried to describe the excitement of riding the line, but when he realized Quizzy wasn't interested he changed the subject. "What's that chameleon on your arm reading?"

"Whatever is your favorite book."

"I'd have to give that some thought. These days it would be something with a happy ending."

"Then it probably wouldn't be anything I would write," she said. "At least not now. Maybe someday." She seemed to force a smile. "I've got a ton of work to do. I just wanted to come out and say hello and to let you know I'm doing a follow-up story on Lucas Ruthlier."

"I'm glad you drove out. I'll go back to the house with you."

They descended the crooked path to the floor of the canyon and walked to the house.

"Would you like to come in for a glass of lemonade?" Alex asked.

"Sure, that sounds great."

The contrast from the heat outside refreshed them both. A lazy ceiling fan moved the air in the living room, evaporating the perspiration from the backs of their shirts. The window shades were open, and the room was awash in soft light. Seven's highchair stood near a corner of a large walnut dining table. Colorful baby toys rested on the tray.

"Are you working on a painting?" Quizzy asked as Alex came from the kitchen and handed her a glass of cold lemonade. "I'd love to see if you are—and you don't mind."

"Yeah, there's a new one in the room at the end of the hallway," Alex said. "I'm hanging it there for a few weeks until it cools off in my mind. Until then I can't tell if I'm really done with it. C'mon, I'll show you."

They entered the room. The three-foot-wide painting rested on a simple homemade easel of two-by-fours leaning against a wall. Two golf tees inserted into rows of drilled holes supported the painting. The colors were subtle, but the vivid contrasts of light and shadows created tension within the piece. The perspective of the drawing converged at the horizon.

"What do you think?" Alex said.

"It looks very good to me," Quizzy replied. "The colors are deceptive. Individually, none of them jumps out at you, but the combination is quite striking."

"Thanks. You have a good eye. I should have guessed, based on the quality of that tattoo on your arm." They studied the painting for a few more seconds until Alex asked, "How did you come by the name 'Quizzy?'"

"My given name is Elizabeth," she said and then smiled, "but my parents called me Lizzy at first. They said I had an insatiable curiosity—reaching and crawling for everything in sight. So, inquisitive Lizzy became Quizzy."

"And now you quiz people for a living."

She laughed. "I surely do." She looked away from the painting to Alex. "You have a nice home here. Comfortable and tidy—but not too tidy."

"My family has lived at this place for a very long time. There are still pecan trees the original Colvins planted. As a matter of fact, I have pecans out the wazoo. Would you like to take a bag home with you?"

"I love pecans."

"I store them in the shed. C'mon." On the way out the

back door Alex picked up a hammer. They walked through the backyard under the oaks, kicking aside golf balls. "I practice my chipping here," he said.

"Are you any good?"

"No, that's why I practice."

A rusty hasp and padlock secured the newly repaired door on the metal shed. Alex raised the hammer.

"What are you doing?" Quizzy asked.

"I locked the key inside. I'm going to break this padlock."

"Wait a second. Maybe I can save you a lock."

Quizzy walked to her car, opened the trunk, and returned with a leather manicure case. She unzipped it. Instead of fingernail clippers, scissors, and filing tools, there were a half dozen steel picks, some straight, some curved, and some with a flare or hook on the ends. She removed one of the tools and inserted it into the bottom of the padlock, manipulating it until the shackle released with a click.

"Unbelievable! Where did you learn to do that?"

"My uncle was a locksmith. He showed me and my brothers how to get into everything when we were kids. It's a talent that comes in handy now and then."

"I know that's true. I could've used a lock-picker not too long ago. I got the job done, but it wasn't pretty."

"Did you hammer your way in?"

"It was a little more than a hammer."

"Tell me!"

"Maybe some other time. We could trade stories." Alex pushed his forefinger through Quizzy's curls and touched the top of her head. "I think you have one buried in there."

She looked at him with narrowed eyes. "We'll see...." She smiled, but Alex sensed reservation as he handed her a paper bag of pecans.

11

BOBBY WARE WAS on his way up after working five years in the big-window entrance booths that controlled street access into the main campus of the University of Texas. His reward for good attendance was a new job as campus watchman on the night shift. The hours were upside down, but the work was vastly more interesting. And now he was mobile! No longer confined to the glass booth, he roamed the sidewalks and footpaths in his blue uniform. He rousted passed-out frat boys and escorted solo women to parking garages. He shared his considerable knowledge of the surrounding geography with visiting parents, vendors, and service providers who gravitated to the huge campus.

Ware had an eye for trouble. Every few months he'd spot a suspicious car whose occupants didn't fit the common visitor profile, and he'd call in the license plate to the campus police.

On this warm evening katydids buzzed in the trees as Ware patrolled behind the biology building. Not one person in a hundred would have noticed the flicker of light across Professor Sorensen's fourth-floor window, but it alerted the ever-vigilant Ware. He waited and watched below the window for two minutes more, but the office remained dark.

Probably nothing, but best to check it out.

The protocol for investigating a suspicious incident was to call the campus police. But this was only a routine check. No need to bother them yet.

Ware entered the building and ascended the stairs to the fourth floor, avoiding the noisy elevator. He walked down the hall to the closed door of Professor Sorensen's lab, thankful for his rubber-soled shoes. He tried the door, but it was locked. A good sign. With his master key he opened the door just enough to let himself in. His eyes adjusted to the dim light from the street coming through the windows.

Everything was in order here, he thought.

He advanced between the tables of the lab to Sorensen's office door. Like the door from the hallway, it too was locked. Another good sign. He looked through the frosted glass for movement in the dark office inside.

Relaxing, Ware unlocked the door, stepped in, and flipped on the light switch. A quick scan revealed nothing, so he craned his neck to look in the only place he couldn't see: behind the door.

Ware recoiled, and then screamed as a hand shot toward his face and wrapped itself around the back of his neck. He thrashed, but the hand held him close. A wiry man exploded from his crouch behind the door and drove his knee into Ware's jaw. He tried to jerk back, but the assailant still gripped his neck, holding their faces inches apart.

The attacker grinned as Ware tried to focus, but all he could see was a knife buried in the man's neck. A tattoo! His vision locked onto the tattooed knife. The actual knife in the man's hand was only an arcing blur as it swung into Ware's chest.

12

"TWENTY-ONE YEARS. That's how long I've been at that desk." Professor Sorensen sat with her chin in her hands. "I don't know whether I'll be able to work in this office again," she said to Captain Steiner. She motioned to the double-sided pecan desk. The leg nearest to her was spattered with blood. A CSI technician was dusting for fingerprints, and another bustled around the room, dropping grisly evidence items into small paper bags and labeling them.

Sorensen was struck by the similarity of the way both she and the investigators worked: keep the samples uncontaminated; document everything. A third technician snapped pictures from odd angles: standing on a chair, then from tangential angles to the floor. He crouched on his elbows like a dog ready to play, but this wasn't any game. Sorensen was grateful they had finally taken the unfortunate victim's body away.

"And you say that both doors were open?" Captain

Steiner asked. "The one to the hallway and also the one into your office?"

"Yes. I was alarmed when I came down the hall. I could see the lab door was open. I thought we had been vandalized, although I couldn't imagine who would want to come all the way up here just for that. Then I thought about theft. There's quite a bit of valuable equipment in the lab, although it's not the kind of stuff you'd find in your local pawnshop."

"And your office door?" asked Steiner. "Was it wide-open or just a little bit open, or what?"

She looked at the investigator with a wrinkled nose of distaste for the whole proceeding.

"I know this seems trivial, but I need every detail."

"It was wide-open. As soon as I saw my open office door from the lab I thought about the meteorite. It was the only thing of value in here. That and some research on my computer about a bioluminescent fungus project I'm working on. It could have considerable commercial value someday as a substitute for electrical lighting."

Steiner said to the fingerprinting technician, "Jerry, be sure to dust this computer thoroughly. Also get one of the IT boys to find out the last time it was booted up. Be sure to dust the surveillance camera in the stairwell, too. The lens has been painted over."

Sorensen continued. "Fortunately, I had taken the meteorite home when I left work yesterday. I was going to give it back to Alex Colvin today."

She slumped in the chair and in a distressed voice said,

"Oh, God, what if I hadn't taken the meteorite? What if this ... this *animal* was after *it*? He could have just stolen it and left. And that poor night watchman wouldn't have had to die."

"You're not to blame, Professor. Even if the meteorite had been here—assuming that's what the murderer was after—it's just as likely the outcome would have been the same."

Sorensen wasn't comforted.

"Where is the meteorite now?" asked Steiner.

"It's in the trunk of my car. I was going to drive out to the Twisted Tree Ranch and return it today. The physics people and I are finished with our preliminary analysis, although we'll do further investigation on the samples we kept. It's a unique object and it fell at an unusually steep angle. God only knows why. That's a figure of speech, Captain. We are scientists, not theologians."

Despite Professor Sorensen's efforts at objectivity, the watchman's bloody murder in her office profoundly changed her perception of the meteorite. *It's not a religious object, just a rock from space*, she thought. But a crazy church had proclaimed it to be holy. An innocuous natural creation untouched for billions of years by human hands was now a religious artifact. Sorensen felt a pinch of wry amusement, but guilt settled into her stomach. Then came the fear. She could be in danger, too. That harmless space rock had become deadly, now that it had come into contact with man.

***

When something isn't within your grasp, extend your reach. Captain Gregory Steiner had lived by that guiding philosophy for years. He may not have uncovered anything at Sorensen's office that would identify the night watchman's killer, but Steiner knew he had to tighten the screws on potential suspects. People under pressure made mistakes.

He opened the computer application he was using to record the events of the murder investigation. The off-the-shelf project-management software was perfect for tracking his progress. Murder investigations, after all, were just projects with a most unpleasant type of data, he had reasoned when he adopted the application.

The gray machine sitting on his desk contained the stairwell surveillance video from the UT biology building on the night Bobby Ware was murdered. Steiner clicked the play button and forwarded the video until he saw movement and then played the tape at normal speed. A large pink square with legs ascended the stairs. The legged square approached the camera until it overwhelmed its entire field of vision. Circles of black swirled around the screen until the entire camera lens had been spray-painted.

Someone had cut in half a standard sheet of pink Styrofoam insulation and carried it up the stairs in front of him to block the camera. It had been found in the Dumpster outside the building. Steiner penetrated the Styrofoam square with his imagination and saw an amorphous face staring back, mocking him. It was obvious that once the camera had been disabled, the murderer entered the biology lab, where he was later surprised by the curious and unfortunate night watchman.

He ran the tape again and studied the legs protruding below the Styrofoam square. The murderer was an average-size person—almost certainly a man, to be able to overpower the night watchman. The intruder wore dark close-fitting pants over black square-toed boots. Like what a motorcycle rider might wear, Steiner speculated. He entered his observations into the software program.

13

A T ELEVEN IN the morning the air conditioner kicked on, even though Alex had bumped up the thermostat to seventy-eight. His appreciation grew every summer for the sprawling live oaks that shaded the metal roof of the ranch house. He thought about the new houses on the land he had sold for the subdivision. There were fewer trees over there—too few to shade every house. He had snagged a premium price for the lots with at least one large tree. Alex wondered how the sun-baked newcomers could afford to run their air conditioners twenty-four/seven. It would be another three months until October and a break from the relentless heat.

He thought about his Colvin ancestors in the era before air-conditioning, living in their "dog run" houses. Those old houses had been constructed in two sections connected only at the roof, allowing the breeze, family pets, and even farm animals to pass through the middle.

The telephone ringing interrupted his daydream.

"Hello."

"Is this Alex? Alex Colvin?"

Alex didn't recognize the voice.

"Yes, it is."

"Alex, my name is Billy Swillers. How you doin' today?"

"I'm fine."

"Alex, I own and run a marketing company. I have an idea that might make us both a little money. I'd like to run it by you. Is there a time we could get together and discuss this idea of mine?"

"Depends. What's on your mind?"

"Well, it has to do with the water comin' out of that spring on your land. I read all about it in that story in the *Austin Chronicle*. I think a lot of people would buy that water if they had the chance."

Alex frowned. *Huckster*, he thought. "What did you say your name was again?"

"Billy. Billy Swillers."

"Yeah, Billy. I don't want people coming out to my place to buy anything."

"Oh, no, it's nothing like that. I got a little ranch, myself. I wouldn't want people traipsin' around my place, neither. No one would be bothering you at your place. I'm talking about bottled water. I know some people that own a bottling plant in Austin. I'd like to tell you all about it. Whaduya say about gettin' together, and I can give you the lowdown?"

Alex furrowed his brow. Most hucksters weren't ranchers, assuming the guy wasn't lying about that. "Just send me something I can look over. If I'm interested, I'll get back to you."

"Well, the thing is, Alex, there're some confidential details that I'd just as soon not send by mail or e-mail. Also, when I said this could make us a little money, I probably should have said 'a lot of money.' Whaduya say we get together and I'll tell you all about it."

Cutting cedar trees in the summer sun had turned into hot, dreary labor. Alex was ready for something new to occupy him, when he wasn't caring for Seven or painting. And he needed the money. Payments on the pickup, maintenance around the ranch, and even the reduced taxes on a wildlife refuge stretched his budget. And Seven—didn't she deserve the best? With Trina gone, Alex had dredged up his old plan to sell off a chunk of land. Swillers's lure of money had piqued his interest. It might be worth listening....

"All right. I suppose that would be okay."

"That's super, Alex. What's your schedule like? Are you free today anytime? I'd like to buy you lunch or dinner."

"I'm here with my daughter today. Maybe next week."

"You know, right now I'm close to Green Mesquite barbecue. Have you ever had their sliced brisket?"

"Can't say I have."

"It's to die for! They got a secret recipe. The owner is a buddy of mine, and he won't even tell me. Whaduya say I pick up some brisket, potato salad, and cole slaw and bring it out to your place for you and your girl? I kinda need to see the place if we decide to move on this plan, 'cause we'd need to figure out a way to get your springwater to the bottling plant. How's that sound to you, Alex?"

Alex had eaten only a day-old doughnut for breakfast. The thought of a heaping plate of barbecue enticed him. "All right, I suppose that would be okay, Billy. Bring some extra pickles, though."

"Good deal. I'll be out there in about an hour."

"Do you need directions?"

"No, I know where your place is. It's become pretty well-known lately."

***

Wealth had spewed into Billy Swillers's grandparents' lives when oil was discovered on their west Texas ranch in the thirties. The second round came to Billy and his brother in the nineties, when gas was discovered in the played-out oil fields.

Swillers never had less than a half dozen deals working at any given time. Most of them revolved around oil and gas or real estate, but he had flipped vacation condos, a chain of bowling alleys, shrimp boats, road construction equipment, hunting dogs, and hundreds of vehicles.

Every quarter, Swillers received a high-six-figure royalty check from the gas wells on his property, enabling him to funnel cash into his other operations. Most of them didn't make money, but every so often a deal came through that covered the expenses of the rest. He wasn't formally educated but had a comptroller's understanding of business finance and microeconomics. He had just sold his latest endeavor for a modest profit: a breeding operation of greyhounds and Dobermans. Sheep and goat farmers wanted a dog that was fast enough to run down a coyote and tough enough to kill it. He called them Doberhounds.

He parked his black Infiniti sedan behind Alex's pickup and rang the doorbell. Swillers was thin below the waist and thick above. An Italian leather belt held up his blue jeans, but the seat of his pants still hung loose. His gray dress shirt, with sleeves rolled to the elbows, was a tight fit, the result of endless business meetings at fine and not-so-fine restaurants. Black Skechers canvas shoes with double-tied laces revealed that Swillers anticipated walking the ranch. He needed to understand the logistics of capturing and transporting enough springwater to Austin to make his deal viable.

Alex answered the door in khaki shorts, a pocket T-shirt, and flip-flops. Swillers held a bulging brown bag of barbecue brisket in his left hand. He extended his right to Alex. A tough-looking dog stood at Alex's side, assessing the stranger and eyeing the bag.

"Set that on the table over there," Alex said. The aroma was heavenly, and they sat down to eat.

"It's too bad your girl isn't old enough to enjoy this barbecue," Swillers said as Alex offered a spoonful of mashed peas to Seven, who was sitting in her highchair. "She does seem partial to the potato salad, though. Here's a picture of *my* girl." Swillers held out his iPhone to Alex, displaying a photograph of a pretty eighteen-year-old.

"She's enrolled in a two-year program at Austin Community College for computer network security. She's a whiz at computers."

When they had finished eating, Alex crumpled the barbecue wrapping and tossed it in the trash, except for a wad he set on Seven's tray. She began to bat it around.

Swillers continued. "That sure is an unusual-looking dog. English bull terrier? I've never seen a snout curved forward like that, 'cept in pictures. What's her name? You think she'd like a bite of this brisket?"

"It's Jessie, and she'd eat the whole bag if you let her."

Jessie jumped to her feet and covered the distance to the table with a few muscular strides as Swillers offered the meat.

Snatching his hand back, he returned to business. He explained in detail his concept of filling a tank truck a few times a week from the spring, hauling the water to the bottling plant in Austin, and distributing it via the plant's regular outlets. According to Swillers, grocery and convenience stores across Texas would soon be selling the product, and if it was successful they would ramp up to go nationwide.

"I'm thinking about calling the product Divinity Springwater," he said. "I'd like to call it Miracle Water, but the FTC probably wouldn't go for that. We have to be careful about what we claim. And now for the best part—the money.

"The going rate for bottled water is around four dollars

per case. I think we can get fifty percent more than that, because our product is perceived to have special qualities—even though we don't make any claims about that. So, our product retails for six dollars per case, we wholesale it for five, and our cost should come in around three dollars. We clear two dollars per case. The bottlers bear most of the costs, so they get the biggest cut. The way I figure it, they need fifty percent of the profit to cover their end of the deal, and you and I would split the other fifty percent."

Seven batted the crumpled paper off her tray to the floor. Alex picked it up and set it back in front of the girl, who grinned at him.

"Go on," Alex said. "What's the bottom line here? How much do you expect to sell?"

"My friends at the bottling plant have been in the business a long time, and know the market like Green Mesquite knows barbecue," Swillers said. "They're thinking that after they get things put into production, there'll be enough demand for a half million cases in the first year. That's just in Texas."

Alex calculated the numbers aloud. "So, if I get twenty-five percent of a two-dollar profit, that's fifty cents per case. Take that times a half million cases and I'm looking at two hundred and fifty thousand per year."

He tried to swallow.

"Yep, you figured right. That's if everything works out like we think. The figures are preliminary, but that's what we ballparked it at."

Alex raised his eyebrows, and Swillers sensed his host's excitement.

"There's one problem," Alex said. "My spring doesn't produce enough water. It flows at a gallon every four seconds—on a good day." He punched in numbers on his cell phone's calculator. Then he read the label on the bottled water with which he had just washed down his brisket, and entered more numbers into the calculator.

"This is a half-liter bottle, so a case of twenty-four bottles is a little more than three gallons," Alex stated. "A half million cases would be over four thousand gallons per day. And that's just for the first year. Your deal, Billy, would cut my spring's output too much in the summer. And that's six months long around here. There're several places downstream that rely on that water to replenish their wells. People have been killed in this part of the world for screwing with someone else's water."

"Believe me, I know that from havin' my own ranch. Here's the most beautiful part of this deal, Alex. We won't be sellin' one hundred percent Colvin springwater. We'll be sellin' water *infused* with Colvin springwater. That's what it'll say on the label. Infused. It's a wonderful word, isn't it? The bottlers in Austin use their regular source of water, and then just add a little of your water into every bottle. You set the limit on how much we can take from your spring, and we'll adjust the infused amount proportionally."

As Alex mulled over the proposition, Swillers said, "Whaduya say we take a walk over to your spring, and you can show me what everyone's so excited about? Can your daughter come along in that fancy stroller?" He indicated the covered contraption in a corner of the living room with a bicycle wheel in front and two in the rear.

"Yeah, she loves to be wheeled around." Then to Seven, he said, "Don't you, sweetie?" The girl laughed and shook her arms.

Alex pushed Seven, and Swillers ambled alongside. Jessie lingered to sniff around the black Infiniti. The midafternoon temperature was creeping into the upper nineties, and they zigzagged their way to the spring, taking advantage of sparse shade wherever it appeared.

"I hear you got a chupacabra living out here," Swillers said. "A trophy like that would be worth a lot of money."

"It's just a coyote with bad hair," Alex said.

"Maybe you shouldn't tell anybody. Let people think what they want. It'd be good for business. I shot a coyote on my place last year. Here's a picture of him."

Swillers punched up a picture on his iPhone of himself kneeling with a rifle and the dead animal's head on his thigh. He held it out for Alex to see.

"You got any quail out here? There's no bird meat better than quail. 'Cept maybe pheasant. My wife's a great cook. You should come out to my ranch sometime and go quail hunting. She could cook them up for us with all the fixin's."

"Yeah, there's quail around here."

"Maybe we could go huntin' sometime. I got a couple of good dogs I could bring up from my place," Billy said.

"The Twisted Tree Ranch is a wildlife refuge. No hunting allowed."

"That's too bad."

When they reached the red-handled spigot, Alex opened it for Jessie, and she lapped the flow midair. When she finished, Swillers cupped his hand, held it in the stream, and bent over to drink.

"That sure has a good taste. I'm feelin' a little better already." He winked at Alex.

They settled into the shade of a small live oak near the clear pool. The cool water filled the eroded depression in the bedrock beneath the opening in the hillside from where it gurgled forth. Swillers leaned against the tree.

Sheltered from the sun, they enjoyed the breeze as Swillers explained to Alex that all he would need to do was allow a small tank truck to pump water out of the pool five days a week. He wouldn't even need to be around when the truck was loading. Once the drivers learned the procedure it would become routine. Alex's involvement would be negligible, except to cash a monthly royalty check for the use of his springwater.

"Send me a contract to look over," Alex said. "I'll run it by my lawyer and think about everything. Just make sure I'm off the hook in case someone gets a bad bottle of water, or the truck runs over somebody, or the bottling company goes belly-up owing money. Otherwise, I don't see any showstoppers from where I sit."

"We'll structure the contract like a mineral rights deal. But instead of extracting oil, we'll be taking water. You and little Seven could end up with a fair amount of extra spending money over this venture."

Billy Swillers could barely contain his excitement at Colvin's agreement. The Austin bottlers already had the production, packaging, sales, and distribution outlets in place from their existing lines of bottled water, so it would take only a few weeks from signing the contract to production.

The "product," as Swillers called it, would resonate with a junk-food-consuming public looking for a no-effort counterweight to their bad habits. Eat yourself silly and chase it with a bottle of Divine Springwater. "That's a recipe for better health," he said.

Swillers had already planned the packaging: the label on each bottle would show a stylized tree with a twisted trunk and a perfect canopy, above it, a tiny dark object with a lavender tail streaking through an azure sky.

1984

THE BIRTH OF Drago Illya Ruthlier depressed his mother as much as it cheered his father. The boy cried more and slept less than most newborns. By his first birthday it was clear that he was as hyperactive as the next-door neighbor's ferret. Lucas and his son visited the park across the street whenever the days were long enough and the weather fair enough. The quaint park meandered through the block along a creek with muddy banks. Downstream it flowed into the Dambovita River, which ran through the heart of Bucharest. Upstream, the creek wound its way back to what appeared to be its point of origin about ten miles east of the central city. An acrid odor sometimes irritated the sinuses of the residents, and the creek reflected a silvery metallic sheen when the sun was overhead. The excitable boy inevitably ended up caked with dirt or mud whenever he played near the creek.

By age two, Drago was assembling jigsaw puzzles designed for children twice his age. At age four he was multiplying numbers. But he also worried Ruthlier. He was unpredictable, and other children avoided him, unsure when the boy would turn hostile and lash out at anyone nearby. His intelligence shone when he focused on a task, but his concentration easily drifted.

On Sundays Ruthlier cemented his bond with little Drago by taking him on reflective walks through the city's cemeteries. Almost the entire population of Bucharest was Romanian Orthodox, and they adorned their loved ones' graves with finely crafted biblical icons. When he held them close, that warm feeling he discovered when he stole the plastic Barney enveloped him. The idyllic cemeteries offered such a selection from which to pilfer!

Irena cared little for the boy. On an autumn evening after a long day at the lab, it was obvious to Ruthlier that his wife, sitting at the kitchen table across from him, was miserable. Irena swirled the ice cubes around the inside of her empty tumbler as Drago watched from the floor.

"Sometimes I wonder if I'm going to be stuck in this goddamned country forever," she said.

She's drunk, thought Ruthlier. "You're the one who was so gung-ho to come to Romania. You and Miruna."

"It's worse than I expected. Christ, even birth control is illegal." She shot a glance at Drago. "I wasn't supposed to get pregnant. Damn black-market pills."

"You were taking the pill? You never told me that! Nothing about you makes sense anymore. You're a mess."

"Fuck you!" Irena shrieked, and then slung ice cubes at her

husband. "There's a lot you don't know. You are so stupid!"

Ruthlier blinked with incredulity. Never before in his life had he been called stupid.

"You think I wanted to come over here? God, no!" Irena's hands were trembling. "I detested this place even before we arrived."

Ruthlier stared at his wife with a puzzled expression.

"Don't look at me like that. You're clueless, aren't you? Do you remember when I first met you in that coffee shop in Chicago and asked about the papers on your table?" Irena said. "I guessed they were about physics."

Ruthlier nodded.

"I didn't guess. I knew. In fact, I knew you had a table full of physics papers before I walked through the door."

"I don't understand."

"That's because you're stupid."

Ruthlier scowled.

"I told you that my parents owned a restaurant named Davidoff's in New York. That they emigrated from Hungary in 1956, when the Soviet Union sent tanks to Budapest to stamp out the revolution. That is true—sort of. We didn't exactly flee Hungary, though. The restaurant we left in Budapest was very successful. Our best customers were the Soviet apparatchiks who frequented every day. We treated them very well, and they returned the favor. Did you know that the most loyal communists are the wealthiest ones?"

"What's your point?" Ruthlier said. "Beside the fact that your parents would take anybody's money. You were just a little girl."

"As I said, you are too stupid to figure this out. Stupid and blind. What a pathetic combination. Let me spell it out for you." Irena took a hefty swallow from her glass. "When the tanks rolled into Budapest in '56, a wave of partisans fled for their lives, mostly to New York. The KGB asked my parents if we would slip into that wave. They supplied all the cash, and then some, for us to start our new restaurant in New York. There were many others like us who worked for the homeland under the cover of the immigrant wave. It was a perfect opportunity to overwhelm a fledgling FBI. From our new restaurant in New York City my parents gathered information on events and people."

"Your parents were spies?"

"Not just my parents. I am their protégé."

Stunned, Ruthlier sat silently as images from his marriage flooded over him. Illogical events came into focus. Motivations became clear; false loyalties exposed. His pursuit of the God particle and its potential to manipulate gravity had blinded him. His marriage hadn't just rotted away—it was a sham from the beginning.

A hot nausea churned his insides. He had sacrificed everything—citizenship, family, love. He had been duped into defection and then exploited. His career was managed by the same people who had planned his marriage, and now it was obvious that it amounted to professional servitude. Coupled with the tragedy of the zero-gravity experiment, the revelation pushed Ruthlier to the verge of exploding like the Soviet rocket.

He stared at his wife. *She's enjoying this.*

"And there is nothing you can do," she said. "Someday, hopefully soon, I will get a new identity and another assignment in the West. If I am revealed, the Securitate will come for you, and Drago will go to the orphanage."

"If you leave, Drago and I will find our way out of here. I'll expose you!" He slammed his fist onto the table. For the first time in his life he had been humiliated. He was a fool.

Irena laughed. "You are property of the state—a state that forbids individuals to own property! Don't you think that is delicious? Romania will never let you go! Even if you managed to contact someone who cared in the West, what would you tell them? That as Fred Zimmerman you faked your own death and defected to aid the communists, and now you wish to re-defect? They would throw you in prison as soon as your feet touched capitalist soil. If you presented yourself as Lucas Ruthlier, the Romanian son of American parents, the United States would demand that Romania grant you asylum. But Romania wouldn't hesitate to reveal your true identity and your defection. Any way you go about it, it's prison if you return to the West. And by the way, dear husband, if you ever tell anybody about my real occupation, I'll have your throat cut."

Drago began screaming on the floor.

It was a Friday in February when Irena disappeared from her husband's and three-year-old Drago's lives. The sky was gray, and the park was slushy from melting snow. Ending another routine week, Ruthlier picked up his son from his apartment building's day-care center, which to him was the most worthwhile function of communism.

141

As soon as they entered their apartment Drago began to cry. It looked as if a thief had come through, picking random items off shelves and tables. In the bedroom, Irena's clothes and other personal belongings were gone. In their place were stark, bare spaces of closets and shelves, empty as the void he could see in the boy.

Drago cried all night as his father reassured him that they would be okay, and that *he* would never leave. The next day Drago killed the neighbor's ferret with a rock when it came to sniff him.

Four years after Irena had abandoned them, Lucas Ruthlier and his son's escape from Romania in 1989 was surprisingly easy. It was less a result of guile and planning than it was historical good fortune.

The Soviet Union fell apart.

The government of Romania disintegrated into anarchy as the addictive needle of cash and guns was yanked. After decades of repression and poverty, angry Romanians poured into the streets. The twenty-five-year reign of President Nicolae Ceausescu and his wife, Elena, was overthrown. Captured by revolutionaries, the president and first lady were given a two-hour trial. They were dragged to his palace wall and shot, she screaming obscenities at her executioners until they pulled the silencing triggers. The couple fell before the cameraman could load his film.

Cronies and high officials of the former government and Securitate services were disposed of with equal fervor. Tutors of the privileged—Ruthlier's cover—could be regarded as complicit, so he stuffed a few essentials into two suitcases. There was no time to dispose of the heavy trunk in the storage compartment beneath the stairs. Aside from saving the plastic dog, once again he would have to begin anew on assembling another prized collection.

By far the most valuable possession to leave Bucharest with Ruthlier was the doped lavender crystal, set into an unassuming silver ring on his right hand. "Tourmaline," he said to anyone who inquired about the stone.

In the confusion of the transition, Lucas Ruthlier and his son took a train west to Hungary. Ruthlier persuaded a sympathetic border official who also had a young son to let them pass. "I am a simple mathematics tutor unfortunate enough to have taught the children of very high government officials," Ruthlier pleaded. "If I am caught it will be very bad for me. The boy, who has already lost his mother, would go to a state orphanage. Please help me and my boy, sir."

The border official, aware of the heartbreaking stories that were surfacing about Romanian state orphanages, flipped through Ruthlier's documents. He wrote a thirty-day visa, enough time for Ruthlier to take another train to Budapest, make an appointment at the American embassy, and retell the same story. With his documented fake American heritage, perfect English, and mathematical teaching skills to support his family, Lucas Ruthlier was soon granted asylum in the United States. The Securitate had been dissolved along with the rest of the Romanian government. No one was left who knew or cared about either Lucas

Ruthlier or Fred Zimmerman.

Ten years earlier, as Fred Zimmerman, Lucas Ruthlier had driven through Texas on the way to the rendezvous of his Chevrolet Impala with Coatee Creek. His impending defection—even if he didn't call it that—to the communist cause hadn't suppressed his enjoyment of the rolling hills, with their gnarly live oaks and creeks cut deep into limestone cliffs. He remembered a toughness to the land, but there was also a tenderness that revealed itself in the friendliness of its people. Good God, they even waved to one another as they passed on the highway!

The continuation of his physics career back in America was too risky. Lucas Ruthlier appeared physically far different from Fred Zimmerman—he was thirty pounds heavier, and a significant portion of that weight had accumulated in his neck and head. His long, wavy silver hair extended backward and puffed out like the hood of a cobra. It was as if he had a perpetual blow-dryer pointed in his face, making his head look even larger. But the penalties were too severe to chance his recirculating in the rarified atmosphere of the theoretical physics community. Discovery of his true identity would mean a very long prison term.

He shelved his dream of proving the existence of God within the fundamental particles of nature. Nevertheless, the effect of that dream could still be achieved. All that mattered to Ruthlier was that the subtleties of gravitational fields could be manipulated. He cared little whether or not people comprehended the nuances of subatomic particle physics. After all, one didn't have to understand the structure of the foot in order to walk. He had completed enough experimentation in Romania to rebuild the crystal technology in Texas. The culmination of his work would be to bring down a target object outside of the Earth's gravity. All he needed was money and time, and the personal computing revolution that was sweeping the country. Integrated with the expanding field of brain research from the medical community, his dream lived.

The ex-physicist was sure that the first person to achieve telekinetic resonance with matter would be hailed as a savior. *I will lead with the wisdom of Solomon,* he thought. *Now is the time to prepare the way.* While he refined his technology, Ruthlier would devote himself to diminishing skepticism for the seemingly impossible events to come. By the time his doped-crystal experiments came to fruition, people would already know his name. He would convince people of the God particle's existence by evangelizing instead of showing them a display of shattered subatomic particle paths on a computer monitor.

Austin, Texas would be fertile ground for his seed of new thought. In a city whose motto was "Keep Austin Weird," another offbeat voice advocating an eclectic message wouldn't arouse resentment or suspicion; to the contrary—it could aid in his acceptance. Ruthlier bought a small 1930s pier-and-beam house, and he blended into a South Austin neighborhood of artists, musicians, and working-class parents. He taught math at Austin Community College and tutored high school students in the evenings.

For Lucas Ruthlier to be ordained as a minister was a simple matter of filing the required paperwork. *God bless America!* he thought, and the Church of the God Particle was born.

He posted flyers around the UT campus and in Laundromats and grocery stores. By the end of the year he had attracted a dozen people to his unpolished sermons in a South Austin mini-mall suite. Donations were modest at first. On Sundays after church, he and young Drago explored places in the city they hadn't yet visited.

Sometimes those were cemeteries.

When seven-year-old Drago received his first physical examination in the West, the neurologist informed Ruthlier that the boy had somehow absorbed high levels of heavy metals and other chemicals into his nervous system. A few years later, when Romania's news reporters could write such a story and live to write again, the source of the poison would be revealed: a leaky aluminum smelter near Bucharest that fed the creek in the Ruthliers' Romanian backyard.

Drago had been affected in a way that spiked his emotions at minor provocations and weakened his concentration on routine tasks. His physical abilities were superb. On the playground, Drago was the fastest boy in his class. He learned to play Ping-Pong in the common room of the school, and his rattlesnake-quick reflexes elevated him to the level of much older children. But he struggled to contain his temper. Once, when he lost a game to a sixth grader, he threw the paddle at him so hard it stuck head-high in the Sheetrock.

Drago's intellectual aptitude suffered, but the boy was still sharp enough to advance through school. His biggest challenge was to suppress his incendiary temper so he didn't explode over trivial incidents. His schoolmates stopped making fun of his accent after he threatened to cut off a tormentor's head with a knife he stole from the school cafeteria.

"I'll shinny up the flagpole in front of the school and mount your head at the top for everyone to laugh at," he had told the boy. "They do it all the time where I come from." He was a loner with no close friends.

He was, however, devoted to his father.

For the next twenty years the Reverend Ruthlier preached his atomic gospel. He refined his sermons, burnished his oratory skills, and grew ever more passionate. Unlike in the lab environments of his previous life, he had the refreshing freedom to say anything he believed. It was *his* church. His flock grew, and his funding grew. Many of the parishioners held advanced degrees, although some of them couldn't sustain a nontechnical conversation. Other people just showed up one time to hear "that crazy preacher with his crazy ideas."

But when the Lavender Fireball fell on the Twisted Tree Ranch, the reverend manipulated the wave of publicity, and church attendance soared. The mini-mall suite couldn't hold them all—but a renovated Nations Home Hardware building would be perfect.

14

A SUMMER BREEZE swirled through the restaurant's courtyard, dropping leaves and twigs into calm corners. A jowly businessman in a dark suit at the next table struggled to spoon his chicken tortilla soup with one hand and immobilize his shifting hairpiece with the other. Alex contemplated whether the man's cockeyed toupee was more pretentious than the white, rippling tablecloths covering plastic lawn furniture. Charlie and Professor Sorensen sat on either side of Alex and were talking about a wagon wheel built into the nearby fence. Quizzy was retrieving text messages from her phone and punching in responses.

The courtyard extended under sprawling pecan trees that were once part of a commercial grove. Now only fox squirrels consumed its pecans, wary of the diners below, as if the people might reach up and snatch one of them by the tail as an entrée. The ambient sound of clicking, scratching claws on brittle tree bark drifted on the breeze and permeated the courtyard.

Climbing to a suitable dining perch after discovering a fallen pecan from the previous autumn, a plump squirrel fumbled the nut from its tiny paws. The pecan fell into the businessman's soup below, splashing a yellow spot on his tie. Alex suppressed a laugh and pondered the correlation between falling objects and human misery. Not calculable, he decided. Besides, the businessman was only perturbed by a falling object, not miserable. Misery would better describe himself when the Lavender Fireball fell. He thought about the night watchman's family, who had also been touched by death.

The businessman summoned the waitress with a wave. He demanded a new bowl of soup and then chastised her ineffective pest control. She walked to the kitchen, rolling her eyes. "Fat bastard," Alex overheard her mutter.

An hour earlier at the Frost Bank, Alex and Charlie had met Professor Sorensen, who had been followed by Captain Steiner. Steiner believed the night watchman had interrupted an attempt to steal the meteorite, and the murderer might try again. "That thing needs to be locked up until the person who did this is locked up," he had said.

The Ranger insisted that no one be left alone with the meteorite. The professor led Alex to her car and opened the trunk. The meteorite was swaddled in plastic bubble wrap, and Alex unceremoniously lifted it out as if it were an evil baby. Charlie produced a 20mm army surplus ammunition box, and Alex dropped the Lavender Fireball into it. Accompanied by Steiner, Alex marched his reviled possession into the bank and locked it away in a safe-deposit box.

From the bank, Alex, Charlie, and Professor Sorensen had driven to the restaurant where they met Quizzy. Piqued by their recent encounter at the ranch, Alex had invited her to lunch. Somehow, he had been candid, yet at ease with her. It was an unusual combination for him—one he hadn't had with Trina. He wanted to help her with the story she was writing, not only to portray his family in a positive light, but also to stick it to the Ruthliers.

The food arrived, and after a few satiating bites, conjecture about the murderer's identity started.

"Captain Steiner warned me against discussing details of the night watchman's murder," Sorensen said. "It could jeopardize his case." Alex saw a subtle look of disappointment cross Quizzy's face. The frustrated reporter would have to settle for bland generalities.

"I think Reverend Ruthlier's weird son—the guy with the knife tattoo on his neck—is suspect *numero uno*," Alex said. "He was creeping around with a metal detector the night ... the night the meteorite hit." Alex felt Quizzy studying him. "I'll bet Steiner is all over that guy."

Because the Reverend Lucas Ruthlier had asked Alex for the meteorite, the speculating diners couldn't help but conjecture that he, too, was involved.

"I don't know," Quizzy said. "It seems a little conspicuous that someone on record as seeking the meteorite would kill so publicly for it. Why draw attention to something and then murder someone to get it?"

"Church of the God Particle," Charlie interjected. "I see the God particle in the news all the time, but I don't know what it is."

"It's a fundamental subatomic particle," Professor Sorensen said. "The worldwide physics community looked for it for more than forty years before they discovered it. Although most physicists hate the name, the so-called God particle finally revealed itself in the intense heat of a Swiss supercollider. Of course, once physicists found it, it was inevitable that they began looking for other fundamental particles. That is the nature of physicists."

"I know that atoms are made of protons, electrons, and neutrons," Quizzy interjected. "Is that what you mean by subatomic particles?"

"Yes, but there are others," Sorensen said. "All matter, such as this plastic table we are eating upon, our bodies, and the air we breathe is made up of trillions upon trillions of atoms. Each atom is composed of smaller particles. There is the familiar nucleus, with its protons and neutrons. That is orbited by electrons. Electrons are thought to be fundamental and indivisible, but protons and neutrons can be broken down further into smaller particles. Also, there are loose particles flying around everywhere. Physicists have given these particles odd names, like quarks, muons, gluons, bosons, and others."

"Is there something controlling them? Something like an atomic traffic cop?"

"That isn't fully understood, Charlie," Sorensen said.

"Because they are so small, the relative space between particles is immense. If you were to expand an atom's nucleus to the size of a basketball, the electrons would be the size of dust specks, and thousands of meters away. As counterintuitive as it seems, what we perceive as solid matter is almost all space between far-flung electrons and other passing particles.

"The hardness of this table," Sorensen said as she rapped her knuckles on it, "is because of the difference in electrical charges between the atoms in the table and the ones in my hand. That's the reason my hand doesn't pass through it. It's not because the stuff in my hand bumps up against the stuff in the table."

"So, what's this have to do with the God particle?" Alex asked.

"The God particle is a special type of subatomic particle," Sorenson said. "A universal field of God particles imbues mass and controls the distribution of matter—everything we perceive and interact with in daily life. Thus, its grandiose name. Imagine that you are a subatomic particle. You don't have any weight until you start to swim through the sea of God Particles. They push back on you; give you resistance, so to speak."

"I'd like to find a God particle," Alex said. "It could be useful. I know a few people whose mass I'd like to eliminate. If I had a jar of God particles could I make people disappear?"

"From a quantum point of view, I suppose you could," said Professor Sorensen. "They wouldn't just drop off the face of the earth, so to speak, but they would disappear from your existence, and you from theirs. You both would be living in separate, parallel dimensions. You might intersect occasionally, but not in any significant way. Like passing cars on the road, so to speak."

"I'm liking this God particle more and more," Alex said. "Where would I look for one? Maybe under that rock?" He pointed to an ornamental chunk of granite near the sidewalk.

"Yes, you could look for a God particle under that rock. I'll wait here and finish my sandwich. Let me know if you find one."

"Will I need any special tools? Maybe an electron microscope?" he asked.

"Not a microscope, but an atom smasher. Particle accelerator is the proper scientific name. They generate the tremendous amount of energy needed to investigate particle physics. But since the size of the explosion is confined to the subatomic level, we aren't blowing up cities in our searches."

"This is all fascinating, but I don't get the connection between the physics of the God particle and the Church of the God Particle," Quizzy said. "How do you get from theoretical quantum mechanics to religion?"

"A twisted mind can conjure up anything," Alex said.

Sorensen continued, "One of the most intriguing aspects of particle physics—and also cosmology—is the idea that something can be created from nothing. In the beginning, to use a biblical reference, there was nothing. It wasn't empty space; there was no space. There was no universe. No time, no light. Nothing. Nothing larger than the size of a single atom, anyway. We know that for sure. It's not a stretch to postulate that there was nothing at all.

"Then came the Big Bang. It was the mother of all explosions—literally. Our beloved particle accelerators are attempting to reproduce the broiling temperatures of the Big Bang—one trillion, trillion, billion degrees. My point is that all matter was created from nothing. Assuming that the laws of physics are immutable, then it's possible that we could *re-create* something from nothing. I suppose some people could label that scenario as a religious experience. It's the possibility of unlimited bounty and resources."

"Or unlimited misery and suffering," Alex added, drawing a frown from Quizzy.

"Like most things, it's what you make of it," Quizzy said.

"Well, I still don't see how all of this ties into the Church of the God Particle," Charlie said. "I mean, what are those people doing on Sundays? Are they out in their backyards building atom smashers? Maybe murdering night watchmen to steal valuable meteorites as a down payment on the ten billion they're going to need? Things don't add up."

"I am a scientist, not a theologian," Sorensen said. "I have no idea what they are thinking in that church. You'd have to ask Reverend Ruthlier."

"That is exactly what I intend to do," said Quizzy.

15

CAPTAIN STEINER TRACKED down Drago Illya Ruthlier the same way Alex had found him—his picture and identity were posted on the Web site of the Church of the God Particle.

The duplex of the wiry man with the tattooed knife in his throat was in the same South Austin neighborhood as his father's home. Steiner guessed from its uninspired design that the building had been built in the sixties. The green wooden sign at the street read simply, "The Oaks." Steiner had come across the building permit for the Ruthliers' new living quarters within the Nations Home Hardware building, and he wondered when they would make the move.

As he walked past Drago's motorcycle parked in front of the building, Steiner's hand brushed against his Glock 9mm security blanket on his hip. Dressed in the standard-issue khaki uniform of the Texas Rangers, he didn't want to test the bullet-stopping ability of his Kevlar vest.

Tipping down his Stetson to block the sun from his eyes, he strode to the door and knocked on it. The door-jamb had been repaired recently.

The door opened six inches, revealing a man in a sleeveless T-shirt with short, disheveled dark hair. Even in the dim light and under two days' growth of stubble, the tattooed knife cutting Drago's throat was riveting.

Good, I woke him, Steiner thought. "Are you Drago Ruthlier?" As if someone else in Drago Ruthlier's apartment would have that tattoo.

"Yes, I am he."

"I'm Captain Steiner with the Texas Rangers. I need to ask you some questions." He knew that Drago had his foot anchored behind the door.

"Show me your badge," Drago said through the door crack.

"It's right here on my uniform, as you can see, sir."

"I can't read it. Move a little closer."

"If you want to read it, step outside." There was no way Steiner was going to expose himself through the narrow opening of the door. For all he knew, the suspected knife-man was holding the same weapon he had plunged into the chest of the night watchman.

"What do you want?"

"As I said, I need to ask you some questions. May I come in?"

"No."

"Then you'll have to come downtown with me."

"I remember you," Drago said. "You ejected me from the Twisted Tree Ranch the night I volunteered to help recover the meteorite."

"Volunteered? You were trespassing."

"I am in the salvage business, among other enterprises. How is that less legitimate than some of the others who were allowed to stay? Like that reporter. What was her name again? Quizzy Shatterling, I believe. What kind of a name is that?"

No stranger than Drago Ruthlier.

Before Steiner could answer, Drago added, "As you asked me to leave that night, I am asking you to do the same now."

Steiner was standing in the sun wearing a bulletproof vest under a hot uniform. He had little patience for recalcitrant pricks. "That's not the way it works, Mr. Ruthlier. Either you let me in right now to ask you some questions, or we go downtown. Your choice."

The door swung open.

The inside of Drago's apartment wasn't what Steiner expected. Either the maid just visited or he was a neat freak, he thought. Because The Oaks didn't appear to have clientele who could afford maid service, Steiner deduced the latter. There were no loose books or magazines lying on any of the tables, no scattered clothes, no dirty dishes. On a shelf there was a framed portrait of Drago's father, Lucas Ruthlier. In a glass case on the wall was a display of six knives.

"What are your questions?" Drago asked. He sat down

on the couch and slouched into a corner cushion. His white, sleeveless undershirt revealed more tattoos on his arms. A dragon with blood red eyes ridden by a headless skeleton crushed skulls underfoot. He stretched out his right leg and rested his bare heel on the couch. His demeanor was indifferent, and his body language shouted that he considered Steiner and his questions unimportant. His dark short hair accented the shadows beneath his high cheekbones.

"Is it all right if I sit here?" Steiner asked, and he motioned to a chair.

"No. I'm trying to keep my furniture clean." Drago slouched even more.

Steiner looked hard at the unpleasant man sprawled on the couch. He imagined drawing his Glock and firing two shots into Drago's chest where he lounged. He envisioned blood spurting from the wounds and from Drago's mouth as he gasped for air. He continued to stare into the man's eyes. Drago shifted on the couch. Instead of pulling his Glock, Steiner withdrew his notepad and mechanical pencil. He said, "What happened to your door?"

"I accidentally locked myself out." Drago was now sitting up straighter.

"Maybe you should hide a spare key."

"Are you finished with your questions?"

"A night watchman was murdered Tuesday night at the UT biology building. What do you know about that?" Steiner asked.

"I know nothing about that." Drago slid back into his

slouch.

"Nothing? Nothing at all?"

"Only what I read in the papers."

"If you read about it in the papers, why did you say that you knew nothing about it?"

"I assumed you meant firsthand knowledge," Drago said.

He doesn't fluster, Steiner thought. "Have you ever been inside the UT biology building?"

"Never."

"Would you be willing to provide a DNA sample?"

"No, I would not."

"Why not?"

"Because I don't wish to. I don't have to give you a reason. I know my rights."

"We can get it with a court order," Steiner said.

"You cannot obtain my DNA without having a reasonable suspicion. Since I know my DNA has not been found in that building, you are chasing your tail. After all, it's a laboratory and a classroom—there must be many people leaving their DNA around. But I am not one of them." He smirked.

"Do you know anyone with a key to the biology building?" Steiner asked.

"No one I know has a key."

"Do you attend the Church of the God Particle?"

"I don't see that my religious beliefs matter."

"I didn't ask what you believe or don't believe. I asked if you attend that church."

"Very well, then. Naturally, I sometimes attend services at my father's church."

"Do you know Woody Reeter? He's the janitor at the biology building. He attends your church, too."

"I'm not sure if I've met Mr. Reeter. I meet a lot of people at church. It's a very friendly place."

"He says he met you." Steiner watched Drago dig imaginary dirt from beneath a fingernail.

"Like I said, it's a friendly place."

Trying to keep Drago off balance, Steiner remarked, "I see you like knives," and pointed to the glass case on the wall.

"Not necessarily. I like collections."

"When is the last time you took one of those knives out of the case?"

"I take them out often for cleaning. Cleanliness is next to godliness, you know."

Steiner asked more questions about Drago's movements on the day of the murder, and then proceeded to question him about his occupation.

"I do many odd jobs," Drago said. When the Ranger pressed him for details, he said that many of his jobs were at his father's church. "We recently moved the congregation into a new building, as any competent detective would know. The design and the construction are mine. My father and I will soon be living there."

"That's nice," Steiner said in an I-don't-give-a-shit tone. "I'm finished with my questions—for now."

"Good. I have important things to do."

Steiner walked to the door of the apartment. Drago remained on the couch.

"One more thing. Have you ever operated a backhoe?"

Drago studied the trooper. Steiner could tell that his suspect was forming his answer carefully. "I may have a long time ago. I worked for a plumbing contractor after high school. We replaced sewer lines in people's yards. We used many kinds of equipment. I can't remember specifically if there was a backhoe, but it's possible. Do you know that I am an expert when it comes to operating around shit pipes?" His eyes roamed up and down Steiner.

Steiner thought about his Glock again and asked, "Have you ever been to the Bee Cave Cemetery?"

"But of course! My father used to take me to many cemeteries around Austin. We find them to be serene and tranquil. Do you have family members buried in a cemetery near here? Tell me where, and maybe I will stop by and put flowers on their graves."

Steiner strained out a laugh. "You're a fool, Ruthlier," he said. "Don't underestimate me. I've put a lot of scum like you in the penitentiary at Huntsville. You're on the list if you killed that night watchman. I might even put your stinking carcass in there for operating a backhoe improperly. Where were you last Tuesday between ten p.m. and midnight?"

Drago set his jaw and narrowed his eyes. "I was here in my apartment watching the TV."

"Can anyone verify that?"

"I live alone, so no one can say that I was here or not

here."

"That's too damn bad. You don't have an alibi."

"I watch a lot of television. I have a premium cable package. That night I ordered *Dracula*. You can check with the cable company. Did you know that Dracula was from my home country of Romania? He is one of my heroes."

"I think he was a pussy, myself. He was always attacking the defenseless." He paused to let his insult sink in. "And just because you ordered a movie doesn't mean you were here to watch it."

"I promise it's true," Drago said.

"Who do you think a jury will believe, knifeman? By the way, you might want to invest in a turtleneck when your time comes in a court of law. That's really a bad tattoo job."

Steiner opened the front door, and on the way out said over his shoulder, "Don't leave town. We'll be seeing each other again." He slammed the door behind him and descended the stairs to the parking lot. *He didn't even ask why I wanted to know about the backhoe.*

He walked to Drago's motorcycle and looked it over. It was a black, off-road Honda with brushed aluminum trim and wheels. The original knobbies had been replaced with street tires. The single-cylinder 650cc engine was powerful enough to push the machine up any incline if it could get traction. Steiner knew the bike was capable of anything except a comfortable cross-country trip. Anywhere else, it could shake a police car. *But it won't outrun a bullet.* The foot of the kickstand was set a few inches over the white line marking the adjacent handicapped spot.

Steiner walked to his car and retrieved his parking ticket book and wrote the citation, his first in years. He stuffed it into the instrument cluster on the handlebars. He vowed that he would personally arrest the bastard if he didn't pay. *Assuming I don't arrest him for murder first.*

16

G OD, I HATE going to church, Quizzy said to herself. An ephemeral image of an old man in white robes flitted through her imagination. *Nothing personal*, she said to her mental image of God.

Her aunt and uncle had been the first to appreciate her aversion to conformity. Steady Methodists living in Lubbock, they raised their niece from the age of nine, when her life was demolished and her parents ripped away from her. The cruel and poorly planned cover-up to the so-called "crime of the decade" fell apart, as did Quizzy.

She had insulated herself from the curious public by escaping into books. Hoping their adopted daughter would discover a context for the catastrophe and find a measure of peace, her aunt and uncle tolerated her exploration into "offbeat" religious faiths. During high school she investigated philosophy and religion using the limited resources of the public library. By the time of her graduation, those books had ceased appearing on her bedroom desk, to the relief of Quizzy's adoptive parents. Their anxiety reemerged, however, when they discovered that their daughter's exploratory hiatus was only because she had exhausted the library's collection of books about non-Christian faiths. Her curiosity hadn't diminished.

Quizzy resolved the book dilemma by enrolling at the University of Texas at Austin. Its vast library, coupled with the emergence of the Internet, provided a boundless hoard of information. But even with these unlimited religious and philosophical resources, she didn't find the answers that satisfied her insatiable curiosity. Why, for example, did *her* family disintegrate? She lapsed into a tolerable, yet unfulfilling agnostic existentialism. And she trusted no one.

Quizzy shut off her car and gazed at the anchor stores in the Southside Shopping Center. A Bed, Bath, & Beyond offered vanities at forty percent off. Pet Step, at the other end of the parking lot, pushed Purina. She walked between cars to the sidewalk in front of the Church of the God Particle. She had arrived well before the services began, so she could explore the place and see what kind of people attended a church with so strange a name.

A Gothic stone façade with opened antique wooden doors had been built in front of the sliding glass doors at the old Nations Home Hardware's main entrance. The big-box retailer had moved down the street into an even bigger boxy building. A church member named Billy Swillers, who was a commercial real estate agent, had persuaded Lucas Ruthlier that he could spread the word from the cavernous vacant building. A church wasn't what the Southside Shopping Center owners had envisioned to fill the vacancy—Sunday churchgoers wouldn't spill into the other weekday businesses. But after a year of no rent during a bad market, the owners relented and signed the contract. Reverend Ruthlier now had space to grow his flock.

Two teenage boys dressed in black slacks and white shirts stood on either side of the Gothic façade and handed out programs. The parishioners appeared similar to the congregations milling outside of most other churches in Austin. Quizzy pulled up the collar of her jacket, trying to remain as inconspicuous as possible. Her plan was to sit through a service, get the feel of the place, and slip away unnoticed. There was no obvious reason for the queasy feeling in her stomach; no one had singled her out. To the contrary, the parishioners entering the building all smiled at her.

She accepted a pamphlet from one of the young men as he gushed, "Welcome!" The budding evangelist exuded too much enthusiasm for her. As she approached the sliding glass doors behind the façade, they whooshed open, and she entered.

All physical semblance of the former Nations Home Hardware ended, although Quizzy sensed a residual commercial ambience, as if money still changed hands in the building. The interior was awash in color. An array of stained-glass panels cast off patterns of green, red, blue, white, and amber. The glass was soldered into designs of atomic nuclei, like a divine 1950s futurama, the paths of its orbiting electrons traced by leaden seams. The peripheries of those panels transitioned into sweeping galaxies with spiraling arms of chipped-glass stars.

A four-foot elevated stage with a prominent center pulpit dominated the far end of the building. Concentric rows of folding chairs with white plastic seats radiated from the front of the stage, divided into three sections by wide, red-carpeted aisles. Quizzy counted the rows of chairs on the polished concrete floor and estimated their total number to be five hundred.

A series of small, brightly painted rooms of different heights and widths concealed the concrete outer walls of the capacious main room. The smaller rooms were strung together as if a crayon carrying six-year-old had slapped them up just before naptime. Exposed ventilation ducts, electrical conduits, light fixtures, sprinkler system pipes, and catwalks crisscrossed above the painted rooms and the main chamber. Plastic signs with room names designated the kitchen, child-care room, meditation room, coatroom, bathrooms, office, and a Sunday school classroom.

The Reverend Ruthlier and Drago's new living quarters extended upward from a massive second-floor platform in a corner of the building near the main entrance. Quizzy guessed that the space had once been an office complex used to manage the Nations Home Hardware floor operations below. The elevated complex had been renovated into a foreboding, secure refuge for the two Ruthliers. Its motif was oil derrick gray; none of the colors from downstairs carried upward. A four-foot walkway with a black railing spanned the living area, and a railed stairway at each end provided access from below. The dark steel and dim lighting implied "keep out" to everyone but the Ruthliers.

People came and went from the main worship hall into the various colorful rooms on the main floor. Quizzy was surprised to see people from UT's administration, Austin business leaders, and a few people from state and local government, including a city council member. *What's the attraction of this place? These are not gullible fools*, she thought.

She circulated around the perimeter of the main hall, twisting doorknobs behind her back to the rooms that were not already open. If a locked room had a window, a miniblind inside covered it. All the closed doors were locked, and most were unidentified. There was one room that beckoned Quizzy most of all. It was tagged, "Office."

Working her way through the crowd, she sidled up to the office. With her back to the door, she watched the congregation in the main chamber. She spotted Reverend Ruthlier's swept-back silver hair contrasting with his dark suit across the huge room as he gestured and explained something to an attentive group. Quizzy feigned leaning against the office door and tried the knob. It, too, was locked, as she expected.

She reached into her purse and pulled out a tube of ChapStick and a thin steel tool. After conspicuously attending to her lips, she lingered at the door and inserted the pick into the doorknob behind her back. When she heard the satisfying click she twisted, and then backed into the office. She pushed the door closed, but didn't lock it. She dared not flick the wall switch on, but there was enough light filtering down from the open ceiling, exposed I-beams, and ventilation ducts for her to see. Shelves with books about Eastern philosophy and religion, along with Christian books, covered one wall. A shelf was devoted to physics and cosmology books and journals. Portraits of Jesus, the Buddha, Shiva, Lao Tsu, the Dalai Lama, and Ronald Reagan hung on another wall next to an inscription from the Koran. A large oak desk and chair dominated the room. Several papers with the church's letterhead lay scattered on top. Quizzy bent over to read one with a boldface title that said, "Platinum Club Donors." The first name on the list was Billy Swillers. She made a mental note to check him out.

A framed picture of Drago Ruthlier standing on scaffolding inside the church with a hammer in his hand sat on the left side of the desk. Quizzy remembered how surprised she had been when a contact at the Austin Police Department had let her look through the immigration file of Lucas Ruthlier after the meteorite blew up Alex Colvin's life. Drago was the son of the enigmatic preacher!

Ruthlier's file had been straightforward enough: a Romanian citizen born of American parents who tutored children of Communist Party officials. He had fled the country and was granted political asylum in the United States with his son in 1990. The file was brief. Too brief for Quizzy, and she hadn't yet closed her reporter's notebook on immigration.

She opened and closed the drawers of the desk fast enough to slide the contents. The first three contained common office paraphernalia, but the unnerving sight of a revolver in the middle drawer made her gasp. She detested guns.

In the corner of the room atop an oak filing cabinet with brass handles sat the most provocative object in the room: A life-size bronze bust of Trina Colvin stared at where Lucas Ruthlier would sit at his desk. Although Quizzy had never met the lone victim of the Lavender Fireball, the bust's accuracy, based on photographs she had seen, astounded her. She marveled at the remarkable details. Hair swirled lifelike across minute forehead wrinkles. Eyebrows and eyelashes showed individual hairs, and even the earlobes contained the subtle pricks of piercing. An engraved brass plate at the base read, "Saint Trina."

She tipped the bust back and read the sculptor's name. "A. Ronson" was hand-engraved on the underside. Righting the sculpture, she stood in front of the bust, staring into its eyes as if they could tell the woman's story of her terrifying last moments. She took the cell phone out of her purse, suppressed the flash, and snapped a picture.

"How did you get in here?" a voice behind her hissed. Quizzy jumped and whirled around. Drago Ruthlier blocked the door, his right hand clenching and opening as if it longed for something to crush. She wondered whether he had seen her cell phone as she dropped it back in her purse.

"The door was open, and I thought this room was part of the open house, like all the rest of them."

"This door was locked."

"But it wasn't. I'm here, aren't I?"

Drago narrowed his eyes and closed the door, trapping her in the room. Although he was better dressed than on the night of the fireball, he looked just as explosive. The sleeves of his white shirt were rolled up to half expose the skull tattoos on his arms. His head, with its short, coarse hair, reminded Quizzy of a porcupine.

She took two steps to her left to put the desk between her and the wiry man. She judged the distance to the drawer with the revolver and wondered whether it was loaded. Abhorrence or not, she would use the gun on Drago if it meant surviving an attack. He reached into his pants pocket and withdrew a dark object. Quizzy steeled herself for a race to the revolver. Instead, he tapped out a short message on his cell phone keypad.

She was surprised how soon Lucas Ruthlier opened the door and entered the room, flipping on the light switch as he passed. Assessing the situation, he looked at Quizzy and then at his son.

"I found her in the office," Drago said with pride and a hint of his childhood accent.

"The door was open, and I thought I was welcome to look," Quizzy stated.

"I'm sure it was locked," said Drago, but Quizzy shook her head to the contrary.

The senior Ruthlier looked at the gun drawer and then

at Quizzy. She fake-smiled, trying to conceal that she had seen the revolver. Not that it mattered. This was Texas. Everyone had a gun. Even preachers.

"Let me visit with Ms. Shatterling for a minute, Drago," he said. "Services start soon. Why don't you do a final check on the lights and sound?"

Drago pursed his lips, stared hard at Quizzy, and left the room, not turning his back until he was through the door. He left it open, and Quizzy relaxed—until she saw him take a seat outside, where he continued to glare at her.

Ruthlier sat down behind the desk and motioned Quizzy to one of the chairs across from him. He opened the middle drawer and placed the Platinum Club donor list inside it, studying Quizzy's reaction.

"So you know my name," Quizzy asked.

"But of course. You wrote the Lavender Fireball story in the Chronicle some months ago. Now you are writing a story on me and my church."

"How did you know that?"

"I didn't."

Flustered, Quizzy attempted to recover. "I write lots of stories. Some things are only mentioned in passing."

"This church is too important and growing too fast to be just mentioned in passing. Its mission is nothing less than to prepare the way for the coming of the next prophet. Your last article was not very flattering to us. Maybe you'll acquire a better understanding for this story."

"That is my goal for everything I write." Quizzy's eyes roamed the room and settled on the bronze bust. "The sculpture is remarkable. Who made it?"

"We consider Trina Colvin to be a saint, as you can see from the plaque. She sacrificed her life for the greater good of humanity. The gift of her death propelled the Lavender Fireball into a media fire*storm*. It was an essential step in the preparation for the Elemental One."

"Alex Colvin doesn't think his wife's death was a gift."

"In the future I hope that he will. Events have not yet crystallized."

"Who's the sculptor?"

"He wishes to remain anonymous."

Ruthlier's blue eyes shone against the backdrop of his silver hair, making his head look bigger than it already was. He had the tense look of a man who planned for every foreseeable contingency. That was understandable, Quizzy thought, considering his volatile son. She wondered whether the senior Ruthlier had been involved in the murder of the night watchman. He sat with his thick hands clasped in front of him on the desk. The angle of his arms resting on the desk pulled his sleeves tight around his wide shoulders and upper arms. The man exuded physical power, a striking contrast to the quick, lithe Drago. Quizzy speculated that Ruthlier's wife must have been tall and thin.

"What of your son's mother?" she asked and studied the preacher for a reaction.

"What of her?" His hands constricted around each other atop the desk.

"Tell me about her."

"She's dead."

"When?"

Ruthlier paused. "She died when Drago was seven. It was a long time ago in Romania."

Ruthlier gazed at the wall for a few seconds. "And now I must go. I have a sermon to give. Are you staying?"

"Yes, that's why I came. By the way, I'm going on vacation to Romania in a few weeks. I just want to poke around the country, see whatever I can. I've always been curious about that part of the world. It was closed off for so long, and now everything is opening up. Maybe I'll look for a vampire. Do you have any suggestions about where I should go or whom I should talk to?" Quizzy thought about the revolver and wished it were on her side of the desk.

Ruthlier ground his molars, and the muscles behind his wide cheeks hardened. He said, "Romania can be a dangerous place. Be very careful. There were many quick executions after the revolution. Much information about the old regime never came out at the trials. There are many Romanians who have deep secrets, and they will do whatever is necessary to keep them. As for whom you should talk to? I couldn't say. I don't know anybody over there now. My advice is to hunt vampires. They are relatively safe."

Ruthlier arose and waited for Quizzy to walk ahead of him through the door. He pushed the lock, pulled the door shut, and twisted the knob twice. He steamed away in silence toward a small set of steps leading backstage. Quizzy looked at the seated congregation in front of her, and then at Drago, still glaring at her.

I've worn out my welcome. There will be another service.

She walked toward the whooshing doors and the light of the sun. "Come again real soon!" one of the teenage door-boys said as she crossed through the façade into fresh air.

Her first task at the office Monday morning was going to be cajoling her editor into approving her just-conceived trip to Romania, even if she had to pitch in some of her own money.

17

TWO HUNDRED EIGHTY-SEVEN thousand dollars, according to the recently concluded eBay auction, was the value of a highly publicized, odd-colored, deep-space meteorite that had killed a human being with a direct strike. The highest bidders, Thomas Loya and his philanthropic socialite wife, Anita, sat across a table from Alex and Charlie in a conference room in Alex's bank. Next to the Loyas sat their steely chief of security, Marcus Sloan. Between them on a table, wrapped in clear bubble packing, lay the Lavender Fireball in its army surplus ammunition box. Joining the buyers and the seller at the table was a bank vice president, who had just verified the wire transfer of funds from Loya's account into Alex's.

At fifty-one years of age, Thomas Loya was an Austin-style millionaire. After college, a nascent Dell computer company had hired him as a call center manager. His ability to grasp the emerging technology, organize the center's operations, and manage people under stress propelled him upward through layers of management. When a competitor offered Loya a similar position, Dell enticed him to stay by granting him a few hundred thousand shares of stock options. During the next decade, as the company's PCs became the world's dominant desktop computer, the stock split and the price soared. When Loya cashed out, he and his wife were set up to do whatever they wished. They bought acres of land in the hills behind the limestone cliffs plunging into Lake Travis. They built a house that passing recreational boaters pointed at and asked how anyone could afford such palatial digs.

Aside from harboring the Loyas' ostentatious personal possessions, the house served a business purpose. The Loyas began buying and selling art locally, then nationwide, and finally worldwide. One wing of their home displayed their commercial collection. Although a meteorite was not fine art, they rationalized that this particular curio was rare enough to appreciate in value, and the notoriety attached to it justified its acquisition.

"Y'all be careful now," Charlie said as the meeting in the bank was breaking up. "One guy has already been killed by someone tryin' to steal this thing."

Thomas Loya said, "Yes, we're fully aware that the murdered night watchman may have interrupted an attempt to steal the fireball. As perverse as it may seem, that murder inflated the price I just paid for it."

It's not as perverse as a meteorite killing your wife, Alex thought.

"Well, I'm sure that you wouldn't want the price to go up even more with another murder," Charlie said. "Especially if it was yours."

"I think we can all agree on that," Loya said. "That's why I have Mr. Sloan with me." Marcus Sloan was the owner of Sloan Security. Alex and Charlie had not yet seen him smile. "Marcus has built the security system in our gallery from the ground up. The place is like a vault. It's locked down unless we are having an exhibition. We deploy security cameras, and there is an armed guard on duty twenty-four/seven."

Sloan nodded, exuding confidence.

Marcus Sloan was the most imposing person in the room. A tall, black ex-marine, he made no effort to conceal the bulge of his sidearm under his jacket. Alex wondered how the bank vice president felt about the outsider's weapon in his institution.

Their business concluded, the men and Mrs. Loya rose and shook hands. Sloan's grip was as hard as his appearance. Ammunition box under one arm, he carried the Loyas' newest acquisition to their silver Cadillac in the parking lot, accompanied by the bank's security guard. Sloan unlatched the trunk of Loya's car and wedged the steel box into a corner so it wouldn't shift during the hour's drive back to the gallery.

Loya's wife, Anita, chatted with her husband in the parking lot, then kissed him and walked to her BMW coupe across the lot. Her appearance was striking: blue skirt and white silk blouse hanging on her tall frame as if she were on a Paris runway, but her disheveled blond hair whipped in the breeze.

Alex and Charlie climbed into Charlie's truck and watched as the fireball-bearing Cadillac sedan pulled into the street.

"Well, cousin," Charlie said, "I guess that wraps up a chapter. A really bad chapter. Are you okay?"

"I feel numb," Alex said. "Two hundred and eighty-seven thousand dollars is a big chunk of change, but there's no way I can feel good about that, knowing the real cost. Especially to Seven."

"You did all you could with what you had to work with."

"Yeah, I know. I'll put part of the money into a trust fund for her. By the time she's twenty-one, it should be enough to open any door she chooses. Hopefully she won't fritter it away. I'd like to invest the rest of the money, but I'm not sure where, yet. Plus, I'll have money coming in from Billy Swillers's Divine Water scheme. I can't put my finger on the reason, but I feel kinda scummy about that."

"You shouldn't do things that make you feel scummy," Charlie said.

Alex reflected for a few moments, and then said, "You know, I thought I'd be glad to be rid of that damn meteorite, with all the misery it's caused. But I'm a little sad to lose it. It's become so much a part of my life. I wish I'd never seen or heard of the Lavender Fireball, but in spite of the terrible things, it's also brought other changes—aside from the money. It completely upended my life and Seven's. She'll never know her mother. But at the same time, it feels like the world has somehow expanded for me. It's weird. That damned space rock—that *interloper*—just ripped apart the fabric of my whole life."

***

Six blocks away from the Loya mansion and gallery, a white pickup truck, the most common type of vehicle in Texas, with all its government field agencies and construction companies, sat in the shade of a small neighborhood park with its windows down. On this day, Drago Ruthlier relaxed in the truck he had stolen the night before. Despite wearing a full-body, official NASCAR Rusty Wallace racing suit, minus the helmet, he was enjoying the windy day.

He sat listening to the radio, flipping between stations. On the seat next to him was a blond wig, a ten-pound Sears crowbar, a pair of oversize Ray-Ban sunglasses, a wide-brimmed straw hat, a lavender (no coincidence) feather boa, Kingsford barbecuing mittens, and a red Kidde dry-chemical fire extinguisher.

The Cadillac sedan approached the cross street to the park. Drago earlier had followed it to Alex's bank, adhered a C-4 bomb to the undercarriage below the front seat, and then waited across the street long enough to see Marcus Sloan place an olive-green container in the trunk. Drago then sped ahead to the park and waited for the Cadillac on its return trip home.

He plucked his cell phone off the dashboard and made

a call to the sedan, now approaching the park. Neither of the car's passengers answered, however. The recipient of the call was a prepaid cell phone strapped to the C-4 bomb. The blast lifted the car four feet off the ground, instantly killing Messrs. Loya and Sloan. Nearby house windows blew in, projectiles arced into backyards, and a black, smoky ball of fire roiled upward from the ruptured gasoline tank. The shattered car crunched to earth and shuddered to a stop as an aluminum wheel, its tire shredded, ground into the asphalt.

Shocked neighbors looked out of their broken windows and called 911 in a panic. They saw a blond woman in a NASCAR fire suit and Ray-Ban sunglasses run from the white truck in the park to the burning car. The athletic woman discharged the fire extinguisher onto the back of the car and then slammed the crowbar into the trunk latch until it popped open. She grabbed the ammunition box with barbecue mittens and sprinted back to the white truck, singed feather boa flailing behind her. She gunned the engine like a real NASCAR driver and squealed out of the park at the opposite end.

***

The brazen bombing inflamed Captain Steiner to the point of making him ponder his sworn duty to uphold the law. A piece of planted evidence might save lives in the future, he rationalized.

He replayed the surveillance video from the bank's

parking lot over and over. Steiner was certain that the blond woman in the grainy video was Drago, but he needed more than his instincts to obtain a search warrant or to make an arrest. He opted for legality and brought Drago into one of the downtown interrogation rooms for five hours but couldn't dig up enough evidence to hold him.

The video showed Thomas Loya's Cadillac pulling into the bank's parking lot, followed by the white truck police later found abandoned and burned. After the Cadillac's occupants entered the bank, the white truck parked next to the sedan, and the bizarre NASCAR blonde got out. She held a small package and dropped her key ring. She knelt to retrieve the keys and, while down, reached under the Cadillac. When she stood up, her package was gone. She reentered the truck and left the scene like an agitated hornet on the breeze, stinger at the ready for her next landing.

18

QUIZZY WAS ON the line. She and Alex exchanged pleasantries. "I'm fine, thanks. I'm calling about business, though," she said.

Alex tried to filter his disappointment. "That so? What's up?"

"You know I've been working on that story about the Church of the God Particle. Well, I went out there Sunday to the old hardware store on South Lamar and poked around a little bit."

"Did you convert?"

"Not yet," Quizzy said with a laugh, "although the place is fascinating." Alex smiled at the lightness in her voice.

"Inside, along one wall, there are colorful, odd-looking rooms that connect. But that's only the downstairs part. Upstairs is just the opposite: dark and foreboding. That's where the Ruthliers live. Their apartments are built on an elevated platform that overlooks the main chamber."

Alex tried to imagine the interior of the church as he watched Seven assemble wooden blocks on the floor. "So did you meet Big Daddy and his evil spawn?"

"Yes, I did. And they totally creeped me out. Everyone else seemed pretty normal. I didn't even stay for the sermon, things got so tense. Drago seemed on the verge of losing it when he caught me nosing around the office."

"Quizzy, you've got to be careful around him. I know you know that, but the consequences could be severe. Maybe fatal. Especially after that car bombing the other day, assuming he was behind it. As I do. What kind of person blows up two people in a quiet neighborhood just to steal a frickin' rock? Albeit a valuable rock."

"A fanatic. That's who does something like that," Quizzy answered. "It's not about the money. Drago is totally subservient to his father, from what I saw. Actually, they're both fanatic, but not dedicated to the same causes. The reverend worships his oddball religion and will do anything to further its ends. Drago worships his father and will do anything to please *him*."

"It doesn't add up, though," Alex said. "The reverend obviously has enough smarts to put together a successful church from a scratch religion. That takes a lot of thought. Forget about the validity of the religion itself. The guy's got to have enough on the ball to pull people together, renovate a building, and also finance the whole thing. He can't be happy about a high-profile car bombing. That just intensifies the pressure to find out who did it."

"High profile murder," Quizzy muttered. "The most

painful kind. I get your point, Alex. As you said, it doesn't add up. If Drago is the bomber, it's hard to believe that his father put him up to it. Which makes me think that Drago is completely out of control. Possibly insane. And believe me, I understand the definition. Maybe he thinks that bringing the fireball home to his father will please him. Like a cat that drags a gutted bunny to the doorstep for his owner to find when he steps out for the paper in the morning."

"All the more reason to be very careful, Quizzy. I've grown accustomed to having you around."

"Really? Thanks, Alex. I'll take every possible precaution," she said with diplomacy. Then she added, "That's a nice thing for you to say."

Alex felt his heart accelerate.

"And now for my official journalistic duties.... Do you have any comment you'd like to make about the theft of the Lavender Fireball? Of course, all the other stuff we just talked about is between us and off the record. But as someone having ... extensive involvement with the fireball, you should have an opportunity to comment. Or not."

Images flooded over Alex as his motherless daughter played in front of him. He thought of the woman on the other end of the phone who used euphemisms like "extensive involvement" to spare him the unpleasantness of "first on the scene at his wife's decapitation." He also couldn't help but think about his future bank account, not unrelated to the fireball.

"No, Quizzy, I don't have a lot to say on the record, except that my thoughts go out to the families of the deceased, and that I hope the authorities solve the cases soon. Is that too mundane?"

"It's your quote, Alex. You can say anything you want. There's something else I need to ask you about, though."

"What's that?"

"When I was snooping around the church, I found my way into Ruthlier's office. He's got a bronze bust of Trina setting on his filing cabinet. I never met your wife, but the details are amazing. I suppose he found some photos of her on the Internet. I got the artist's name off the bottom of the bust and I'm going to try to talk to him. There's a brass plaque that says, 'Saint Trina.'"

"That's just too weird," Alex said as he wrinkled his nose with distaste. "Ruthlier told me in his letter asking me to donate the fireball that he considered Trina a saint. I was hoping the whole thing would just go away."

"So would you like to make a statement about the bust?"

"Just say that my family wishes everyone would respect our privacy as we try to move on after the loss of Trina."

"You got it."

"What do you think the chances are of Ruthlier's toning down the Saint Trina thing?"

"Zero," she said.

"What an asshole."

"Like I said, he's a fanatic. Anyway, that's the end of my official Chronicle business for today. I really appreciate your talking with me, Alex."

"I like talking with you, Quizzy. So much so that I'd like to do more of it over dinner sometime soon. What do you think?"

"I think I'd like that very much."

19

I T WAS A fortuitous Saturday morning, calm, clear, and cool. But far more important to Quizzy than the weather, the semiannual East Austin Studio Tour was slated for the weekend. The event presented an excuse to approach the reputedly prickly sculptor of bronze, Albert Ronson. Quizzy reasoned that leaving her condo at eight a.m. should give the man time enough to eat, drink coffee, or do whatever else he did to start the day. It would give her enough time to jump ahead of the horde of art aficionados and curious walkers-about who would be invading the cornucopia of art studios that spotted East Austin.

The tour was self-guided; one parked in the gentrifying neighborhood east of downtown and ambled about with a map, locating dozens of studios. There was an eclectic mixture of formal retail shops, converted industrial spaces, and old homes with backroom or backyard workspaces.

Albert Ronson's studio occupied a long, narrow warehouse that had started its slide into decrepitude sixty years earlier. Weedy abandoned railroad tracks behind the building once delivered lumber, steel and stone that sweaty men off-loaded onto concrete docks.

Quizzy entered the section of the warehouse where Ronson worked. An igloo-shaped firebrick kiln on the concrete floor dominated the room. Hand tools, ingots, and pieces of molds lay on the dusty floor. Above her, exposed rafters supported a patchwork of corrugated metal roofing in various stages of rust.

"Good morning," Ronson said as Quizzy entered.

That's a good start, she thought. She was the first visitor in the shop, so she had the sculptor to herself. He stood over a workbench holding a sharp metal tool. A clay dragon with small wings lay on its side. She walked to the bench near him and examined the serpent.

"Do you like it?" Ronson asked.

"Yes, very much."

"I hate the damn things. Also wizards and vampires. They're all the rage now. But they pay the bills." Rough hands, burned and cut and healed-over many times, stuck out of the sleeves of a dingy cotton T-shirt that looked like it might double for a nightshirt. Quizzy guessed the man was in his late sixties. He pulled a rag from a pocket of his denim overalls and wiped the sharp blade of the tool.

"Would you like to use that on Harry Potter?" Quizzy asked.

"Him and Tolkein both." Ronson smiled, apparently pleased at having someone other than a fawning dragon-lover to talk with. "Out and about on the tour?"

"Yes," Quizzy answered. "But I made a point to stop here first, because I saw a bust of yours at a church that I liked, and I wanted to ask you about it. I'm Quizzy Shatterling with the *Austin Chronicle*."

Ronson shook her extended hand, but now looked at her with suspicion. "Must have been the God particle church. That's the only church I know of that has one of my pieces. But I don't ever remember seeing you there before," he said.

Oh, shit.

"You go there?" she said, trying not to sound incredulous.

"Yeah, I joined after I made that bust of Trina Colvin."

Recovering, Quizzy said, "I've only been once ... so far. I'm sort of feeling my way around the whole spirituality thing. If you don't mind my asking, what made you join?"

"Well, I find the concept of the God particle interesting. But what really got me intrigued was that sculpture. Reverend Ruthlier brought in a life-size plaster positive for me to work from, and it was damn near perfect."

"What do you mean, a 'positive'?"

Ronson grimaced, and Quizzy sensed the sculptor's impatience with her apparently common question. "A positive is the opposite of a negative. If the nose sticks out it's a positive." He saw Quizzy's clueless expression and elaborated. "Take a mask, for example. The outside of the mask is the positive side, and the inside is the negative side."

"I get it."

"Usually, I have to sculpt a positive likeness of my subject from clay and then make a negative mold from that. Then I make another negative mold using a wax coating and support it with a ceramic shell. I pour in the molten bronze, and after it hardens, I pull away the ceramic. Voilà! I have a bust that is ready for the finishing touches. But for the Trina Colvin piece, Reverend Ruthlier did most of the artistic part by bringing me a remarkable positive likeness in plaster."

"What do you mean by the 'artistic part'?"

"The artistic part is where talent comes in. He said that he sculpted the clay for the plaster bust himself. That's the strangest thing of all. He said his hands were guided by the hand of God. Those were his exact words. I know all the sculptors in town capable of doing that quality of work, and none of them did it. Maybe he hired some out-of-town talent. But why go to such trouble? If I didn't know better, I'd say he took a casting directly from Trina Colvin's face."

"You mean where a person sticks straws up his nose and then gets plastered? So to speak."

"Yes, exactly," Ronson said, smiling. "That produces a perfect likeness, but it's not art. There's no interpretation. A technician can do it. But I know that didn't happen, because Trina Colvin is six feet under. The bust is what made me join Ruthlier's church. Anyone who can create fine art 'guided by the hand of God' gets my attention. No doubt the man is over-the-top in a lot of ways, but like I said, he's also got an interesting concept going with that God particle thing."

191

20

Don't expect too much out of this, Alex told himself again as he splashed aftershave on his face. He bent over in front of Seven, who was sitting on the floor, and tied his shoelaces as his daughter tried to help. "Seven, does Quizzy meet with your approval? Give me a sign, girl!" The child just babbled. Her brown eyes, a heritage from Trina's Mexican side of the family, were riveted on the shoelaces. Alex stood up and fidgeted with his belt. It had been years since he had dated. Charlie had advised him just to be himself. He cringed at the thought. *Don't expect too much out of this.* But he couldn't suppress the thought of having someone else around the house. Sex.... If he took that out of the equation, would he still feel the same about Quizzy? Impossible to know. He was a cauldron of emotional confusion. Would her curious nature and probing questions annoy him into insanity? Impossible to know. Would she mind if he shot vultures from the zip line? He hoped so.

Alex ruminated about whether enough time had passed. What would everyone think? The notoriety of a disinclined public figure had settled on him. What should have been his fifteen minutes of fame wouldn't end. *Who gives a rat's ass what everyone else thinks. I didn't ask for this.* Nevertheless, Alex, like all people—no matter what they said—did care what other people thought about him. He buttoned his brick red shirt and tucked it into his black slacks.

The doorbell rang and Alex greeted Samantha, who had arrived to babysit Seven.

"Wow, Alex, you look nice. Why so spiffy?"

"I'm just going out to dinner."

"Where?"

"To the Oasis."

"Oooh, nice. With Quizzy?"

There are no secrets around here. "Yes, with Quizzy."

"Cool. I hope it's great!"

"Thanks, Sam." He smiled and nodded at Samantha, appreciating her maturity. Not many fifteen-year-olds could be so supportive. Trina had stepped in when the girl's mother died, but he didn't sense any jealousy in her toward Quizzy.

***

Quizzy's green Beetle hummed over the Colorado River on the Mansfield Dam Bridge. To her left hulked the massive concrete edifice as it held back the waters of Lake

Travis. She turned onto the feeder road to the Oasis restaurant and rehashed the single item on her mental checklist: *Don't turn this date into an interview.* She turned on the radio, looked across the vista, and tried to relax for the rest of the drive.

Quizzy parked the car and saw Alex watching from a bench in the sculpture garden. She opened the door and stuck a pointed crimson cowboy boot through the opening, followed by a long leg in faded blue jeans. Alex rose, and she walked to meet him with slow, relaxed strides. She faced the setting sun, and its warm light radiated against her. Mother-of-pearl snaps shimmered down her untucked white shirt. The two at the top were unbuttoned: beacons to the unknown. Her untamed dark hair hung in rippling curls, and instead of the usual wire-rimmed glasses she wore smoky gray acrylic frames. She could feel the black leather purse slung over her shoulder moving on her hip.

She and Alex came together in the middle of the sidewalk. He extended his arms across her shoulders, and they embraced, at first keeping a prudish space between them, then closing it in an aroma of cologne, perfume, and mixing body scents. They disconnected, and she looked into his hazel eyes, level with hers.

"What's new in the countryside?" she said. *God, I'm already asking questions.*

"This is new!" he said, sweeping his hand across both them and the restaurant.

She smiled. "Shall we find a table out back?"

"Out back" was the sunset viewing destination for all

fair-weather patrons of the Oasis. The hostess escorted them past the gift shop, through the deserted inside dining area, and onto the high main patio that faced west into the glowing clouds of the sunset. The waterscape of Lake Travis opened three hundred feet below them, shining like blue chrome all the way to the opposite shoreline two miles away. From the cliff-top patio Alex and Quizzy gazed upon the vast, placid expanse. It extended outward, scratched and speckled white by the tiny wakes of minuscule power boats and triangular sails.

Cascading down the cliff from the main patio like wooden waterfalls, the multiple decks of the Oasis supported hundreds of tables impaled by sun umbrellas, their canopies sprouting like colored canvas mushrooms. Patrons faced west as the sun burned into the horizon on the other side of the lake. Alex and Quizzy followed the hostess down several flights of stairs to their table. Alex sat down next to the deck's railing, and Quizzy sat as far away from it as possible. She ordered a margarita, and he a beer. They marveled at the fiery, painted sky.

Alex stood up and peered over the railing. A vireo flitted from branch to branch in a treetop below him.

"Geez, it's straight down into the treetops at the bottom!" he said. "Take a look at this."

"No, I'm just fine here. Unless you want me to throw up. Remember? I don't like heights." A waitress, unfazed by daily spectacular sunsets, brought their drinks and said in a workaday voice that she would return to take their food order. Alex started to propose a toast, but his beer bottle was still capped. He tried to twist it.

"Crap," he said. "I need an opener."

"Not a problem." Quizzy reached into her purse, felt around, and handed a black Swiss army knife to Alex.

"Lock-picking tools, a multipurpose pocketknife—what else do you carry around with you, Ms. MacGyver?" he asked as he pried off the bottle cap. "Got a gun in there?"

"Never. I only keep the knife to open bottles, carve satanic totems, and defend myself from Drago."

"You shouldn't joke about that," Alex said.

"Okay, I don't carve satanic totems."

The waitress reappeared, took their order for fajitas, and vanished once more behind the edge of their deck.

"How are things at the ranch?" Quizzy asked. "How is Seven doing?"

"She's doing pretty well, I think. After the accident ... she wouldn't sleep through the night and cried all the time. Anything would set her off. But she's settled down lately. Samantha's been a big help. She spends a lot of time with her. Sometimes my mom comes down from Dallas for the weekend. Trina's folks in San Antonio are a huge help, too."

"And Charlie and Flora?" Quizzy asked. "Are they still seeing each other?"

"Yeah, they're tight, as Charlie likes to say. Flora's PET scans have all been negative. Her son is riding the zip line. Charlie bought him a kid's harness. I guess you could say things are returning to normal at the Twisted Tree Ranch. It's a new kind of normal, though."

"And you?" Quizzy asked. "How are you doing?"

196

"Pretty well, I guess. I cut a lot less cedar these days, although those trees are like weeds; there's always plenty to get rid of. I exterminated a colony of fire ants in the backyard so I can chip golf balls in peace. Also, I'm selling a fair amount of paintings. Almost all of them are landscapes of the ranch. I was getting so many calls, I signed up with a gallery. I hate paying the commission, but I don't have the time or the inclination to deal with all the potential customers, bless their hearts. The gallery owner says I have a fresh approach and a morbid, yet fascinating subject in the so-called magical ranch. At least he's honest about it."

Quizzy placed her hand over Alex's. "Other than the fire ants and your patrons' morbid tastes, I'm happy to hear you're doing well. I know you've had a tough time of it."

Her hand sent a warm surge through his body. "No doubt about that," Alex said after a moment. "Even my finances are looking up. I sold the unlucky fireball to that poor art collector. I feel kind of guilty about that, but we all went into the deal with eyes wide-open. He and his security chief knew the risks, but I still feel awful. My God, they didn't even last an hour with that cursed rock. If I'd known it was going to get them killed, I would have just donated it to a museum somewhere. I'm lucky it wasn't me or Charlie that got blown up."

"And now the meteorite is missing," Quizzy said, "although I'd bet the Ruthliers have it. I talked to Captain Steiner on the phone earlier today. He's reluctant to discuss the investigation, but the frustration in his voice came through. He can't get a warrant to search the Church of the God Particle. There is a very high standard of evidence required for a judge to sign off on a search warrant for a church. It's constitutional hallowed ground, so to speak."

"What a mess," Alex said. "I wouldn't be surprised to see the Ruthliers on death row at the end of this whole deal. Obviously, the bombing was premeditated."

"I hope they don't end up there," Quizzy said. She looked away from Alex to the sunset.

"I think the Ruthliers deserve the needle if they bombed and stabbed their way to possession of the fireball."

Quizzy removed her hand from Alex's. She shrank away as if the fireball's heat were searing her flesh.

Choosing something less political, he said, "With all the misery the fireball has caused, there's one other thing that looks like it's going to work out, though."

"What's that?"

"I signed a contract to sell water from the spring on the ranch. There's a company in Austin that's started to bottle and distribute it. The stuff should be hitting the shelves in grocery stores in the next few days," Alex said. He shifted in his chair.

"Why?" Quizzy asked.

It wasn't the reaction he was anticipating.

"Why? Well, for the money."

"I understand that's what happens when you sell something. But why would anyone want to buy your bottled water when there are already a dozen other brands on the shelf in every grocery store in town?"

"It's not just in Austin that we'll be selling it. It's all over Texas, and then, if things work out, nationwide."

"Out of your nice little spring? It was barely dribbling the last time I saw it."

"We're going to use the ranch's springwater to *infuse* another source."

"I don't understand," Quizzy said.

"Only a little bit of Twisted Tree water would be added to every bottle. That allows us to maximize the small amount of water we have available from the ranch."

"I understand the technical aspect. But why?"

"Twisted Tree water is magical. Or at least, people think it is, which is all that matters."

Quizzy's shoulders slumped, and she sighed.

Alex said, "You look like my mother when she caught me cheating at Crazy Eights after she taught me to play."

"Please tell me that you're not selling your water as a magical cure for cancer!"

"We're not claiming anything. People can infer what they want."

"Oh, Alex."

"Look, we're just putting a product into the market-place. People can make their own decisions about whether or not to buy it." Anxiety spread outward from his stomach.

"That's just crap, Alex. It's another caveat emptor scheme aimed at the ignorant. It's the worst kind of capitalism. Desperate people will seek out your so-called magic water instead of getting legitimate treatment. It's just another version of snake oil."

He was torn. The uneasiness of the deal with Swillers bothered him, but it was his business, not hers. *Why did I even mention this?* "I don't agree. We're not claiming anything. It's a free country. I'm free to sell something as long as it's not unhealthy or dangerous, and people are free to buy it. That's the way America works." He regretted the words as soon as he had spoken them.

"Please don't lecture me. It's a scam. You say it's infused. Infused with what?"

"Other water."

"What other water? Where does this other water come from?"

Alex pursed his lips. "It's Austin city water," he said.

"You mean tap water."

"Well, yeah. But Austin's city water is perfectly clean and healthy. It's tested all the time."

"Spare me. It's a rip-off."

"Well, I guess you're entitled to your opinion." Alex couldn't think of any good reason to defend the deal, aside from financial. It was becoming clear to him that Swillers' money had clouded his judgment. When he signed the contract he had been worried about providing a secure future for Seven. But now he had the windfall from the meteorite sale....

"Yes, I am entitled to my opinion, and that's it," Quizzy said. "Tell me, who came up with this crazy idea? I thought you were too decent a guy to have thought up a scheme like this." Quizzy took a long drink from her margarita.

Alex slumped and replied, "A marketing guy contacted me. He had everything set up with the bottling company. I just supply the springwater."

"Who is this guy? Did you even check him out?"

"Off the record?"

"Of course off the record, dammit! This is just between you and me, Alex." People at nearby tables glanced at them.

"His name is Billy Swillers."

Quizzy choked as a swallow of margarita went awry.

"Do I need to page Dr. Heimlich?" Alex asked in a feeble attempt at humor.

"Billy Swillers!" she coughed out. She lowered her voice to a forceful whisper. "Billy Swillers was the name at the top of the Platinum Club donor list I saw on the desk in Ruthlier's office. He's the number one contributor to the Church of the God Particle! Christ, Alex, what have you gotten yourself into?"

Interrupting their argument, the waitress arrived, balancing a tray with their food on one upturned palm. She set the sizzling cast-iron plate in its wooden base on the table and then placed their individual plates in front of them. Sensing the tension and her intrusion, she stated the obvious, "Hot plate," and left.

Alex lowered his voice, but said forcefully, "I can't help what Billy Swillers does with his money!" But he knew that his argument was hopeless.

"Maybe not! But if you don't give it to him, he won't use

it to support murderers!"

"I'm not giving it to him. We are in a business deal. A contract. I signed up— I'm obligated."

"Okay, if you want to talk legalese, try this on for size. You might be complicit in murder."

"What? That's pure bullshit! There's no way I could be tied in with any of that."

"Maybe not legally, but you're still tied into it, or at least into anything those bastards do in the future." Alex and Quizzy glared at each other like two hardheaded protestors on either side of a death-penalty picket line.

"I should go," Quizzy finally said. "This isn't working out at all." She pushed back her chair and stood up.

"What about your fajitas?"

"Give them to Mangy." She slung her purse over her shoulder.

Alex stood also. "We shouldn't leave it like this. Maybe we can talk more after we both cool off."

"Maybe. I'm leaving for Romania on Friday. I was going to tell you all about it. Maybe after I get back." She ascended the steps to the deck above, avoiding the railing along the drop-off, and then walked out of the restaurant.

***

Quizzy sat in her car staring across the parking lot. Only the people admiring the sculptures on the lawn kept her from screaming in frustration out of the open window. She pushed the ignition button. *We could have done that differ-*

ently. It didn't have to end like that.

She jammed the Beetle into reverse and chirped the tires as she roared out of her space.

***

"You're home early," Samantha said when Alex shuffled through the door. "Seven is sleeping. So, how'd it go?"

Alex scowled and said, "Hungry? Want some fajitas?" He dropped the Styrofoam container on the table.

"That bad, huh?"

"It was a disaster."

"Oh, sorry to hear that. I know it was important to you. Sort of your coming-out party and all of that."

"Don't remind me."

"Well, at least there's some good news," she said.

"What's that?"

"You only owe me ten fifty."

He asked Samantha whether she would stay another hour or so, since she had already planned for it.

"I'd like to cut back some cedar from the edge of the creek," he said.

"It's dark," replied Samantha.

"I have a light."

21

AILY TEMPERATURES HAD already pushed into the nineties by Memorial Day Weekend. On the Saturday following Alex's dinner disaster with Quizzy, a couple of dozen partiers gathered at Professor Lillian Sorensen's home in the hills east of the Colorado River. Her husband, Ed, a vice president of a local biotech company, perennially hosted the holiday ritual. He stood before the veranda altar of a hulking black-and-chrome barbecue grill, its burner hoods open to the blue afternoon sky. A stained orange apron with a Longhorn logo shielded Ed from flying grease as he orchestrated burger flipping with a wooden-handled spatula. Clouds of aromatic white smoke billowed upward. Hot steel grills seared the flesh and skin of meat darkened with crispy brown patinas. A high-def television sat on a table next to the barbecue grill, showing a PGA tournament in Ohio.

Among the guests were Alex, Charlie, and Flora. Charlie

had eaten a light breakfast, and the sizzle of grilling meat lured him to the veranda. He complimented Ed on his culinary skills, careful not to interfere with another man's barbecuing technique. Beneath the veranda, Professor Sorensen's home workshop occupied a utility room containing HVAC equipment, electrical panels, and a water heater.

When the game ended, the other revelers, sated with barbecue and beer, sloshed to their cars to navigate their way home. Charlie escorted Flora with his arm around her waist. She stepped onto the front porch, and her hair shone when she moved into the sun.

Professor Sorensen said, "Flora, you look wonderful. I'm so happy to hear how well you're doing. I commend you for fighting your illness."

"Thank you, Professor. I may have had a little help from Alex's springwater, if you listen to the gossip."

Sorensen put her hand on Flora's forearm. "I don't believe that," said the professor. Turning to Alex and Charlie, she said, "I'm so happy you all could make it over this afternoon. It feels like I bonded to you all after that awful night of the meteorite. It's too bad Quizzy couldn't come. We've been talking quite a bit lately about meteorites and science in general. She's an information sponge."

"She's in Romania," Alex said, "She's doing a story on the Church of the God Particle. The Reverend Ruthlier emigrated from there before he blessed Austin with his murderous presence."

"Oh, my, her trip sounds risky. You need to keep a close

eye on that girl, Alex," she said. "And what have you been doing with yourself, now that the meteorite isn't your responsibility any longer?"

"Not too much. I'm in a little business project to bottle some of the ranch's springwater."

"Why?"

"It's a long story. Too long for here and now," he answered.

"Too bad you can't use glass. The world is overflowing with plastic water bottles. Millions every day just in the United States. All made from petroleum products. Plus the gasoline and carbon emissions to transport the stuff around. Why don't you think about going into home water-filtration systems instead?" She wrinkled her brow. "But enough of that. You didn't come here for a lecture."

Seeing Alex starting to mope, Charlie interjected, "How's your phosphorescent Amazon slime project coming along, Professor?"

"It's actually a fungus, and it's progressing rather well, thank you. As a matter of fact, if you all have a few minutes to spare I'll show you something you might find interesting." The three affirmed they had the time, and Sorensen said, "Wait here, then." She left for a minute and then returned with a jar half full of a viscous yellowish-green liquid.

"Refined Amazon fungus goo," she stated. "Follow me."

She led them down a staircase that opened into her workshop below. Charlie, the owner/operator of Colvin Machine Works and a man who appreciated a well-equipped shop, said, "You must be very proud of this place." Sorensen grinned.

Fluorescent tubes under white metal hoods hung from the exposed ceiling joists. Pine workbenches with vises bolted to them, and cabinets full of hand tools were pushed up against the walls. Alex could see lab beakers, test tubes, and a Bunsen burner through the glass doors of a vertical cabinet. A white double-eyepiece microscope crouched at the end of one of the benches, next to a computer, monitor, and printer.

"It's my refuge," Sorensen said. "I'm a tinkerer as well as a researcher. This place has enough bare-bones equipment to keep me entertained when I'm not at the office."

She unscrewed the metal lid of the jar and set it on the workbench. From a drawer she withdrew a small bristle brush, and from the printer she pulled out a sheet of typing paper. Dipping the brush in the gooey liquid, she painted a stroke down the center of the paper.

"You're not wearing gloves," Flora observed. "It's not toxic?"

"Not in the least," the professor answered. "You could spread it on bread and eat it, although the nutritional value is minimal."

"Like a peanut butter–and-fungus sandwich," Charlie said.

"How does it taste?" asked Alex.

"Like lightning bugs," Sorensen said. Charlie thought she might really know how a lightning bug tasted.

The professor reached up to a shelf and retrieved a

207

black plastic cube about four inches square on a side, with a standard electrical cord extending out the back. She set it beside the paper she had painted. There were two electrical screw lugs and a dial on the top of it.

"This is a transformer from an electric train set my son had when he was young. He's a marine biologist in Galveston now," she said with pride. "Since he's not using it these days, he said I may."

Two red insulated wires were attached to the screw terminals. She plugged the cord into a wall outlet, turned the dial up to fifty mph, and touched the red wires from the screw terminals together several times in quick succession. A tiny bluish spark snapped each time the wires touched.

Sorensen lowered both wires onto the end of the painted fungus swath, which had dried to a clear sheen on the paper. The end of the swath burst into a bright yellow light. The ball of glowing light slowly progressed up the painted stripe, but the paper did not burn. After the glowing ball passed over a section of the paper, its normal white color reappeared. As the glowing section of the fungus swath advanced, Sorensen laid her bare hand on it.

"Very minimal heat, as you can see."

She removed her hand as the glowing light crawled to the end of the painted swath on the paper. It phosphoresced a few seconds longer, and then the light extinguished as it consumed the last of the fungus fuel.

"There you have it, lady and gentlemen: a cool, harmless, biological light source that can be stored for many years until it's needed. All it takes is an electrical current to start the process. The applications for emergency lighting are tremendous. Batteries that are now required in the event of commercial power failures could be eliminated. All those emergency lights in hallway recesses and stairwells have to be inspected over and over to ensure their batteries are charged. It's a huge cost to maintain them, and they are only as reliable as the inspection routine. With this bio light you just install the stuff and leave it.

"The UT engineering people are testing a mechanical sparking device that will ignite the dried goo. A sensor would detect a commercial power failure and trip a spring-loaded device that generates a spark, and voilà: Let there be light!"

"I'm impressed, Professor," Alex said. "Not that *I* would ever do such a thing, but what's to keep someone from stealing your idea?"

"We've been through some terrible, yet fascinating experiences, Alex. I feel we've formed a common bond of trust among us. I have the utmost confidence that what you have seen here today will remain in this room. Besides," Sorensen said with a Cheshire cat smile, "UT has filed the appropriate patent applications with the feds."

22

EVEN PREACHERS RELISHED Fridays. The Reverend Lucas Ruthlier relaxed in a blue nylon jogging suit, tennis shoes, and his electrode-implanted neoprene skullcap. He stretched his legs on top of his desk, and his leather office chair creaked backward to its limit. He folded his arms across his chest and closed his eyes, comforted by the watchful gaze of Saint Trina's bust across the room. Drago puttered around outside the closed office door, adjusting overhead stage lights. Ruthlier so enjoyed these private moments when he could practice quieting his mind using the EEG machine that had been wheeled next to his desk.

There was only one nagging distraction: What to do about the boy? He could bring down everything, mused the preacher. His routine was just now settling into an uneasy calm after the disastrous car bombing. Disastrous at least in terms of the scrutiny it had brought from the seemingly ubiquitous Texas Ranger captain. However, in terms of personal satisfaction it had been fulfilling in the utmost. He now possessed the Lavender Fireball! To Ruthlier it was the quintessential prize, heralding his coming ascension as a miracle worker and prophet—if he could tap its power. His imagination overcame him, and he luxuriated in a daydream of unrivaled power and influence. His dream, though, soon drifted back to consternation about his son. Over time, Ruthlier knew the jaws of calamity would consume them both if Drago didn't control himself. Talking to him seemed futile.

When his son first told him about the car bomb, the preacher had snapped. He railed at Drago in an incendiary lecture about his recklessness. But joy replaced anger when Drago presented him with the ammunition box and popped the lid. Ruthlier gazed at the meteorite with its mineral veins reflecting the sunlight. Drago beamed at his father's joy, and Ruthlier realized that his just-concluded lecture was wasted. The preacher would have to temper his euphoria. But tempering euphoria was unnatural. In the meantime, they needed to stash the fireball.

Half-asleep at his desk, Ruthlier reminisced back to his boyhood days of studying at Father Lucas's home in Kansas. The priest's house cat would wander in front of a textbook, wanting to be petted. Ruthlier—Fred—would push the cat away, but it always returned. The pattern repeated until he either had to pet the animal or put it out of the room so he could finish his studies. The cat knew that in the boy's heart he wished to pet it more than he wished to push it away, so it kept coming back.

Ruthlier's education and research had at one time been preeminent in the field of physics, but he could never again resume that aspect of his work. No matter. He had gleaned the nature of God, and he would soon demonstrate His power— manifested in himself. That assumed the next phase of the experiment went as planned. The Church of the God Particle was Ruthlier's vehicle of earthly support, both in goodwill and in finance. Nothing was more important than the cause, not even his son. So be it. Throughout history, many have been sacrificed for higher causes. But the thought of losing Drago churned the preacher's insides. *Lord, please don't make me push my son away—or worse yet, make me choose between his life and my work for You.*

The preacher had a following. He would tell his flock what they needed to hear, and they would tell others. When he arrived as the Elemental One, he would find receptive minds.

Ruthlier finally quieted his imagination as he reclined in his office. The faraway whine of Drago's electric drill on the stage lights was almost musical. It represented another incremental step of progress toward the great goal. Images of exploding subatomic particles danced in his mind as he drifted toward semiconsciousness. He dreamily watched as the four scrolling lines danced across the EEG screen. The sensitive, rare-earth electrodes in the neoprene cap picked up his brain waves, even through the luxurious crown of his silver hair.

Ruthlier emptied his thoughts and focused on the image of the Lavender Fireball's nickel-and-iron atomic nuclei immersed in a sea of electrons. He imagined traveling deeper into the mix until he beheld just two nuclei. He halved them, and then halved them again. Deeper and deeper into the subatomic particles he pushed his mind's eye, until he visualized a God particle. The lines on the EEG screen began to squiggle in a cohesive pattern as the synapses in his cerebral cortex fired in unison.

Lucas Ruthlier was ready to tap the power of the meteorite! It was time to reap the dividend of years of focused practice with the EEG machine. The next connection would be directly to the fireball—a human being connected with an object captured in space. An object whose energy had been multiplied a billion-fold when it was pulled into earth's gravity field using the doped crystal, the parabolic dish, and the power of Ruthlier's mind.

The phone on Ruthlier's desk rang, shattering his vision. His legs jerked in surprise, knocking a letter opener off the desk.

"Goddammit, this had better be important!" he roared.

The sound of Drago's drill stopped.

Ruthlier gathered himself and punched the hands-free speaker button on the phone. "Hello," he said in a husky voice as he bent over to pick up the letter opener off the floor.

A familiar voice said, "Reverend Ruthlier?"

"Speaking."

"This is Quizzy Shatterling. I was hoping you could clear up a few things regarding the story I'm writing about the Church of the God Particle."

"I don't have time, Ms. Shatterling."

"When would be a good time, then?"

"That time does not exist."

"I want to give you a chance to comment on information that came to me during my recent trip to Romania."

There was a long pause, and then, "I have nothing to say to you, Ms. Shatterling."

Quizzy plowed ahead. "I talked to a man named Robi Cojocaru. He was your neighbor in the old Working Peoples Apartments in Bucharest. The same building in which you lived. Did you know Mr. Cojocaru?"

There was another long silence as Ruthlier adjusted to the probability that his heretofore delightful day was about to crash down around him.

"No, I don't remember anyone with that name."

"He had a ferret. He said your son killed it when his mother left."

Ruthlier pulled his feet down off the desk and sat upright, rubbing his temple with a meaty hand. He said, "I don't know such a man. My wife died."

Quizzy drilled deeper. "Mr. Cojocaru said that your wife suddenly left one day. And there are no official records of her death. Nothing in the state archives, no cemetery records, nothing."

His anger rising, but still suppressed, Ruthlier countered, "All you have discovered is that there was bad record keeping in Romania during the last years of communism. Does that surprise you?"

"Yes, it does surprise me. The one thing the old state bureaucracy seemed to do very well was keep records."

"My wife is dead, Shatterling. That is all I have to say. Good-bye!" He hit the release button on the call and took a deep breath. He picked up the letter opener for the second time and turned it over in his fingers.

"Bitch!" he shouted and hurled the instrument at the wall. It ricocheted off the oak veneer to the carpet. The phone rang again and Ruthlier thwacked the speaker button.

"Hello!"

"One more thing," Quizzy said before he could hang up. "Mr. Cojocaru said they found a crate full of cemetery artifacts in the storage compartment beneath your stairs. Do you know anything about that? Where did those things come from?"

Scowling, Ruthlier lashed out at the disconnect button again. He kicked back his chair from the desk and began to pace the room. He reached down, grabbed the bent letter opener from the floor, and threw it at another wall.

***

Drago removed his ear from the other side of the office door and returned to the stage scaffolding. Fuming at the meddling impertinence shown to his father, he grabbed an electrical cable and flicked the release on his knife. The blade snapped open. He sliced downward on the cable and then ringed the insulation with deep cuts. He yanked the covering away a layer at a time to expose the bare conductors. She must be stopped, he thought. They all must be stopped.

23

A LEX WASHED DISHES and gazed out the kitchen window. He thought of Trina, and about how upset she had been on the last day of her life when he shot at the vultures from the zip line. He shook his head, smiling through the pain. As if to excoriate his nerve endings a little further, a Texas Ranger patrol car rounded the driveway curve and stopped in front of the house. Through the glare of the windshield, he watched Captain Steiner put on his hat and then adjust it without looking in the mirror. Jessie rose and waited in silence at the front door. Alex glanced at Seven in her playpen. He opened the door before the officer could ring the bell.

"Come in, Captain. What brings you out to the countryside?"

Steiner removed his hat and wiped his spotless black cowboy boots on the mat before he entered. His wide leather utility belt with its holstered Glock, Maglite, and handcuffs punctuated his crisp brown uniform like the black markings on a Doberman. All he needed was pointed ears. He cautiously offered the back of his hand for Jessie to sniff and then petted the top of her head once. For the first time Alex sensed nervousness in the trooper.

"Have a seat," he offered.

"I need your help with the two homicide cases I'm working on that may be connected to the fireball," Steiner said. "I need your permission to do something that's going to be very unpleasant."

"Most everything about this whole affair has been unpleasant."

"Yes, for all of us, but for you most of all. If there were any other way to move forward with this case, I wouldn't be here now. But there isn't."

"So, what's up?"

"The evidence we've collected up to this point has not risen to the level required to obtain a search warrant for a certain place I would like to take a closer look at."

"Would that place be the Church of the God Particle?" asked Alex.

"I'm sorry, but I am not at liberty to say," Steiner said, but with a confirming smile. "We've received new evidence that strengthens our argument for the warrant, but it's still not enough. That's where you and your family come in."

"I still don't understand."

"I need to start from the beginning," said Steiner. "Of course, you remember after your wife's funeral what happened to your family's section of the cemetery."

"Yeah, it was torn to hell by vandals."

"Maybe. There is no way to say this delicately, so I'll just say it. It's possible that your wife's grave was dug up. We'd like to exhume the body to find out for sure, and to see if it's been tampered with."

For a few seconds Alex didn't respond. An array of thoughts flashed into his mind. Was he joking? Not Steiner. At least, not about this.

"That's crazy. Why would anyone want to do that?" Alex sank deeper into his chair. He pictured medieval grave robbers toiling with picks on a moonlit night, bare fingers protruding from holey gloves in a death grip on wooden handles. He couldn't shake the sound of a shovel slicing into fresh earth.

"Like I said," Steiner said, "new evidence has come to our attention. I'd rather not go into details."

"I'm afraid I'm going to need some, Captain, if you expect me to dig up Trina."

Steiner said, "Yes, I suppose so. I expected as much. I would do the same." Alex sensed that Steiner was evaluating his trustworthiness. "You understand, Alex, court cases are won and lost on how the state proceeds. It's important that information doesn't get out, either to tip off anyone or to prejudice a future jury. What I'm going to tell you has to stay between us."

"Agreed."

"Very well, then," Steiner continued. "You know, of course, that Ms. Shatterling went to Romania recently."

"I do." Alex thought back to his and Quizzy's blow-up at

the Oasis. He wished he could rewind the clock and repair that encounter.

"She tracked down Lucas Ruthlier's neighbor when he was living there," Steiner said, "and she interviewed him. Among other things, the neighbor said that Ruthlier left a box of religious artifacts that appeared to have been taken from cemeteries. Ms. Shatterling returned with pictures that the neighbor had taken of the objects before he donated them to a religious charity. They looked like they were from tombstones, mausoleum doors and gates, and there were a few wrought-iron fence ornaments. The common link between the artifacts was that they all represented a saint or a prophet or some other religious figure."

"I still don't understand the connection to Trina," Alex said.

"To get my search warrant for the Ruthliers' church and their living quarters, I need to find evidence that either one of them knows anything about the meteorite's disappearance. Ruthlier has a bronze bust of your wife in his office. I am told it is an extremely accurate reproduction. It would have been very difficult to achieve that likeness, according to an art expert we consulted with." He looked at a photograph Quizzy snapped of it with her cell phone. "He thinks it could be a death mask made by using plaster of Paris applied to your wife's face."

Alex's lips curled in revulsion.

"Sorry," Steiner said. "I'm planning to tell the judge that the fireball and the bust of Trina are both religious icons in the mind of the reverend. If he's fanatical enough to go grave robbing, er ... disinter a corpse, then he's capable of murder in order to get his hands on the meteorite that is the icon of icons, at least in his warped noodle. And as a bonus for the judge, Quizzy has already discovered evidence that Ruthlier apparently gets his jollies by vandalizing cemeteries. I need evidence that he opened your wife's grave in order to make the bust of your wife."

"If you dig up Trina, what would you be looking for?"

"We'd look for evidence that the body was somehow used to facilitate the making of that bronze bust. We'd look for plaster or modeling clay residue around the facial area. Also, plastic or rubber."

Alex shook his head as his thoughts coalesced. "I still don't see how exhuming Trina's body helps you with your murder cases."

"If I find evidence that Ruthlier or his son tampered with your wife's grave to acquire a religious icon I think I can persuade the judge that the Ruthliers would murder to acquire the iconic meteorite. That would get me my search warrant for the church."

"Do you have that photograph of Trina's bust? Can I see it?"

Steiner pulled a photograph from his shirt pocket. He said, "Remember what I said about confidentiality," and handed the photograph to Alex. It was dark, but clear enough. He stared at it for a long time. He turned it from side to side, as if he were trying to look at the sculpture from different angles.

"Whew," he said, and then exhaled. "That's really weird. It's uncanny. It's a perfect likeness, as far as I can tell from this picture." He paused for words. "I feel violated. It's as if he stole her from me. Quizzy told me about this before, but I never saw the pic. This isn't right. Plus, all that crap about Trina being a saint for his wacko religion." Alex lapsed into silence, then hardened with a quiet resolve. After several seconds he said, "What do you need from me?"

"You'd have to go to the Travis County medical examiner's office in Austin and sign some papers. We'll make all the arrangements and take care of everything else, including reburial. And, of course, the county will bear all the expenses."

Alex shook his head. "Man, what a stinking mess. I just want to get on with my life. Me and my daughter. I'm a little overwhelmed by all of this. Let me think about it. Also, I need to talk to Trina's parents in San Antonio. I'll have to tell them everything."

Steiner nodded. "Just make sure they understand the legal mumbo jumbo."

"I'll get back with you," said Alex.

24

MARVIN MOLEY HAD rolled out of bed two hours early so he could prepare for Trina Colvin's exhumation. He hadn't dug up a grave for many years. In the interests of privacy, six thirty in the morning was the optimal time for an exhumation in the latitude of Bee Cave, Texas. The light was good enough to dig, but curious spectators would have to make an effort to go to the cemetery and stay warm—not that they could see anything over the privacy screen Moley had erected the day before.

Sightseers could see only the top joint of the yellow backhoe arm oscillating back and forth. In a different area segregated from the public by another screen, Alex, Charlie, and Trina's parents could see everything. The drone of the backhoe's engine usurped the calls of awakening birds and intruded upon the morning tranquility of the cemetery.

Each bite of the backhoe's bucket into the soft earth

scraped at the psychic scab that covered Alex's anguish. Trina's parents held hands on top of a blanket covering their legs, and her mother dabbed her eyes with a Kleenex. Alex fixated on the backhoe arm as it swung from side to side. It was a pendulum marking time until the final, gruesome conclusion of removing what should have been a forever-undisturbed coffin. On each trip the yellow steel boom dipped lower as the claws of the bucket cut deeper, and then dumped dark earth beside the burgeoning hole.

It took Marvin fifteen minutes to dig within inches of the casket lid. He throttled back the backhoe's engine, and another man in overalls jumped into the hole and probed the dirt with a steel rod until it tapped against the lid. He looked relieved when no one tapped back. The man indicated the depth of the dirt layer on top by spreading his thumb and forefinger. He climbed out of the hole, and Marvin began digging out the sides. When he finished, he repositioned the backhoe and exposed the casket's ends. Marvin and the other man, now wearing surgical masks, reentered the hole and carefully finished digging around the casket with shovels. The sound of shovels scraping away earth that Alex had imagined a few days before was now real.

Marvin and his assistant passed heavy nylon straps under the casket and looped them over the backhoe's bucket. He revved up the engine and lifted the casket out of the grave.

The eternal rest of Trina Colvin had lasted four months.

The backhoe suspended the casket over the work crew

like a metal dinosaur lifting a lifeless carcass for its young to inspect. Clumps of dirt fell away as Marvin, guided by the men on the ground, lowered the casket into an open, larger container. Once the container had swallowed the casket it was sealed with its own lid, and the men slid it into the back of a white delivery truck. A man dressed in blue coveralls with the words "Travis County Coroner" emblazoned across the back pulled down the door of the truck's cargo bay and padlocked it. He then drove his macabre load out of the cemetery and headed toward the morgue in Austin.

Captain Steiner walked to the segregated section where Alex, Charlie, and Trina's parents sat that had a clear view of the unearthed grave. He informed them that this part of the ordeal was finished, and that he would be in touch with the results of the autopsy as soon as they were available. Marvin Moley restarted the backhoe and began to push dirt back into the empty grave. He would have to dig it out again in a few days to rebury the body, but in the meantime the curious public would be deprived of an attractive nuisance. The small crowd that had watched the disinterment procedure was dispersing.

"Are you ready to go, Alex?" Charlie asked.

"I'd like to stay a little longer, Charlie. Can you catch a ride back to the ranch with Trina's parents? I'll be along in a little while."

"Are you okay?"

"Yeah, I'm all right. I just want some time by myself."

Alex watched Marvin finish pushing dirt into his wife's

grave. With the absence of the coffin there wasn't enough to fill the hole completely, just as there was no way to fill the reopened hole in his heart. After the last of the dirt was scraped into the grave, the backhoe and its master rumbled away to the maintenance shed. Alex was left alone, sitting in the morning sun in his folding chair.

He looked around at his family's section of the cemetery. His vision lingered at the graves of his grandparents, aunts, uncles, and cousins. Some retained the Colvin name, and some had acquired other names through marriage. His family's history was rich with stories of tenacious men and women who had contributed to progress and better living. Even the family misfits who had scratched out hardscrabble lives added colorful tales to the Colvin lore.

What will be my legacy?

There was no avoiding the cursed notoriety of Trina's bizarre death. That would follow him forever. But would he overcome that notoriety and rise above the morbid jokes that freakish tragedies spawned? Selling adulterated water with magical powers from a meteorite that killed his wife wasn't going to get him there. He might make a pile of money, but at what cost in the end? *In a hundred years, when my great-grandchildren look upon my headstone, will they joke about my life? Or will they say I overcame a family tragedy and did something worthwhile?* He remembered the hard questions his mother had asked him after his father's funeral. Questions about his passion, his vision of the future for himself and his family, and his commitment to bringing those ideals to reality.

Alex thought about the good fortune most of the people had enjoyed who rested beneath the granite headstones of his family's plot. Much of that fortuity was conveyed by birthright. A Colvin probably had genes for good health and a sound mind. A Colvin probably received a good education and, maybe most important of all, support and association with positive, successful relatives.

He thought about the less privileged in other parts of the cemetery who had burned all their energy just surviving and holding their families together. These unfortunates were of the ilk who would waste precious money on a bottle of deceptive water. Money for a false hope of better health.

And that's going to be my dismal legacy? Taking advantage of gullible people with warped expectations? Have my standards sunk to only what I can legally get away with? Things were becoming simple and clear sitting in the cemetery.

"Hello, Alex."

He came out of his thoughts and slid around in his chair.

"Quizzy!"

She stood behind him. "Am I intruding?" she asked tentatively.

"No! It's good to see you." Never had Alex said anything truer, and he smiled broadly at her. He had no witty line, no snappy greeting, just a warm feeling for the woman standing before him. "I was just thinking about ... everything," he said. "I didn't know you were here today."

"I felt that I should be. This wouldn't have happened," she said as she swept her arm across the scene of Trina's grave, "if I hadn't gone to Romania. I'm sorry you got dragged further into these murder cases."

Alex rose from his chair and faced her. Quizzy's dark curls shone in the crisp air as the rising sunbathed her uncovered head in morning light. She rubbed her hands together in front of her, apparently as much from nervousness as to warm her hands.

Alex shook his head. "It's not your fault. This whole affair has a life of its own. We're all riding a wild bull. I guess we'll ride it until we tame it or it kills us. I intend the former."

"Maybe it will just buck us off," she said.

"I don't think so. We're stuck." Alex smiled, trying to reassure her. "I've ridden a few bulls. I know how it's done." He noticed her shivering. "C'mon, I'll walk you back to your car."

***

Quizzy flipped down her sun visor as she drove east toward Austin. Murder touched so many people in so many ways, she thought. And it changed them all. Its repercussions radiated outward like strands of a spider web, ensnaring random passersby. Three people killed intentionally in order to possess an object that killed an innocent mother in an apparent accident. In the center of the web lay the enigmatic preacher with his incomplete past.

Quizzy knew that as she ferreted out the preacher's secrets, she drew his attention. If his attention got her the story—good. *But what if it gets me killed?* Where was the tipping point? And then there was Alex. Quizzy was drawing him deeper into the web by mere proximity to herself. Yes, murder changed everybody it touched. Alex, especially, judging from what she saw at the exhumation. Maybe it was the morning light, but his face appeared softer. He seemed introspective, but he was also reaching out to her.

25

TRINA COLVIN'S VIOLATED casket had convinced a judge to grant Captain Steiner his search warrant. Tempering his anticipation, Steiner parked his cruiser in front of the Church of the God Particle. Four other Austin police cars and a SWAT mobile unit followed his lead.

Steiner thought back to his difficult conversation of the previous day that had launched the search of the church. In Steiner's downtown Austin office Alex Colvin had sat across from him at his metal desk. Pictures of Steiner's wife and teenage boys in football uniforms hung on the paneled walls. Daylight streamed in from a single window overlooking busy Guadalupe Street.

"Thanks for coming downtown, Alex. Like I said on the phone, the results of your wife's autopsy are in." He thumbed a manila folder on the desk.

"Did you find any plaster residue on Trina's head? Was my wife's grave tampered with?" Alex shifted in his chair, trying to get comfortable.

Steiner fidgeted with a mechanical pencil. "Alex, I have some strange news. We couldn't even find your wife's head. It wasn't in the coffin with the rest of the body."

Alex grimaced, closed his eyes, and tilted his head back. He righted himself and asked, "So what's that mean?" Steiner could see Alex heating up.

"It means that your wife's body was tampered with. Of course we verified with the mortuary that the head was included in the burial."

"So, where's my wife's head?" Alex shouted.

"I do not know, sir."

***

The church's front windows were spotless, as if they had just been recently washed and squeegeed. The last trooper in the search team drove around the building and watched the back door to make sure no one smuggled anything out.

Steiner's first inclination had been to crawl over every square inch of the place during the next Sunday service. But his better temperament, shaped by years of law enforcement experience, prevailed. He realized that Lucas Ruthlier was not a fool just because he had raised a son who was. Finding the Lavender Fireball at the Ruthliers' place of worship and residence would be good fortune beyond reasonable optimism. The reverend was too cagey to risk bringing down his church and self-proclaimed sacred mission by hiding the meteorite in the church, no matter how much perverted comfort its presence might evoke. An unsuccessful search in front of devout families at a Sunday service without an arrest would be a public relations disaster for the Texas Rangers.

Steiner knew the case was dragging, and he needed to agitate his prime suspects. Although the senior Ruthlier was measured and cunning, his son was reckless. Perhaps in his wild impulsiveness he had made a colossal mistake and brought the ultimate incriminating present home to Daddy.

Steiner cupped his hands against the front glass of the building and peered inside. Enough light filtered in for him to discern the vast main congregation room. Above it, darkness veiled the second floor living area, where he presumed the reverend and Drago were still sleeping. There were two black metal stairways leading up to either end of a walkway spanning the front of the living quarters. Steiner knew that Drago was the primary renovator for the church. He made a mental note of the son's dismal architectural imagination. *But he's one hell of a creative car bomber*, Steiner had to admit.

One of his officers pounded on the sliding glass doors while Steiner made a phone call. The detective chose to call Drago, hoping to startle him into doing something stupid. It was impossible to predict what that might be, but he cautioned his men to limit their exposure from inside the building. Steiner couldn't rule out the possibility of a panicked Drago rushing out of his upstairs apartment shooting wildly, throwing knives, or even lobbing a bomb. Drago had the high ground, but there was nothing Steiner could do about that.

"Mr. Ruthlier," he said when Drago answered, "this is Captain Steiner of the Texas Rangers. I have a warrant to search your building. I am at the front door with a contingent of officers, and we need immediate access. Perhaps you can hear us knocking." The other officer continued pounding on the frame of the glass door, sending reverberations through the cavernous building. "Please come to the front door immediately and let us in. Otherwise we will enter with force."

"Fuck you," was all Drago said before he hung up.

"Break it down," Steiner told his men. "Don't let that glass fall on your arms." Steiner apprised the officer at the back door of what was about to happen. Two men dressed in SWAT gear carried a steel battering ram to the front door, but instead of swinging it at the door they just threw it through the glass. Shards flew and shattered when they hit the concrete floor. One of the SWAT men cleared away the remaining glass hanging from the doorframe, and the policemen ran into the building swinging automatic weapons, shotguns, and spotlights toward the second floor.

Steiner shouted into a bullhorn the words beloved to him: "This is the police! Come out with your hands up." He repeated the command until Reverend Ruthlier emerged from an upstairs door in his bathrobe and bedroom slippers. He stood on the elevated walkway with his hands raised. His silver hair was disheveled, and he squinted in the spotlights at the gun barrels pointed at him.

Steiner shouted, "Where is Drago? Where is your son?"

Without lowering his hands, Ruthlier motioned his head at the other door farther down the railed walkway. "Drago!" his father shouted. "It's okay! Come out! Come out now, son! Make sure you keep your hands raised! Just stay calm and walk out the door with your hands up. Everything will be all right."

The door opened, and Drago stepped onto the walkway with his hands above his head. Barefoot and wearing gray cotton sweatpants and a T-shirt, he stared at the police below. Steiner made sure Drago saw him smiling. "Both of you keep your hands raised and come down the steps. We have a warrant to search this building," he ordered.

The elder Ruthlier barked, "You'll pay for that glass! You'll pay for this whole episode! There was no reason to break that door down coming in here."

"You might want to talk to your boy about his phone etiquette," Steiner said.

After the Ruthliers descended the stairs, Steiner instructed his officers to search them. They discovered the preacher's cell phone. Who carried a phone in his bathrobe? Steiner wondered. "Have a seat," he said, and pointed to the nearby folding chairs the congregation used during services. He handed the senior Ruthlier a bundle of paperwork stapled at the corner and then read from his own copy.

"I have a search warrant that directs the state of Texas to seize any and all objects with origins not of the planet Earth; cemetery artifacts; objects associated with or belonging to the deceased person Trina Colvin; explosive materials and/or other bomb-making supplies or instructions; knives with serrated blades; plaster of Paris or any other mold-making materials; fire-retardant suits; barbecuing mittens; and women's clothing: specifically, but not limited to, blond wigs and feathered boas."

"You must be joking," the reverend said.

"Do I look like I'm joking?"

"You are wasting your time," Ruthlier said. "And mine. I'm going to make a call on my cell phone. Please instruct your officers not to shoot me as I reach into my pocket." He hissed the word "officers." Ruthlier opened his phone and dialed a number. "It's happening. The police are here searching the place. You know what to do." Ruthlier listened as the person on the other end talked. Finally, Ruthlier said, "Very good. I knew I could count on you." Ruthlier hung up and looked at Steiner.

Drago had sunk into a Silly Putty slouch in his plastic folding chair, his sinewy, tattooed arms folded across his lean chest. He smirked at Steiner and tightened the ligaments in his neck, making the dark blue dagger dance on his flesh.

At that moment Steiner knew his search was not going to turn up anything useful.

***

After he hung up from Ruthlier's call, Billy Swillers, the number one contributor to the Church of the God Particle and magic-water dealmaker, called his attorney first. The attorney who was summoned to the church in order to ensure that the police complied with the law. Swillers then blocked his caller ID delivery and began calling the news departments of Austin's local television stations and the daily newspaper, the *Austin American-Statesman*. He intentionally omitted Quizzy Shatterling's weekly alternative publication, the *Austin Chronicle*.

"The police invaded the Church of the God Particle in the Southside Shopping Center and have taken it by force!" Billy announced to each of the media outlets. "As a citizen who cares, I thought you should know!"

Billy's last round of calls was to the most fervent members of his church. "I just thought you should know!" was his refrain once again. "I'm going down there to see if I can help!" he told them. Naturally, they went too.

Thirty minutes after Steiner's men had thrown their battering ram through the sliding glass door of the church, the parking lot of the Southside Shopping Center was packed with vehicles of the news media, more police, church supporters, and church detractors who saw a cult in every religion that wasn't their own.

***

The police, under the supervision of Steiner, finished searching the upstairs living quarters and allowed the Ruthliers back into their apartments. Drago changed clothes and, at his father's instructions, isolated himself in the church complex, but it was obvious he utterly failed to calm himself.

The reverend traded his bathrobe and slippers for an expensive cobalt suit and black leather Italian wingtips. To the throng outside, he presented a show of sweeping up broken glass and dumping it into a rubber trash container near the shattered door. From behind the police line the cameras broadcast the image of an embattled preacher not above menial tasks. Especially poignant was the tiny but profusely bloody cut on his finger that seeped scarlet through the snow-white bandage Ruthlier's lawyer had somehow produced. After he swept up the glass, the reverend and his attorney walked through the broken front door to accommodate the straining press.

"We are not a wealthy church, and the police have assured me they will replace this door. If they don't, we'll just have to scrimp and save a little bit more," said Ruthlier with a plastic smile, his thousand-dollar suit breaking the cool morning breeze.

Steiner scowled. What a lying sack of shit! He hated doing public relations work, but he could see the distasteful necessity for it expanding like the hot air of the reverend's words. Steiner looked over the jammed-up parking lot. A group of people were stapling and painting signs. People in other groups nearby argued with one another. He was glad he had called for backup from the Austin Police Department.

"Why are the police searching your church?" one of the reporters with a microphone shouted to the reverend.

"These are times of stress and uncertainty," said Ruthlier. "The collective subconscious of the race of man has summoned divine help. The Elemental One is coming! It has been predicted, and the probabilities are overwhelming. Inertia to maintain the status quo manifests itself as an attack on the messengers of change. This church and I are two of those messengers. You can see for yourself the resistance to our efforts at spreading the word about the true nature of the universe." He gestured at the shattered glass door.

Another reporter shouted over his peers, "Is this search related to the car bomb murders?"

A reporter holding a furry microphone added, "Or the murder of the night watchman at UT?"

"Let me assure you that neither I nor anyone else involved with the Church of the God Particle knows anything about those murders—or any other illegal activity. As I said, our sole mission is to reveal the holy word about the nature of the universe."

Steiner shook his head and conceded that Lucas Ruthlier knew how to use the media.

Ruthlier's attorney stepped in front of the preacher, absorbing the event's focus. "That's all the questions we have time for," the attorney said. "The reverend has to get medical attention for his hand."

As the men walked back inside, a reporter shouted one last question: "Reverend Ruthlier, what exactly is the God particle?"

With a final manipulation of the press, Ruthlier said, "I

invite you all to attend our Sunday services to find the answer to that question." Then he disappeared into the bowels of his church.

Steiner straightened his Stetson and then adjusted his dark brown tie and the collar on his waist-length leather jacket. He walked toward the assembled reporters and motioned to the first one who saw him to come over. Like a colony of fire ants preparing to devour a fighting horned toad, the rest of the reporters swarmed toward the officer. As the reporters elbowed one another for better access, he began speaking.

"I am Captain Greg Steiner with the Texas Rangers. I want to say a few things about the events of this morning. We, of course, have a lawfully executed warrant to search this church, signed by a Travis County judge. When we arrived here this morning we were denied access by the residents, so we had no choice but to use force to gain entry into the building.

"The search warrant is part of the murder investigation of the car bombing of Thomas Loya, an art collector, and his chief of security, Marcus Sloan. We also believe that the murder of the University of Texas night watchman Bobby Ware is connected to the other two murders.

"In no way does this lawful search have any bearing on the religious beliefs or practices of the Reverend Ruthlier, his church, or anyone who worships at this church. This is a murder investigation. Nothing more and nothing less." Steiner waited for the barrage of questions.

"Is Reverend Ruthlier a suspect in the murders?"

"Reverend Ruthlier is a person of interest," Steiner answered.

"But is he also a suspect?"

"As I said, he is a person of interest."

"What about his son?"

"He is also a person of interest."

"You made a statement several days ago that the exhumation of Trina Colvin's body was related to these murder investigations. Is the search of the church today a result of something you found from that exhumation?"

Steiner thought carefully, then said, "This is an ongoing murder investigation. I'm not going to get into evidence that may or may not have been uncovered during the course of our investigation." He winced at his choice of words.

More questions followed about impending arrests and the reasons for the murders. Even though he disliked talking to the press, he had done it enough to have become steady in his demeanor and judgment. Steiner ended the questioning and retreated toward the church to supervise the remainder of the search. As he neared the broken door, he noticed Quizzy Shatterling scribbling notes. News of the raid had spread fast.

More people were in the parking lot. Most were there for the show, but two camps of opinionated protesters were forming and shouting at one another. One side held signs such as, Keep Government Out of Religion, and the other held the opinion, The Church of the God Particle Is a Cult. Steiner asked the sergeant in charge of the Austin po-

240

lice contingent whether he would post a couple of men near the protesters in case their verbal enthusiasm devolved into using the signs as weapons.

Inside the church he looked up at the roof structure. It was suspended by hundreds of steel beams and cross members. Intertwined among those were exposed HVAC ducts, electrical junctions, and conduits. There was no way his men could justify tearing all that apart in their search. The repair bill would be tens of thousands of dollars. That was not in the budget.

By noon the search was finished. As Steiner had predicted at the beginning, nothing of real value was discovered. Still missing was the prize meteorite, the crucial evidence that would link the Ruthliers to the car bomb murders. His men carried out two computers and a few boxes of low-value office supplies that, in theory, could be used to facilitate making a plaster casting.

"Put a towel over that," he instructed one of his men carrying the bronze bust of Trina Colvin toward the press corps. Drago stood far away in a corner and sneered at Steiner as he exited the church, following a trooper carrying the final box.

26

THE FRUSTRATED DRIVER in the Jeep next to Alex tapped his horn, hoping that his southbound lane of Interstate 35 downtown traffic would inch ahead less slowly. To Alex's right the pink granite dome of the state Capitol provided a welcome visual distraction from the dusty glass of the rear windshield ahead of him.

Thirty-five views of the Capitol dome from all directions had been sanctified in 1983 as "unobstructable" by a city council ordinance. The council had panicked when a developer erected a nearby edifice that blocked the dome from a popular vantage point, so they passed the Capitol Corridor View Ordinance. No building in Austin could be erected that obstructed any of the proclaimed "view corridors" to one of the most beloved structures in Texas. Consequently, some of the most valuable downtown real estate parcels were undeveloped parking lots.

But economics and politics were not on his mind, and

Alex was enjoying his protected view of the dome as he crept along the upper deck of the congested superhighway. He didn't even mind answering his cell phone in such slow traffic.

"Hey, Alex. This is Billy. How ya doin' today?"

Alex felt a pulse of revulsion upon hearing Swillers' voice. *Oh well, I need to talk to him.* Alex told Swillers that he was "doin' fine" except for the traffic jam.

"Alex, I was wonderin' if maybe you could help me out with something. Don't you know Quizzy Shatterling, that reporter from the *Austin Chronicle*?"

Cautiously, Alex said, "Yeah, I know her."

"Well, she's been pokin' around the Church of the God Particle, doin' research, askin' a lot of questions. Alex, the church is one of the main investors in our Divine Spring-water project. It's in all our best interests if Shatterling doesn't disrupt things any more than she already has. She even gave the police false information about something she turned up in Romania, of all places. I'm sure you saw on TV the other day that the church was raided. They didn't find a thing, but it sure stirred up a hornets' nest."

Alex reflected on the television coverage and his disappointment that Steiner hadn't arrested either of the Ruthliers. "Yeah, of course I saw it." *And the lunatic who runs your goddamn church dug up my wife's grave and stole her head!* He refocused. "Billy, we need to talk."

Swillers was ready to talk, but not to listen. "So do you think you might have a word with her?" he asked.

"Billy, I can't tell Quizzy what to do or what to write.

243

Nor would I, even if I could."

"But she's liable to screw up the whole deal." Alex could hear the frustration in his voice. "Someone needs to muzzle that bitch!"

Alex felt a hot surge of blood rushing into his face. "Billy, you listen to me. Your church has caused me nothing but grief." He thought of Captain Steiner, and the promise the Ranger had made to him about the confidentiality of the murder investigations. He stopped himself from lashing out at Swillers about the results of Trina's autopsy. "All I wanted was for me and my daughter to get on with our lives after the death of my wife. That hasn't been possible, and I blame your God particle church for that."

"It's a wonderful church, Alex! With a new message for the times!"

"It's not the message that's disrupting my family's lives, Billy. I don't even know what the hell that message is about, and I don't really care. The problem is the loose nuts running the place. For God's sake, Billy, they're murder suspects!"

"That's not true!"

"Of course it's true! It's common knowledge that they're suspects."

"No, that's not what I meant. I mean they didn't do it." Alex didn't reply. "It's a smear campaign!" Swillers sounded like he was ready to cry.

"Listen, Billy. There's something else I want to tell you. I'm pulling out of the water deal."

There was a moment of silence.

"What do you mean, you're pullin' out?"

"Just what I said. I'm calling off the whole thing. I can't live with it. It stinks."

"*Bull ... shit!*" Swillers yelled in two distinct words. "You can't pull out! People have invested in this deal! You can't just walk away!"

"I can, and I am. I've given it a lot of thought. I can't stop you from going ahead on your end, but as of now, I'm done. You can continue producing your Divine Springwater. All you have to do is keep diluting the springwater you've already taken from my place. You can dilute it forever. Right down to the last fucking God particle. It's the same scheme as what you set up in the beginning, just the proportions of my springwater to your tap water will have to change. You'll have to *infuse* less."

"You can't do that!" Swillers sputtered. "You signed a contract! We'll sue your ass off!"

"I don't think so, Billy. Terms of any contract are null and void if they stipulate something illegal. Now that I've had a chance to really look at this thing, I'm ready to say that the Divine Springwater scheme is a fraud perpetrated on the public. Maybe you should report me to the attorney general or the FTC. See what they have to say about the whole thing."

"*Fuck you!*"

"Goodbye, Billy. Make sure you tell whoever is running your chimp show not to send the water truck out to my place anymore. I'll just turn it away."

Alex severed the connection. Traffic was moving again,

and the Capitol passed from view behind an unpatriotic building. He lowered the window and breathed deeply. Even diesel fumes were preferable to Swillers's foul phone air. He felt refreshed.

***

Swillers had put together hundreds of oddball deals in his life. Some had made money, some hadn't, and a few had lost money. But for every one of them he had fought tenaciously to make it work. He considered the Divine Springwater project to be one of his best ideas yet. His frustration turned to anger. Swillers set his phone on the desk in front of him. "Damn, Lucas ..." was all he could force out.

The reverend looked at him and said, "I take it that didn't go well." He then looked at his son leaning against the wall. "Drago, don't do anything rash. Do you understand?"

"Of course, Father."

27

THERE WERE ONLY a half dozen swimmers in the long Barton Springs pool, even though the sun was shining. Quizzy traversed the considerable length of the spring-fed pool with a leisurely backstroke. It was her last lap, and the exertion warmed her body inside her one-piece suit, goggles, and swim cap.

The endorphin high of the workout cleared her head, and she imagined herself living at these springs ten thousand years earlier. The nearby office towers and high-rise condos of downtown Austin faded away in her mind, and the lush floodplain of a free-flowing Colorado River replaced them. The springs fed the creek, the creek fed the river, and the river fed the gulf. The evaporated water from the ocean rained over the land, replenishing the aquifers and recharging the springs, completing the cycle. How beautifully simple.

Quizzy finished her last lap and hoisted herself out of

the water onto the concrete walkway. Next to the bathhouse overlooking the public pool, she could see Alex leaning against Philosophers' Rock, the life-size statue in front of the bathhouse. Cast in bronze, three old men sat on a boulder conversing about an opened book one of them held. It reminded Quizzy of the tattoo on her forearm: the chameleon in wire-rimmed glasses reading a book whose title was illegible.

Alex hoisted Seven out of her stroller, set her in the arms of one of the metal men, and then snapped her picture. "Wave hi to Quizzy!" he said.

Seven waved at everyone and to no one in particular. Quizzy, sans swim cap and wrapped in a towel, stood on the concrete at the edge of the pool and waved back. She entered the bathhouse and reappeared a few minutes later dressed in jogger's pants and a sweatshirt.

They walked downstream along the trail, where the creek flowed into the Colorado River at Lady Bird Lake. Across the expanse of serene water, the glass-and-steel skyline of downtown rose into the warmth of the Texas sunshine. Kayakers and canoers paddled in the calm water, while a UT crew team stroked a beeline down the center of the narrow lake. The view mesmerized even Seven, and the three of them settled onto a bench, out of the way of joggers and walkers relishing the perfect weather.

"I like it that the water from my little spring finds its way here," Alex said.

What's left of it after it's bottled, Quizzy thought. "When you called me, you said that you wanted to talk to me about Billy Swillers."

"Yeah, he called me yesterday, asking me to lean on you to ease up on the story you're writing about his church."

"Why would he ask you that?"

"I don't know. I guess he thinks I have your ear."

Quizzy thought a second and said, "That bothers me. No one 'has my ear' except maybe for my editor. Why would Swillers think that you could influence me?"

"I don't know. I didn't ask."

"What did you tell him?"

"That I didn't have your ear."

"Good answer."

"Listen, Quizzy. Swillers was really worked up. I think he wanted me to pass on an implied threat."

"Ruthlier tried that before I went to Romania. Look where it got him."

"Ruthlier is still a free man, though. They're dangerous people, Quizzy. I know we've talked about this before, and I know you're going to write your story, but you need to take every precaution you can."

"What's that supposed to mean?" she said in a rising voice. She calmed herself and said, "I'm not angry with you, Alex. I know you're trying to help. But what am I supposed to do differently?"

"I don't know. Just limit your exposure to them whenever you can."

She looked at him. "That's going to be difficult. I intend to go to a service at their church."

"Oh, Christ."

"Those people are not Christians," she said. "Anyway, I have to go there again. I can't write a story about a church and its allegedly criminal preacher and not ever attend a sermon. Besides, there will be plenty of other people there. The Ruthliers wouldn't dare try anything funny."

Alex ran both hands through his sandy hair, and Quizzy read the consternation on his face. He let out a sigh. "'Try anything funny?' That's a nice euphemism. I wish you wouldn't go."

"Alex, if they're so dangerous, why are you in business with them?"

"I'm not. I fired them. That's one reason I wanted to talk to you today. I told Swillers I was out of the deal."

"Whoa! Why didn't you say so? I thought you had signed contracts, and the bottled water was in production. What made you change your mind?"

"I did sign a contract, and it is in production. But the more I thought about the whole affair, the more it stank." He told Quizzy about the rest of his phone conversation with Swillers.

"Maybe you should be the one taking precautions," she said.

"You're probably right. But as you said, what to do? The Ruthliers are going to screw up and make a mistake. Steiner is all over those guys. He's on a mission to put them away for a very long time. Hell, they're probably headed for a double date with the needle."

Quizzy sighed and said with a dismissive wave, "That's not a joking matter."

"I'm not joking. No matter what you think of capital punishment, the Ruthliers qualify, according to my law book. That's assuming they were behind the car bomb, as I do. Those murders were premeditated and carefully planned."

Quizzy slumped on the park bench. She looked at Seven, who had fallen asleep in the stroller. With wet eyes she looked at Alex and said, "I can't escape from it. It follows me around and twists me up like I'm a piece of clay."

"What do you mean?" he said. Quizzy sat up, knotting her hands in her lap. "What follows you around?"

"Death. Dealing with death. The death penalty. Alex, you don't know who I am, do you?"

He shrugged. "I think I do."

"Shatterling is the name of my uncle's family," she said. "I went to live with them when I was nine. They raised me after that. Before then my last name was Simmons. My father was Jonathan and my mother was Claire. Claire Simmons." She said the name feeling as if she were a grieving relative reading it from a tombstone. She waited as Alex searched his memory.

"The name sounds a little familiar, but I can't recall anything more."

"I'm glad you don't know the name. Maybe there's hope, after all." She laughed, but she heard the resignation in her voice. "My mother got the needle, as you so cavalierly put it. Courtesy of the state of Texas."

"Your mother was executed?" His face contorted with incredulity.

"My mother killed my father when I was nine. There was a trial and then eight years of appeals. My family wasn't poor, but we didn't have the kind of money it takes for drawn-out legal proceedings and high-priced lawyers. That and all the money they spent on me for shrinks. It wouldn't have mattered for my mother, though. After eight years the appeals ran out, and so did my mother's time. End of story—end of her life. Like I said, I had been adopted by my aunt and uncle long before the time my mother was ... executed. They raised me until I came to college here at UT."

Alex said, "I remember my parents talking about it one day when I was a teenager. It was on TV, too. It's coming back to me.... You saw it happen! You had to testify against your mother!"

Drained, she nodded. "My mother was schizophrenic. The shrinks for the prosecution didn't see it that way, but she was delusional. I have to believe that to explain what she did. To explain what happened to me."

"She shot him, didn't she?"

"Yes. My parents' marriage had gone bad. My father was seeing someone else. My mother wanted a divorce, but he wouldn't agree to it. He thought their staying together would be best for me," she said, her eyes watering. "They got into a big argument in the driveway. My mother couldn't take it, and she snapped. She ran into the house, got his pistol, and went back out. I watched, terrified, through the living room window.

"My mother tried to cover everything up. She tried to

use me as her alibi. She told me to say that a mugger surprised us and shot my father. The cover-up is what got the crime elevated to a death-penalty case. The whole story fell apart, of course. Nine-year-olds aren't capable of lying like that. She hadn't even understood that. It's like she didn't know me—or even understand children, for that matter. There was a nightmare trial with a guilty verdict, and then eight more years of slow-motion hell with the ultimate worst outcome."

"Oh, God, Quizzy, that's horrible. I can't imagine." Alex massaged the side of his head with his fingertips. "Do you have any brothers or sisters? Someone else who went through all of that with you?"

"Nope. Just me."

"I'm so sorry. Thank God for your aunt and uncle. I'm sure your father is pulling for you now, though."

She wrinkled her forehead in puzzlement. "I thought you weren't much into that religious stuff."

"I'm not, but I think people live on after they die."

"That's religious."

"Regardless, I'm sure your father wants you to stay safe."

"Why? Because I'm all that's left of a murderous family?"

"You're being too hard on yourself. Trust me on this."

"That's my problem. I don't trust anyone. Ask my shrink."

Alex said, "Your distrust makes you a great reporter, if that's any consolation."

"What?"

"As a journalist, you don't trust what anyone tells you. You take the extra step to verify everything."

"In that case I'd settle for being a lousy reporter."

Seven awoke, looked around, and then began to squirm in her stroller. Alex lifted her out, and she toddled a few steps to Quizzy. "Look at you!" she said and took the child's hand. Alex joined them. Seven explored for a few minutes while Alex and Quizzy decompressed with small talk.

"She needs to be changed," he said. "Let's head back to the pool. I'll take care of her in my truck." Alex put one arm around Quizzy's shoulders, and pushed Seven in her stroller with the other.

When Seven was in a dry diaper and strapped into her car seat playing with a Snickers wrapper, Alex hugged Quizzy good-bye and asked, "When are you going to the Church of the God Particle?"

"This Sunday."

"Do you mind if I tag along with you?"

"Really?"

"Yeah, I think it might be a good idea. I'm a little curious to see what all the fuss is about, anyway."

"Absolutely," Quizzy said with a broad smile. "If you're sure you want to go...."

"Yes, I'm sure. Trust me."

28

"WORMS OR MINNOWS?"

"What?"

"Are you going to use worms or minnows?"

"Worms today."

"Good. Dig some for me." Lucas Ruthlier handed his son a spade he had just removed from the trunk of his Lexus. Carrying fishing poles, a minnow bucket, folding chairs, and a tackle box, they walked through the weeds down to the water and set up the chairs. They had dressed in nearly identical clothing—work boots, cotton shirts, and work pants—but they could never be confused with each other.

The elder Ruthlier was thick and moved with power. His silver-haired battering-ram head was a beacon that demanded attention. His son's disturbing throat tattoo also demanded attention, but then it repulsed. Drago, with his short-cropped hair, darted through the weeds searching for good worm dirt.

Ruthlier pulled a hunting knife from his pants pocket and removed it from its leather sheath. He walked to Drago. "Here, use this to cut down that carton."

Drago took the knife from his father and halved a cardboard Tropicana carton with a circumcising cut. He threw the top onto the ground, and then proceeded to turn over several shovelfuls of rich, dark soil under a rotting elm tree. He picked out a dozen fat night crawlers and put them in the bottom of the cardboard container, and then crumbled a few handfuls of dirt into it.

When Billy Swillers had purchased the small ranch years earlier, he bulldozed an earthen dam across the small creek that bisected the property. He buried a galvanized culvert high in the center, so when the pond was full, the water overflowed back into the creek bed. Most of the time the creek was dry, but it flowed often enough to keep the pond respectably full. Swillers kept it stocked with bass and crappie and invited his best friends to avail themselves of the plentiful fish.

It was a splendid day in central Texas. The air was motionless, and the intermittent buzz of flying insects drifted over the glasslike surface of the water. Relentless heat would soon enough desiccate plants, animals, and people.

But today is today, and it should be enjoyed to the fullest, mused the reverend. At least, as much as possible. He looked at Drago sitting a few feet away and feared that leisurely nature outings might be far down on a future list of available activities remaining for his son. The Texas Ranger was closing in, relentlessly investigating each lead, eliminating escape routes like a boxer cutting off the ring. He couldn't be allowed to stop the mission. The path for the Elemental One must be unobstructed.

Ruthlier gritted his teeth at the irony of Captain Steiner's mission. The man was sworn to uphold the law, presumably to better society. Yet Ruthlier was certain that the captain's small-minded endgame of apprehending Drago and himself would cause greater harm in the long run. People like the Ranger had become cynical, he lamented. Too many false prophets, schemers, and power brokers cloaked in the robes of religion had disgraced themselves. In the age of mass media and blurred time zones, news of their misdeeds had jilted so many. Long ago, Ruthlier had vowed that by the time he absorbed the energy of the meteorite and revealed himself to be the Prophet, his congregation would be open and accepting. The rest of society would eventually follow when his new abilities were comprehended.

Drago slouched in his lawn chair, floating in and out of consciousness like his red plastic bobber undulating on the ripples of the pond. Ruthlier marveled at how his son could be so tranquil in the face of the looming threat. But he knew that Drago could become an aroused predator in an instant. He had proved that beyond any doubt. His fixation on delivering the fireball had unveiled cunning and ruthlessness, wisdom notwithstanding. He had murdered three people, two of them with a spectacular car bomb, attempting to please his father.

Even though Drago was as relaxed as the turtle sunning itself on a log at the far end of the pond, the preacher understood that his son was uncontrollable. He had been reckless. Perhaps his intent was well-meaning, but his judgment was atrocious.

Despite the warm sun on his chest and the fishing pole in his hand, Lucas Ruthlier could not relax. He was about to undertake his greatest experiment. Its success depended upon his mind's focus. But he was preoccupied. He was going to be tested; he could feel it. The time was growing near when he would have to make hard decisions. Decisions that could determine who lived and who died. He didn't know how his choices would manifest themselves, or whose life would be in his hands, but the preacher knew that even his own life was in play. There could be only one guiding principle—the mission to create himself as the Elemental One was paramount. All else dimmed in importance. When the time came, would he have the courage to do *anything* that was necessary? Could he sacrifice his son, or eliminate whoever else obstructed his mission? The thought of losing Drago knotted his stomach. He had promised all those years ago that he would never abandon the boy.

Those questions weighed on Ruthlier as the afternoon wore on. The bass and catfish he and Drago yanked out of the pond did little to ease the preacher's stress on a day he needed to be stress-free.

"Drago, it's time to do what we came out here for.

We've fished long enough."

"I understand."

They loaded their gear back into the trunk of the Lexus, except for the spade. From the backseat Drago pulled out one of the recliners they had used on their church's roof and a small wooden table. Ruthlier slung the spade across his shoulder. The men walked into the woods a few hundred feet; Drago dumped the recliner and table, and Ruthlier gave him the shovel. He began to dig in silence. After a few scoops the blade chinked against something hard. His son went to his knees and dug around the object with his hands. When it was half-uncovered he pulled it out of the hole by one of its handles. Grinning, Drago held up the metal ammunition box with one hand, as if he were a warrior showing off a vanquished foe's severed head.

Beaming, he presented the olive-green box to his father. The preacher tried to suppress his excitement, but he knew Drago could see his joy. He and the Lavender Fireball were reunited! Ruthlier's hands trembled with anticipation as he accepted the box, and he held it to his chest. He then set it on the ground and pulled open the lid.

He gasped at the sight of the meteorite inside. He lifted it out and cradled it like a newborn. The iridescent blue and green veins of minerals within the iron and nickel shimmered in the afternoon sun against the dark contrast of its craggy recesses. To the preacher the rock was fragile, as if it were alive, regardless that it had already survived a fiery supersonic impact. He set it on top of a small wooden table next to one of the recliners, and then he climbed into the recliner and lay back. Nervous tension gripped the preacher's body. The fireball was holy. The time he had labored his entire life for had arrived.

Ruthlier prepared himself to connect with the fireball. *Will I survive?* He tried to imagine the flood of energy that would soon be coursing through his body. Like radiation, it would assault the DNA strands in his cells, migrating proteins in genes that controlled the tissue of his brain and nervous system. His genome would be forever altered in an epigenetic explosion.

He motioned Drago to stand farther back, and then he closed his eyes. Clearing his mind of everything else, Ruthlier imagined a God particle and the four lines of an EEG screen moving in the synchronous pattern he had practiced so many times. His mind emptied, and a warm feeling of well-being cascaded through his body.

Ruthlier reached out to the fireball on the wooden table and placed his hand on top of the dark rock.

Lavender stars exploded in his head, and he felt a rush of energy permeating his body. Motionless in the recliner, he gave himself over to the kaleidoscope of visions and feelings passing through his brain. A singular image of a God particle intensified and shimmered in his mind's eye, and he floated into its core. Darkness enveloped him.

***

Drago stood leaning over his father in the recliner, staring in alarm at him. Ruthlier opened his eyes and looked from side to side. "How long was I out?"

"A few minutes. I wasn't sure what to do."

"There is nothing to do. It's beyond your control. Beyond my control now."

Drago took a quick breath. Nothing had ever been beyond his father's control before.

Ruthlier got out of the recliner and stood in the soft grass, looking around as if he were seeing the place for the first time. He pointed to the ground.

"That twig. I'm going to raise it."

Drago watched as his father stared at a small, branched twig in the grass. The lines on Ruthlier's forehead deepened as he concentrated, and his breath came in short huffs. As he labored, perspiration soaked through his collar.

The twig remained in the grass, unmoving.

"That's not possible!" the preacher cried with exasperation. "Maybe less mass.... A leaf!" Drago watched as his father bore down with his concentration on a dried leaf.

Nothing.

His father whirled around, frantically searching for something even smaller he could affect. Despair crept over his father's face, and his focus evaporated. With a stricken expression, he picked up the meteorite off the table and shoved it at Drago. "Let's get out of here."

Drago placed the fireball back into the ammunition box, and when they got to the car he loaded their gear into it. Ruthlier quietly slid into the passenger seat and Drago started the engine. He looked at his father. He had never seen him so crestfallen—not even when his mother had abandoned them in Romania. As they drove back toward Austin, Drago tried to squeeze the life out of the steering wheel with white-knuckled fingers while his father stared dumbfounded out the window.

29

THE STOLEN MOTORCYCLE purred down the blacktop as the cold night air chilled the rider. At this speed, a startled deer springing out of the bar ditch would be devastating. Drago locked the machine's throttle and used both gloved hands to snap shut his jacket collar. He grasped the handlebars once again and lowered his helmeted head. He twisted the throttle open, accelerating the bike to more than a hundred miles per hour. Damn the deer and screw the law. At one a.m. on deserted County Road 1440, he was more likely to encounter the former.

He blew by his destination—a ravine filled with scrubby mesquite trees—and decelerated. He turned the bike around and guided it off the road among the thorny trees.

Satisfied that the bike couldn't be seen from the road in the moonlight, Drago killed the engine, dismounted, and knocked down the kickstand with a well-worn boot. He walked a hundred yards away from the road through the open field and stashed his helmet, using a persimmon tree as a marker so he could find it on the return trip. From his backpack he pulled out a gray wool stocking cap, covered his head, and then resumed walking parallel to the road. If a car were to appear he could crouch behind the scrub and avoid its headlights. After fifteen minutes he angled left and crossed the road. On the other side of the ditch he ducked between two strands of the barbed-wire fence delineating the property of the Twisted Tree Ranch.

The maintenance trail that Alex and Charlie used to haul supplies and cattle feed to the top of the ridge angled up its back side. At the top, the massive oak tree for which the ranch was named overlooked the canyon in front of it. Drago covered the distance in twenty minutes. Everything he needed was in his jet-black canvas backpack.

Far below in the canyon, the front of Alex's ranch house shone in the light from the pole next to the carport. There were no lights burning in the house. The creek was a dark ribbon meandering along the floor of the canyon. Four months earlier Drago had searched next to it with the metal detector, looking for the meteorite.

He thought about slipping into the house and killing the owner in his sleep, but there was the bull terrier to contend with. Besides, his other plan was much more elegant. Drago sat down on a rock and breathed the cool night air. He touched his neck and felt the blood pulsing beneath his dagger tattoo.

He envied the sleeping man in the quiet house below.

No nightmares for the prick Alex Colvin. At least, not nightmares of a mother cutting her son's throat. Countless nightmares, all the same. How many times had he awakened thrashing and screaming as his mother hovered over him with a knife? The terrifying image had plagued him since he was a little boy—since he heard his mother proclaim she was going to cut his father's throat. So then why not his own? And then she vanished from his life, leaving behind a haunting apparition to stalk him when he slept.

The worthless psychiatrists never succeeded in banishing his maternal demon. She terrorized him until he became a reactionary cluster of tangled nerves. He grew to resent other people who were not also persecuted. It was so unfair. Everyone should have to overcome a hellish torment. The particulars were unimportant; it was the struggle that built character. Look at how it had hardened him—how it had instilled a machinelike efficiency into a superb physical specimen.

On his eighteenth birthday, Drago's mother had again attacked him in his dreams. It seemed that nothing could keep her at bay. He drove downtown and slipped a panhandler a few dollars to buy him a bottle of tequila at a seedy liquor store. After he poured a cup for the other man, Drago finished the bottle. *I cannot defend myself against my mother's dagger*, he reasoned with inebriated logic. *Embrace it. Absorb it. A blade that is embedded cannot cut.*

In an attempt to cover the smell of tequila on his

breath, Drago had chewed a stick of gum as he walked to a nearby tattoo parlor. In excruciating detail he described to the artist the knife that tormented him, down to the drops of blood trickling off the blade. Three hours later he staggered out of the tattoo parlor with his newly inked skin and high hopes that his knife-wielding mother would let him be.

She wouldn't.

***

The shining steel cable of the zip line fastened around the muscular, twisted trunk of the huge oak tree and then stretched out over the edge of the cliff before disappearing into the darkness of the canyon. Drago scrutinized the design. The two roller assemblies were secured around the base of the oak tree with thin chains and rusted padlocks to prevent anyone from taking an unauthorized ride. He studied the attachments of the thick stainless-steel cable to the tree.

They have made it easy for me.

From the backpack Drago withdrew a hacksaw and a thick towel he had shoplifted from the Bed, Bath & Beyond in the Southside Shopping Center. He began sawing the eyebolt of the turnbuckle. He draped the towel over the blade to muffle the noise. With slower and slower strokes, he sawed two-thirds of the way through the bolt. He examined his work, caressing the weakened metal.

Drago removed a lump of modeling clay from his pack

and forced a thin wedge into the cut. He spread a layer of silver paint on the clay patch to complete the job. No one would be able to detect the tampering unless he was inspecting the turnbuckle up close. He was sure his father would be pleased with the end result—once he calmed down. Soon there would be one less meddler.

Drago stared at the ranch house. It didn't matter who rode the zip line, he thought: the asshole rancher, his hick cowboy cousin, or the bitch reporter. They all needed to go.

He gathered his tools into the backpack and retraced his path down the maintenance trail. Looking across the moonlit ridge, he thought about the chupacabra legend of these hills. *I'll cut its throat if it fucks with me.* Drago followed his footprints back down the ridge, across the road, stopping to pick up his helmet under the persimmon tree.

The last thing he did before climbing onto the bike was to change into another pair of boots he had removed from the bike's leather side bag. After a glance in both directions to make sure no cars were on the road, he started the machine, pulled onto the blacktop, and sped for Austin.

When he reached the city limits, he drove behind a Taco Bell and threw his old boots into the nastiest-smelling Dumpster he could find.

30

RUTHLIER HAD SPIRALED into a depression. He moped around his apartment above the church for a week, and his next sermon was uninspired. He repeated the self-hypnosis procedure to modify his brainwaves dozens of times while touching the fireball, always with the same results. He didn't understand why he couldn't assimilate the power in the meteorite, but he refused to capitulate. Years of research and sacrificed lives demanded that he continue with another plan.

The realization that he would never become the Elemental One was slow and painful. But Ruthlier was a pragmatist, and after the worst period of his life he resigned himself to the alternative that another person should take his place. That no one would step forward into the next phase of human evolution was an unbearable thought. His life's work could still be achieved. The reverend controlled access to the fireball. Whoever was to be consecrated would be from his church. The influential preacher would then lead the Chosen One through the perils of a disbelieving, hostile society. The reverend would be with him step by step.

Reverend Ruthlier was eager to see how his newest sermon would be received. He had been practicing his oration for weeks in front of the EEG machine. The sermon was painstakingly crafted to send the minds of his congregation into a state of blissful receptiveness.

One other important thing was new in the Church of the God Particle: the collection plates. The old ones had been sterling silver embossed with a lacy design around the rims. The new plates were simply white-glazed ceramic. Ruthlier had commissioned Albert Ronson, the sculptor of Trina's bust, to craft them. Each plate had a chip of the Lavender Fireball embedded in its base, exposed to the touch of anyone who held the plate. The preacher would be watching for sudden changes in demeanor as the plates were passed among his parishioners.

***

The adolescent door-boys hadn't lost any of their enthusiasm since Quizzy's last visit to the Church of the God Particle. With feverish smiles they handed her and Alex the morning's program when they passed through the whooshing sliding glass doors. She prayed this visit would be less dramatic than her last.

Why do I not want to be seen at this place? She was

dressed to be inconspicuous: flat shoes, dark jeans, white cotton blouse, and a beige sweater tied loosely around her waist. She guided Alex to an open space in the mingling crowd where they could look around and orient themselves.

"Oh, my God, this place is huge," Alex said. He surveyed the vast room with rows upon rows of folding chairs on the polished concrete floor. The colorful stained-glass panels assembled against the outside windows shone in the morning sun. At the front of the room the lacquered pecan pulpit on the stage awaited the main event. Reverend Ruthlier was dressed in a dark suit, talking to a group of people in front of the stage. Drago was not in sight.

Alex noted the colorful painted rooms along the sides of the building, but the most intriguing feature of the immense structure was the dark, looming overhang of the second story living quarters.

"That's got to be where Ruthlier and Drago live," Quizzy said when she saw Alex staring at the iron beams supporting the floor. High, narrow windows designed for looking out overlooked the cavernous main room and the crowd below.

"It's a defensible fort," Alex said. "I wonder what goes on up there?"

"Nothing good, I'm sure. Look, there are two doors. One must be Ruthlier's apartment and the other Drago's," Quizzy said.

The crowd was moving into the seats, and the reverend had disappeared.

"Let's sit down. It looks like it's showtime."

The houselights dimmed, and a spotlight appeared on the pulpit. Another light shone on a curtain at the side of the darkened stage. Quizzy wondered whether Drago was operating the lights. From behind the curtain a wide figure draped in a flowing lavender robe emerged into one of the lights. The robe covered Ruthlier's shoes, and he appeared to float across the floor as he moved to the pulpit, where the spotlight beams came together on him.

"Welcome, friends! Welcome to the Church of the God Particle! I give thanks that we are here together."

Quizzy gave thanks that the congregation didn't break into applause. She wondered how a human being could make silver hair shine so brightly. *What does he use on it?*

The effervescent preacher proceeded through the mundane business of church matters. He announced next week's potluck dinner, an art supplies fund-raiser for the neighborhood elementary school, and a request for canned goods for the local food bank. The program progressed to a song about opening one's heart, sung by a guitar-playing young woman dressed in a white robe.

The woman was still onstage, singing, when Quizzy noticed a tapping on the back of her chair in sync with the beat of the music. She turned around to see a parentless six-year-old girl in a blue dress pretending that she was the drummer.

With a stern look, Quizzy said to the girl, "Your tapping is making me crazy." The girl stopped, contemplating the implications. Quizzy turned her attention back to the stage.

When the singer finished her second song, Ruthlier returned to the pulpit and announced that at the end of the sermon a collection plate would be passed, and that he and God appreciated everyone's generosity. "Embrace the plate and feel its energy. That energy will be directed for the utmost good."

As Ruthlier began his sermon, Quizzy removed a notepad and a pencil from her handbag and made notes. She produced a small pair of binoculars and focused them on the preacher. After a few minutes she shifted her view and looked around at the crowd. So much for remaining inconspicuous, she thought. But none of the churchgoers seemed to notice the binoculared woman peering at them. They were fixated on the preacher.

Ruthlier's billowing robe, punctuated at the top by his enormous head, shone in the lights only slightly less than his silver hair. There were insignias on the robe's chest and sleeves: the same interlocking, multicolored tubular design that adorned one of the stained-glass panels by the front windows. As he moved his arms the emblem undulated on the lavender cloth. It was impossible not to look at it.

Quizzy gave the binoculars to Alex, who then began his own observations of the preaching man at center stage. After a few moments Alex pivoted his head like an owl scrutinizing a crowded nightscape. Quizzy opened the program given to her by one of the grinning adolescents at the front door. The title of the day's sermon was "Catch the Bus."

Ruthlier began, "Imagine it's night and you're waiting at a bus stop. It's raining, but you have an umbrella, so you are dry and warm. The pleasant patter of gentle rain on your umbrella drowns out the street noise. It also quiets the cacophony of hectic thoughts in your mind built up during the long day.

"As you relax in the rain you close your eyes and begin to daydream about who you are. Not about your likes and dislikes, but about your deepest and truest identity. It is an identity that is unique, like a vibration or tone that you feel deep within yourself that permeates your being and emanates outward. It is your pure essence: the pattern of energy that is you."

Quizzy looked around at the congregation. Most of them sat motionless with their eyes closed.

"Now imagine dividing your energy pattern in half," the preacher said. "Keep dividing your bundle of energy again and again. Every time you divide your energy bundle in half, slow down time to half its speed. Keep dividing your energy and slowing down time until you reach the size of a single atom and time is barely moving. This piece of your energy bundle is minuscule, but it still contains millions of swarming particles.

"Imagine an atom nearby. The piece of your energy bundle is the same size it is. But we must get even smaller than an atom—a million times smaller. Slice off a piece of your energy bundle so small that the nearby atom is a million times bigger.

"Now you are finally small enough to see a single parti-

273

cle of energy within your bundle. It is the essence of you."
Ruthlier delivered "you" with enough force that people in
the front row flinched.

"That single particle whirls and corkscrews, pulsates
and shimmers. It is a God particle," he said as he jutted out
over the pulpit. "The God particle moves with amazing
quickness compared to that lumbering, behemoth atom we
left behind earlier, with its electrons sizzling in and out of
reality in a field around it."

Quizzy turned her head toward Alex, who was deep in
thought. She elbowed him in the ribs.

"What?" he said. "I'm trying to concentrate on what he's
saying. It's like I'm in the land of giants. I feel so … small.
It's like I'm a little bit outside my body."

"I just wanted to make sure you were still on the planet," she said.

"Which planet?" Alex turned his attention back to the
preacher.

Ruthlier continued. "Your shimmering God particle is
alive—an agent of the Almighty. No, it's not an agent; it is
part of the Almighty Himself. It knows what it is. It is
aware. It cannot be destroyed or violated by any means. It
has individuality, but it comes together with other God
particles like a flock of birds on the wing, moving in con-
cert, all of them acting as a single entity.

"This flock of trillions of God particles is not just part of
God; it is also part of you. You are one, together. Your
shimmering energy bundle of God particles is imbued with
your identity and is powered by the ceaseless energy of the

274

Almighty. It swarms within you and also outside of your corporeal body. It swarms through other nearby atoms, imprinting your essence upon them, and their essence upon you."

"He's making me itch!" Quizzy said in a whisper. "My skin is crawling, listening to him describe all those swarming particles."

Alex slowly turned his head toward Quizzy and rolled his eyes to focus on her. "What?" he said.

"Never mind. Are you okay?"

"Yes, fine." He closed his eyes.

He's sluggish, she thought.

"Just as a single God particle cannot be destroyed," Ruthlier preached, "neither can your identity. It is preserved and expressed by the trillions of individual God particles within your energy field. Like a single bird in the flock, each has free will to fly anywhere it chooses. That is the nature of Nature.

"When a bird separates from the flock, as it may freely do, the flock still retains its identity. So, then, do God particles come and go from different swarms of consciousness, combining and recombining, sharing their identities along with your identity in an endless subatomic dance. That dance builds your cells, your organs, and the consciousness that you know as yourself.

"But that is only the beginning," Ruthlier droned. He preached about how innumerable God particles combined into ever more complex structures. Gesturing for greater effect, he described how all people's God particles combined to form the consciousness of the human race, and added to the consciousness of plants, animals, and even rocks and water, created the planet Earth.

"The pattern repeats itself with other stars and planets and space itself to form our Milky Way galaxy. The final configuration of the pattern is the totality of God's infinite universe!" He threw up his arms and exclaimed, "Hallelujah!"

"Hallelujah!" responded the congregation with one voice. Even Alex cried out.

Quizzy studied Alex. *Is he really into this?*

Ruthlier paused to catch his breath. Changing pace, he now spoke in a quiet voice, and everyone strained to hear.

"In that way we are all connected with one another and everything else, no matter its vastness or its insignificance." He gestured toward the insignia of connected tubular rings on the shining robe covering his wide chest. As he moved his arms the emblem swayed and undulated.

Quizzy glanced at Alex. His eyes were half-closed. She was sure that Ruthlier would make a good hypnotist. *My God, that's what he's doing!*

The congregation was rapt, their imaginations fired by the vivid depictions from the preacher in the lavender robe illuminated in the pulpit spotlight. Quizzy suppressed her imagination, intent on maintaining her independence of thought.

Ruthlier flashed a politician's smile and continued. "Now, after that lengthy pontification, remember, you are still waiting for that bus in the rain." The congregation let

276

go a subdued laugh. "Once again, dive into that pattern of energy that is you. Find that swarm of God particles that is flying in and out of your body, and also through the interior of that giant, lumbering atom I talked about earlier."

"Alex, you're in la-la land," Quizzy whispered. He didn't acknowledge her. *Keep an eye on him when the sermon ends.*

"Our lumbering atom has twenty-six protons and thirty neutrons in its nucleus," said Ruthlier. "This configuration makes it an atom of iron. It is an infinitesimal piece of our imaginary bus's front fender that is en route to pick you up and get you out of the rain.

"From your subatomic vantage point alongside your tiny God particles, you can see the electrons of the huge iron atom moving in their fields. The fender's other atoms and electrons are doing the same thing. As they move, they also appear and disappear into other physical dimensions. To us, in the dimension of time and space we occupy, the electrons look like they're blinking on and off.

"Compared to your God particles those electrons are very slow, but compared to you in your flesh-and-blood body standing at the bus stop they are extremely fast. In fact, those electrons are so fast that in our everyday human world they materialize in and out of our perceived existence billions of times each second. Their blinking is so fast that to you at the bus stop, the approaching bus is solid and constant, and the rain is steady.

"You may say," Ruthlier said, "'This all seems so complicated just for me to catch a bus. Why do we need all these God particles when we already have trillions of atoms in every square inch of matter?'" The preacher leaned forward over the pulpit. Quizzy thought back to when he stood on the rock leaning into the crowd at the Twisted Tree Ranch during the chaotic night of the fireball. Then he was competing for attention with the unfolding events of that night. Now he had captured his congregation's full focus.

"We need all of those God particles for good reason," he continued. "They form the energy fields that are imprinted with our unique identities." He swept his arm across the congregation. "God particles are the means for you to express yourself in the physical world! Your God particles signal our iron atom and all other atoms when and where to blink on and off."

Then, with all of his preaching power, Ruthlier roared, "God particles control how and when events materialize. Because all of our basic identities are imprinted on an ocean of God particles, and those God particles determine how and when things materialize, we therefore create how and when things materialize and events will occur!

"*We* create our reality and then experience it with our physical bodies. We also create our physical bodies exactly the same way—a billion times a second, so that it seems seamless and natural as we experience the flesh and skin of ourselves."

Quizzy swept the binoculars across the crowd. The preacher had them riveted. Alex sat motionless. *Ruthlier is one hell of an orator,* she thought. *And he has a mysterious subject.*

"Things and events materialize for each of us according to how we imprint those ubiquitous God particles. Are you an optimist who believes you deserve the best that life has to offer? Or are you a pessimist who believes hard times are normal? For the optimist the bus is running on time, and there is a seat available next to another pleasant traveler. For the pessimist the bus is late, and it will splash water out of the gutter on the pants he just had cleaned.

"Is your life a vicious cycle of events conspiring against you, or is it a virtuous cycle of good things coming your way? And when bad things come, as they must for you to experience what it is to be human, do you learn from them and grow into a more resilient creature of God?" Ruthlier stopped talking and looked out across the capacious room, taking time to collect his final thoughts of the sermon.

"I am just a man who tries to speak in a way that conveys the laws of nature. It is undeniable that these seem strange and counterintuitive. I am woefully inadequate for the job, but it is my life's work to at least open the door. Every Sunday behind this pulpit you have heard me say that the Elemental One is coming. *He* will sweep the door off its hinges.

"I am merely a weak light on a path that He will illuminate like the noonday sun. His arrival has been foretold throughout history, and again recently with the fall of the Lavender Fireball. The Elemental One will one day appear alongside the fireball. In spirit, this church also stands alongside the fireball; therefore, He will appear to you!" In a hypnotic finale of his sermon, Ruthlier opened his arms to everyone.

One of the white ceramic plates arrived, and Quizzy accepted it from an elderly man next to her. It was heavy enough that she slid her hand underneath it. There was a small bump protruding from the bottom of the plate. She passed the plate to Alex, who then passed it on, holding it in a similar fashion. Quizzy noticed the reverend looking their way as the plate went by. Alex said, "Wow, I don't think I ever heard anyone speak like that before. I was really zoned in."

"I'm glad to see you're back. I was a little worried about you."

The drumming had resumed on the back of Quizzy's chair. She was trying to observe Ruthlier and his interaction with the crowd, but the distraction grew, and she turned around. Instead of the little girl, she faced Drago leaning forward in the chair behind her. She gasped at the sight of his sneering glare and ugly tattoo. Alex jerked around to investigate.

"Welcome back, Shatterling. Did you enjoy my father's sermon?" Drago said over the noise of clapping as the elder Ruthlier gazed out over the congregation. Quizzy couldn't tell whether Drago wanted a serious answer, or if he was just trying to provoke her.

"It sucked," Alex said. "Just like you." He put his arm across the back of Quizzy's chair between her and Drago. The applause subsided, and many in the crowd arose and stretched.

"Irritable this morning, aren't we?" Drago said. "I just stopped by to welcome you like a good Christian, even if that is not what we are here. We got off to a bad beginning, so I'm trying to be a little friendlier."

Suspicion gripped Quizzy. Memories of Drago's volatile disposition played through her mind like a highlight video. Finally she said, "Answer me one question, Drago."

He stared at her with flinty green eyes. "Ask," he said.

"What happened to your mother? When I visited Romania, your neighbor there said she just disappeared one day."

Drago recoiled as if he had been shot. His face reddened and his hands began to tremble. He sprang out of his chair and stood, sputtering for words.

"I'll cut you both to little pieces," he hissed, then whirled away, kicking the leg of a chair with a pointed black boot.

"I guess he doesn't want to be friends anymore," Alex said. "Are you ready to get out of here?"

"I believe I am."

A steady rain was falling as Alex drove his truck away from the church. The satisfaction of seeing Drago lose his composure had given way to contemplation, and he drove in silence.

"Are you okay?" Quizzy asked. "Besides being threatened to be cut into little pieces?"

"Yeah, I'm all right. A little angry, I guess. I can't quite put my finger on the reason. It's not just Drago."

"He really flipped out back there."

"He's in a constant state of flipped-out. It's just a matter of degree. But I think what's bothering me more is Ruthlier's sermon." He turned onto the street and scratched his head. "I don't know why, but I'm angry that it made some sense to me. I was expecting the usual bullshit of a money-grubbing charlatan. I still think he is one, but his philosophy or theology or whatever you want to call it holds together. At least for now. Maybe I'll think about it more and realize it's full of holes. It's a big gulp to swallow, as Charlie would say."

"Let me tell you something I learned in Journalism 101," Quizzy said. "When you disagree with or, worse yet, are in conflict with someone, there is a tendency to demean him and his work. And vice versa: If you appreciate someone's work it's easier to overlook his character faults. I must guard against both of those tendencies in my profession. My editor is expecting—demanding—an objective story about Ruthlier and his church. I have to separate, as much as is possible, the philosophy of the church from the preacher's megalomaniac and murderous methods."

"Maybe that's what's bothering me," Alex said. "I prefer my adversaries to be one-dimensionally bad."

"You've got to separate the messenger from the message," Quizzy said. "Just look at the history of religion. The most heinous acts imaginable have been perpetrated by religious leaders. Torture, treason, terrorism, fraud, pedophilia, perversion ... you name it."

"Don't forget war."

"Yes, of course war. Nevertheless, those tragedies don't

negate the overarching message, whatever that may be, for any particular religion. Degrade and tarnish, yes. But not negate. Not if enough people believe in its core message."

"Maybe," Alex said. "But after enough perversion and tragedy, you'd think a religion would fade away."

"Some do. There are lots of dead religions—for whatever reason."

"Oh, well, whatever the reverend's message may be, I'm sure of one thing: He won't let anyone or anything stand in his way of advancing it. He'd kill for his cause. Correction—has killed."

They drove a couple of blocks farther down the narrow street when they passed a city bus stopped to take on passengers waiting in the rain.

31

THE SATURDAY AFTER his church visit Alex fired up the barbeque grill at the Twisted Tree Ranch. The guests began arriving at noon. Quizzy drove her Beetle, the Sorensens came in their Volvo sedan, and Samantha rode her mountain bike. Charlie, Flora, and her son, Troy, rode in on horseback from Charlie's place. Troy was dressed like a smaller version of Charlie—both wore boots, jeans, and denim jackets, but Troy also wore a riding helmet.

Flora Flores, appearing as strong as the horse whose reins she held in her gloved hands, pulled down the brim of her Longhorns baseball cap as she faced into the summer sun. They dismounted and Charlie tied up the horses with enough rope for them to graze under the trees in the backyard.

Texans said that any day is good for barbecuing, and this was one of the best; by early afternoon the temperature had climbed into the nineties, but it was pleasant enough in the shade under the live oaks. Alex fired up his stainless-steel Weber gas grill and laid out quarter-pound patties of unadulterated, prime ground beef. Ed Sorensen hovered over the grill with a Shiner Bock, offering unneeded cooking tips.

"Let Alex cook however he wishes," the professor said, and she hooked her husband's arm and led him away to join the others.

After lunch and before grogginess set in from the burgers, beans, and beer, Alex queried the group: "Who's up for a zip line ride?"

Troy and Samantha volunteered with enthusiasm, the Sorensens and Flora looked unsure, and Quizzy shook her head in a definitive no. Seven shouted gibberish.

"Probably the best way to do this is to have someone wait at the end of the line to help people get unhooked and out of the harness," Alex said. "Flora, would you mind doing that? After a few people go, someone can take your place at the bottom, and you and whoever else wants to go again can walk up the trail to the top of the ridge."

"I don't mind at all. I know I don't want to be the first to go!"

"It just looks scary." He looked at Samantha and said in a pleading voice, "Sam, would you mind watching Seven here in the front yard until I come down? I'll relieve you then, and you can walk up with Flora."

"Sure, Alex," she said, but disappointment showed in her eyes. Turning to Seven, she pointed at the suspended cable overhead and said, "Let's watch Daddy ride the zip line!"

The procession snaked up the trail, stopping occasionally to rest and appreciate the view. Alex led the way, packing the climbing harnesses on his back. The Sorensens followed in their hiking shoes and windbreakers, then Quizzy with her long strides. Charlie brought up the rear, walking just behind Troy, who was still wearing his riding helmet. Jessie roamed among them, sniffing the trail where other animals had recently passed.

"What's that sticking out from the rock over there?" Troy asked.

"It's the handle of an ax. I keep it up here for when I cut cedar," Alex answered. "Someday I'll show you how to use it." *I need to show you the lawn mower, too.*

The trail threaded its way between boulders and trees, then steepened the last fifty feet, where it rose alongside the limestone outcropping of the cliff. By the time the hikers reached the twisted tree at the top, everyone except Troy was out of breath.

"It's spectacular up here!" Professor Sorensen said as she took in the full-circle vista from the top of the ridge. Jessie rolled onto her back in the grass and wriggled.

Alex unlocked the chained padlocks around the trunk of the tree, freeing the roller assemblies. "Who's first?" he asked.

"I'll go, I'll go!" Troy shouted. The Sorensens looked at each other with trepidation, and Quizzy stepped farther away, lest someone should volunteer her.

"You da man, Troy!" Alex dug through his backpack and

pulled out the small harness and a small pair of leather gloves. "Here you go."

Troy had ridden the zip line before, and he stepped into the harness and cinched it tight under Charlie's supervision. Charlie lifted the boy off the ground with one arm and snapped the harness's main lanyard onto the first roller assembly. The lanyard supported the boy's weight, and Charlie held him steady as Troy interlocked his gloved fingers over the top of the roller housing. Alex watched Quizzy struggle with rising anxiety, yet he sensed her reporter's instincts documenting the procedure as the boy prepared to launch.

"Are you ready, Troy?" Charlie asked.

"Yes!"

"Away, then!" Charlie nudged Troy down the line toward open air.

"Yeeee-haw!" Troy screamed as he hurtled away from the cliff top into the canyon sky. He picked up speed, and the line began to sing. The Sorensens watched in amazement. Quizzy peeked with horrified fascination as the screaming boy receded.

Down into the valley he flew, his mother waiting anxiously at the far end of the line. There the cable was bolted around another oak tree on the opposite canyon hillside. The slope of the line flattened as Troy neared the terminating tree, and the ground rose to meet him.

He was still screaming when his rollers slammed into the sliding block of wood attached to the thick bungee cord. The cord stretched like a rubber band, stopping Troy three feet from the tree, and then it recoiled, sending him back out onto the line a few yards. He rolled back down, and Flora helped him unhook from the line and get out of his harness. He jumped up and down and waved to the tiny figures at the top of the ridge.

"Yee-haw?" Alex asked Charlie. "Where could he have learned that?"

Charlie just shrugged.

"Who's next?" Alex asked. "Professor? Ed?" He didn't bother to ask Quizzy. No one volunteered. "Okay, then, it looks like it's me!" He took out the adult harness and gloves from his pack.

"I have a question," the professor said. "How do you get the roller assemblies back to the top of the ridge?"

"Someone has to tie a long rope on them and walk back up the trail, pulling them along the zip line," Alex replied.

He started to step into the harness when Charlie said, "Alex, why don't I go next? That way I can walk Flora and Troy back up the trail and also pull the rollers as I come."

"You're always thinking, Charlie."

Alex handed him the harness and gloves, and he put them on. He stood at the top of the cliff and reached up to grab the cable. Pulling down on the line, he tried to snap the lanyard from his harness onto the roller assembly but couldn't reach it.

"Here, let me help," Alex said. He jumped and hung on the steel cable, pulling it down a few inches farther. Charlie maneuvered the carabineer at the end of the lanyard into position.

The turnbuckle snapped.

The cable and the broken eyebolt shot forward, ripping the roller assembly out of Charlie's hands. It flew into Alex's forehead and then whistled over the edge of the cliff into the abyss.

Lights exploded into Alex's vision. He staggered backward, fighting to stay conscious. He felt his foot on the edge of the cliff, arms wind-milling to keep him upright. Charlie caught a flailing arm, and Alex felt the steely power of his grip.

Like a drawn bow, Charlie bent and tensed, setting his front foot on the cliff ledge. For an eternal second he balanced, struggling to gain leverage. *Don't take him over*, Alex thought. Charlie heaved backward, pulling himself and Alex onto the rock.

They collapsed onto Jessie, who was standing behind them. The bull terrier yelped as a bone cracked. Alex looked up to see a fuzzy Quizzy with her mouth agape and the Sorensens in shock. Far below him, Flora wrapped Troy in her arms and cried.

Alex stood up on rubbery legs, and Quizzy ran to him, grasping his upper arm. Blood dribbled down his face as he started toward Jessie.

"This turnbuckle has been sawed, Alex," said Charlie. He held up the end of the severed eyebolt.

A hot wave of anger swept through Alex. There were no boundaries now. If the Ruthliers would come for him, they'd go after Quizzy, too. She was even more of a threat to them from her upcoming Chronicle story and her cooperation with Captain Steiner. Alex's termination of the water deal probably disrupted funding for the Ruthliers' church. No one was safe. The brazen murder attempt had been indiscriminate. They could have killed anyone. The realization that he would have to fight for his and Quizzy's survival slammed into him as hard as the eyebolt from the severed turnbuckle.

The murder of the night watchman and the car bombing had revolted Alex as an observer, but now he and Quizzy were targets. No longer could he rely on Steiner and the rule of law to protect them. Alex would assume that responsibility, and the legal consequences faded.

***

Captain Steiner exploded when he heard the zip line news. Like scavenging dung beetles, he and his team crawled all over the top of the ridge looking for traces of Ruthlier stink. Steiner took the murder attempt as a personal challenge. He summoned the Ruthliers to his interrogation room and grilled them about their possible involvement, but nothing more than the Ranger's frustration came out. Steiner had no doubts as to who concocted the zip line homicide plot. But charging people with attempted murder required more than a hunch. "You're going to fuck up," he told Drago as he crowded him in the doorway of the interrogation room on his way out, "and then I'll have your worthless ass."

32

PINTS WERE HALF-PRICE at Uncle Billy's brew pub. Alex, Charlie, and Quizzy sat at the farthest table from the door, and glanced through the open windows at passing pedestrians on the sidewalk, guarding against anyone overhearing their conversation.

"How's Jessie doing?" Quizzy asked after a sip of pale ale.

"She's has to wear a cast for six weeks," Alex said. "She took the brunt of the fall from Charlie and me."

"To a damned fine dog," Charlie said, and they all clinked glasses.

"We've got to do something," Alex said. He touched the side of the cold glass against the square bandage covering the sutures in his forehead. "We're sitting ducks. And I'm not even sure why."

"Because the Ruthliers are insane, evil scum," Charlie said.

"It has to do with the story I'm working on," Quizzy said. "It doesn't paint a pretty picture of the Ruthliers. There is something about Lucas Ruthlier's past in Romania that he wants to keep secret. I'm sure his wife isn't dead. Alex, I'm not trying to be flip, but we know that he's also a graveyard kleptomaniac—in addition to being a religious zealot. And Drago is a robot who is programmed to please him. He has no other setting."

"That's all good to know," Charlie said, "but I'd rather be ignorant and alive than informed and dead. We need a plan of defense."

"I think Steiner is close to an arrest," Alex said. "He just needs a break. He's restrained by the law in what he can do. We are not restrained, at least not as much."

Charlie said, "Steiner and his boys have already combed over every crime scene. I don't see how we can help him there."

"He needs the fireball to turn up in the Ruthliers' possession," Alex said. "That would break his case wide-open."

"Knowing Lucas Ruthlier," Quizzy said, "he has it now. His compulsion to be around religious artifacts is too strong. He had to leave a box of them behind in Romania. The temptation to reacquire the meteorite would gnaw away at a person like that. It's almost like a sexual urge." She glanced at Alex. "Captain Steiner already used up his search warrant," she continued. "Ruthlier knows the odds of his getting another one are zilch, especially for a church. I'd bet the fireball is safe and sound in his apartment."

"Hell, it's probably sitting on his coffee table!" Charlie

said.

Finally, Alex said it. "So all we need to do is somehow discover the meteorite in Ruthlier's place...."

"Steal that rock!" Charlie said. He filled up everyone's glasses, and each of them contemplated what was being suggested.

"We wouldn't even have to steal it. All we'd have to do is find it at the church and then call the cops," Alex said. "Finding it may not even rise to the level of burglary. Besides, he doesn't own the meteorite. It belongs to that art collector, or at least to his estate. His wife is the rightful owner of the fireball."

"I love your convoluted logic, but don't kid yourself," Quizzy said. "It's still burglary. Or at least breaking and entering. Let me get this straight—you want to break into someone's home and then give the booty to the law and ask them to ignore how you got it."

"Yeah, that's about right," Alex said with feigned nonchalance, "but I still don't think it's burglary."

"Whatever. You know, that's how they finally nailed O.J. He broke into a hotel to retrieve some trinkets he claimed were stolen from him. You're as nutty as him and Drago sometimes."

"I'm not out to kill people."

"But Drago may kill you if you break into his daddy's church."

"He's trying to kill me anyway. What have I got to lose?"

They all took a gulp of beer.

"We've chased this pig all the way around the pen,"

Charlie said. "We're back where we started. We're in the crosshairs. We need to take the initiative. I'm not worried so much about what the law will do. For anything really bad to happen to us, a jury would have to convict us for stealing a rock in an attempt to protect ourselves. Talk about a sympathetic motive! We're just getting justice for a grieving widow. It's not like we're doin' it for the money. We would be a defense lawyer's dream case. Plus, the Ruthliers live in a danged church. We can always say that we were making a late-night visit to be nearer to God!"

"You're right. It would never come to trial," Alex said.

"Maybe we could get Anita Loya to authorize us to recover her property," Quizzy said. "That might give us a little better legal footing. Not much, but a little. There's only one thing we cannot do," she stated, "and that's carry a gun into Ruthlier's place. Legally, it would change everything—boost the severity of the case. The punishment is way more severe."

"She's right," Charlie said. Then to Quizzy: "But didn't you say Ruthlier kept a pistol?"

"Yes, I saw it in his office desk."

"And he would be within his legal rights if he shot us while we were inside his home," Alex added.

"They give you a medal for that in Texas," Charlie said.

Alex thought of Sweet Pea at home in his locked nightstand drawer.

"We've also got to assume Drago has any number of lethal weapons," Quizzy said. "After all, he put together a car bomb." Alex looked at Charlie. The C-4 secret was still

294

theirs.

"Okay, so if we do this—steal the fireball—we need to make sure no one is home when we go in," Alex said.

"I think I know a way to make that happen," Quizzy said. "We would need your help, Charlie." They ordered another pitcher of pale ale, and Quizzy described her plan. When she finished, they dissected it to minutiae.

"Every risky operation has an escape plan," Alex stated afterward. "We need one, too."

As the group quieted in thought, Charlie began to rub his chin. He stared out the window with a vacant expression. "I just had a very strange vision," he said. "But we might be able to use it. We'll need Professor Sorensen's help, though."

"I don't want to drag the professor into this," Quizzy said. "It's our little party. We need to keep it small."

"I'm almost afraid to ask," Alex said to Charlie. "But ... what did you see?"

"I had a glimpse of Quizzy all lit up in a purple glow," Charlie answered. "Like she had some kind of aura. She was sitting on the floor and then started glowing."

Alex raised his eyebrows and exhaled. "Where do you come up with these bizarre things?" he said.

Charlie shrugged his shoulders. "I can't help what I see in my mind, any more than you can control your dreams."

Alex nodded and rubbed his temples.

"I don't understand how Professor Sorensen fits in," Quizzy said.

"We need her bioluminescent goo to make you glow."

"And why would I want to glow?" Quizzy asked. "Other than to fulfill your vision."

"It's the plan B escape," Charlie said. "Assuming we're going into Ruthlier's church and home to find the meteorite, we need a backup plan. Plan A is to break in when they're not there, steal the meteorite, and get out. Plan B is if we get caught in the act."

"I'm still not clear on how it's going to help us if Quizzy is glowing," Alex said.

"Let's say plan A goes bad, and the Ruthliers catch you inside their particle church," Charlie said. "Quizzy would discreetly ignite Sorensen's goo that she has painted all over herself. She mysteriously lights up like it's the Fourth of July. Then she rants and raves like someone possessed. Flops around on the floor. To the kooky Ruthliers, something unexplainable and divine is happening. They'll back off—Ruthlier is a true believer. You just need to buy a little time until the cops arrive. They'll already be on the way, because I will have called them. If plan A goes bad, I'll know right away, since I'll be keeping tabs on the Ruthliers after we spook them out of their church," Charlie said. "I'll send in the cops. We just need to buy a few minutes until they get there."

"I still don't like the idea of involving the professor," Quizzy said.

Charlie said, "Professor Sorensen wouldn't have to know what we're doing. She could help without ever realizing what we were up to. But she's as sharp as one of Drago's knives. She'll be suspicious and try to figure things out." He looked at Quizzy. "If she calls you, you'll have to act ignorant." Then to Alex he said, "You can act normal."

"Very funny." Alex drained the rest of his beer. "Let's get out of here. It'll take us the rest of the day to replace that eyebolt."

"What eyebolt?" Quizzy said.

Alex and Charlie exchanged uneasy glances.

"Do you mean you guys are resurrecting that zip line after what happened?" Quizzy asked with an incredulous expression. "Are you insane?"

"Probably," Charlie said.

"It's a matter of principle," Alex said. "We are not going to let those goddamn terrorists run our lives."

33

THE LENS OF the stairwell camera once again functioned. Days after the murder of the UT night watchman, it was scrubbed clean with acetone. Woody Reeter, the janitor who thought he had seen the Lavender Fireball bleeding in Professor Sorensen's office, had cleaned it. Now the functioning camera recorded Charlie Colvin as he ascended the stairs to see Professor Sorensen.

Charlie's timing was bad. Classes were changing, and students scurried through the halls and up and down the stairs. Dressed in holey jeans, tennis shoes, and T-shirts, they eyed the conspicuous cowboy as he entered the lab room.

I should've brought my rope, Charlie thought. *Really give 'em something to stare at.* He walked through the lab and into Professor Sorensen's office in the back.

She was seated at her desk wearing reading glasses,

grading papers. She made a red "X" next to an answer on a grad student's test. She smiled with pleasant surprise at seeing Charlie.

"Have a seat." She motioned to a maple chair worn smooth from years of use by puzzled or pleading students. "To what do I owe the pleasure of your visit to my place of quiet learning? Quiet usually, I should say."

Charlie knew he couldn't have been sitting more than a few feet from where the body of Bobby Ware was discovered. *They did a nice job of cleaning up the place.*

"I need a big favor, Professor. I need a couple ounces of your Amazon glowing goo, or whatever you call it."

"That's not so easy to come by. Whatever for, Charlie?"

"Well," he said, trying to think of a way to evade the question, "I can't really say what it's for. I suppose I could make up a harmless story, but I won't. Please take my word, though—it's very important."

"That's not much to go on."

"I know, and I apologize for that. It's for a very worthy cause; believe me. I don't want to beat around the bush. But the less you know, the better."

Sorensen wrinkled her forehead and drummed her fingers on her desk. "My life's work is the pursuit of knowledge, and having it withheld irritates me," she said. "But I saw you risk your life at the edge of a cliff to save your cousin's. I know you're in a fight for your lives, and maybe Quizzy's, too."

Sorensen swiveled her chair and pulled open the door on a heavy floor safe behind her. "Things have changed around here," she said. "I had this safe moved in after that most unpleasant business with the meteorite and the night watchman. The dean said I needed to tighten up my procedures." She scowled. "The bureaucracy I must endure.... How much bioluminescent liquid did you say you needed?"

***

Anita Loya had aged since Alex had last seen her at the bank when they transferred the meteorite. As she stood framed by a massive front door, her eyes had a droopy, tired look, and her blond hair had lost its luster. He could relate—he wasn't so perky himself these days. She invited him inside and offered him a seat on the living room couch.

Behind her sprawling Lake Travis mansion was the recently renamed Thomas Loya Memorial Gallery. The widow had added "Memorial" after her husband's body parts, along with those of his security chief, had rained down when Drago Ruthlier's C-4 bomb exploded beneath their Cadillac.

"You said on the phone that you wanted to talk about the fireball," Loya stated. "That you might know where it is."

"Yes," Alex said. He wasn't encouraged by the disdain in her voice when she said "fireball." "I might know where it is, and I might be able to recover it."

A door opened and a tall man wearing khaki Dockers and a tight-fitting white golf shirt entered the room.

"This is the gallery's new chief of security, Jimmy

Razure," Anita Loya said. Alex shook the man's hand. Razure said in a voice devoid of warmth that he was glad to meet him. Alex was unconvinced. He thought Razure was even meaner-looking than the last chief and hoped that he was luckier.

"You said you might know where the fireball is," Razure said, revealing that he had been listening to the conversation. "I don't understand. Do you know where it is or don't you?"

"Not exactly, but I have a hunch," Alex answered.

"Everyone has hunches. Tell me yours."

"I think the Ruthliers have it in their church."

"And?" Razure said.

"And I might be able to recover it," Alex said.

"You mean steal it."

"I didn't say that. Besides, it's already stolen."

"I don't have time for word games," Anita Loya said. "Why are you here? What do you want from me?"

Alex told her.

34

CHARLIE CARRIED A shoe box under his arm that contained a roll of electrical tape, insulated wire, a switch, a nine-volt Duracell transistor battery, and a Gerber baby food jar full of Sorensen's jungle goo.

In the parking garage elevator under her downtown condo building, Quizzy pushed the button for the nineteenth floor. After a quiet ride Alex followed her and Charlie down the hall and into Quizzy's condo. He wondered whether he would survive the weekend. When he had left Seven with her grandparents in San Antonio that morning he had to fight back tears. He told them it must be something in the air bothering his eyes.

Like all new visitors to the condo building, the cousins gravitated to the windows and the views of downtown. The early afternoon air hadn't yet loaded up with humidity and was crisp and clear. The pink granite of the Capitol dome shone with its defining reddish tinge.

"Quite a roost you have up here, Quizzy," Charlie said. "You're on top of the world."

"Except for my upstairs neighbors, I guess I am." Charlie opened the balcony door, and he and Alex walked out. The wind twisted Charlie's mustache as he leaned on the shaded railing of Quizzy's north-facing balcony.

"I never go out there," Quizzy said from the other side of the door. "I love the views, but at this height I prefer being enclosed by steel and glass."

Alex walked down the hallway past the bathroom and laundry room. The sight lines were open, clean, and simple. He could stand in the living room and see the entire apartment except for the rooms down the hallway. Stainless-steel appliances on black granite countertops complemented the airy kitchen.

"Are we ready to get started on our dress rehearsal for tomorrow night?" Alex asked.

"I need to change," Quizzy said, and then went to the bedroom at the end of the hall. She reappeared a few minutes later, barefoot and wearing loose-fitting jeans with a long-sleeved white cotton blouse, shirttail out.

"There're a few bugs that could chew up our plans, especially with the electrical connections," Charlie said. "They're fragile, so we need to make sure the joints are solid. It all starts with the battery."

He took out the little rectangular Duracell from the shoe box. "This has to go on the back of your belt, Quizzy." He held it against the small of her back with one hand as she stood under the living room ceiling light. With his other hand Charlie fidgeted with the roll of electrical tape.

"Make yourself useful, Alex," Quizzy said with a playful smile.

Alex took the adhesive tape from Charlie and stood behind her. He lifted her shirttail and inserted his fingers under Quizzy's leather belt, pulling it away from her waist. The heat from her body warmed his fingers as he looped the tape around the battery and the belt.

"Next we need to fasten the electrical switch to your leg," Charlie said. "You'll be able to activate the circuit by kneeling or by pressing your knee against a wall or a piece of furniture."

He removed the switch from the shoe box, looked at Quizzy, and then handed Alex the device. "You two seem to be in a groove," he said to his cousin. "You can do this."

Quizzy sat on the edge of the couch and pulled her right pant leg up over her knee.

Alex knelt at her foot as if he were fitting a shoe. He put one hand around Quizzy's bare calf, and with the index finger of his other hand he stroked a tattoo of two kissing bumblebees.

"What inspired this?" he asked.

"My nature."

Alex looked upward along the length of Quizzy's leg and torso and met her eyes.

"Tape away," she said. He placed the mounting flanges of the switch on her shinbone and circumnavigated her upper calf with several wraps of tape.

"It's a good thing you shave your legs," he said, "or this

tape would be hell to remove."

"Actually, I only shave that one."

"I don't think I believe that," he said, and inserted his hand under the cuff of the other pant leg to feel smooth skin. "Told you."

"Good grief, you two," Charlie said. "I'm going to let y'all work through the details of whatever you think needs to be done here. Alex, you know how the circuit works. Be sure you give it a thorough testing, though." He grinned at them, picked up his hat and jacket, and started for the door.

Quizzy intercepted him and hugged him hard.

"Thanks for all you've done, Charlie," she said, blushing.

"Don't mention it, Quizzy. Everything's going to work out just fine," he said, but Alex could see the forced smile.

Quizzy shut the door behind the departing cowboy and turned to Alex. He stood, and she walked up to him. He put his arms around her waist and breathed in her closeness.

"You're trembling," he said. "Are you okay with this?"

"With this, very much so. But, Alex, I'm so scared about tomorrow." She put her arms around his neck. "What we're planning is so dangerous."

He pulled her closer and they kissed. Doubt and nervousness evaporated as they embraced, and a warm longing flowed through entwined limbs. They kissed deeper and fell onto the couch. Alex brushed his hand against Quizzy's breast. He moved along her sternum to the vee of her blouse. He kissed her again and opened the first button.

"Let's get this off so we can get down to basic wiring," he whispered.

"Is this the part where you electrify me?" she said.

They sank deeper into the couch. Gallows humor slowly and sweetly evolved into a focus that pushed out all thoughts of the danger they faced.

***

Alex and Quizzy stood in the center of her balcony holding hands, marveling at the enveloping lights of the city. They stayed on the high terrace for only a minute, but it was a milestone for Quizzy.

When they reentered the stability of the living room, Alex taped a wire along Quizzy's right arm, down her back, and to the switch below her knee. He softly brushed Sorensen's bioluminescent goo on her arms, neck, and chest. He tested the circuit by pushing the switch. The goo glowed white, just as it had in the professor's demonstration. The glow crawled over her body, and Alex followed every inch of its progress with his fingers. The goo burned itself out long before the couple did.

Later in the evening they drove to the ranch, where they spent the night. After a lazy, romantic morning they climbed the trail up the side of the canyon, where Alex showed Quizzy how to chop cedar limbs with the ax he kept beneath the rock shelf.

Exercise in the brisk canyon air kept at bay their creeping apprehension about the impending assault on the Ruthliers' stronghold that night.

35

I N MOST WAYS Drago was unpredictable. Nevertheless, he could be relied upon for two habits: one was to do whatever pleased his father, or at least, in his contorted reasoning, what he thought would please his father. The second was to sit in a relic of a chair at a broken-down sidewalk table outside the Continental Club on Thursday evenings.

Clients of the nearby SoCo Tattoos strolled in and out, modeling their inked illustrations. Live music from inside the club pounded the walls, seeking escape through the open front door. Drago sat behind his out-of-place Honda among the Harleys on the street in front of him.

Across the street at Jo's Hot Coffee, Charlie sat outside at a wobbly table with a bottle of beer. He would have preferred another draft, but too much of the first one had sloshed out because of the unsteady table. Normally he would just find a sturdier table, but on this night, location was more important than comfort. He sat one row back from the street, watching Drago from under his pulled-down Stetson. His truck was parked three blocks away, even though Jo's shared a parking lot with the Hotel San Jose next door. Charlie didn't know whether Drago knew his truck, but best not to chance it.

Charlie looked at his watch. On the opposite side of the block, Anita Loya's chief of security, Jimmy Razure, would be smearing mud over the license plates of Loya's black BMW coupe. Anita Loya would be adjusting her brunette wig. Before yesterday, when they had met to finalize their plan, Charlie had never known anyone who seethed in a vengeful rage.

Loya's BMW appeared on Congress Avenue and drove down the hill to the Continental Club. The flashers came on as Razure double-parked next to the line of motorcycles in front of the club.

From his lookout station across the street, Charlie watched as Drago examined the BMW with the smoked-glass windows that had stopped in front of him. Anita Loya opened her door and stepped into the street. She reached into her Black Goat sweater and withdrew a folded piece of paper. She peered at Drago over the top of her sunglasses and smiled at him, and then pushed the paper into the in-strument cluster on the handlebars of his motorcycle. As a puzzled Drago stared, the woman quickly retreated into the BMW through the still-open door.

Drago sprang to his feet and shouted at the vehicle as it pulled into traffic, "Hey! Who in the hell do you think you are?" But he was left standing in the street, shouting. He stomped over to his Honda, pulled out the paper, and unfolded it. Charlie already knew what it said:

Drago,
I need to see you in a quieter place. We have much to talk about after these many years. Meet me in the lounge of the Hotel San Jose at 10:30 tonight.

Your mother,
Irena Davidoff Ruthlier

Across the street, Charlie watched Drago squirm. He had expected to enjoy the drama, but it left him hollow. He punched a number on his speed-dial.

"Anita Loya just drove off," he announced.

"Great," Alex answered. "We'll be in touch."

***

Drago stared up the Congress Avenue hill, hoping the black BMW would reappear. But what if it did? *My mother? After all these years?* If she stepped out of the car, he knew he could bury his knife in her heart before she took another step. Maybe it would end the nightmares. But what if she were coming to claim him? Feelings of childhood disbelief and hate erupted, conflicted with hope. His thoughts swirled in a vortex of confusion. Out of the maelstrom a thread formed: *Perhaps there is an explanation for my abandonment.* He read the note over and over.

Drago paced the sidewalk in front of the club, gazing across the street at the Hotel San Jose, checking his watch over and over. He glowered at patrons going into the club, making sure they got a good look at the tattooed knife slicing his throat. He was in the mood to shock.

It was only nine thirty. Could she be at the hotel now waiting for him? He pondered going over, but if he disobeyed, would she leave? He opened his cell phone and started to make a call but aborted it. The note hadn't said anything about his father. Drago sat down and held his head in his hands. Renewed hate for his mother gripped him. What kind of mother would bring her child such distress? He touched the speed dial once more, but this time allowed the call to go through to his father's apartment.

Drago told his father about the BMW, the woman, and the note.

"Christ!" Ruthlier exclaimed. "That's.... I don't believe it! What did she look like?" Drago described the woman. "It could be her," his father said, "but it could be a lot of women. What color were her eyes?"

"She wore sunglasses."

"In the dark? What about the license plate of the car?"

"I couldn't read it because of the mud."

"Was the rest of the car dirty?"

"No, it was spotless."

"Ugh ... I don't like any of this," his father moaned. "It's too far-fetched. I'm coming down there—armed. Wait for me where you are. I'll be there in ten minutes." The line clicked before Drago could say anything.

***

Across a large vacant lot dotted with plastic bags and other trash, Alex and Quizzy watched the rear of the Southside Shopping Center from behind a nearby apartment complex. They heard a chain drive gnash as an electric motor labored, and the Church of the God Particle's articulated rear door slid to the top of its guide rails. Lucas Ruthlier's Lexus drove through the open door and down the concrete ramp outside. The car tore out of the shopping center's parking lot as the door closed behind it.

As the Lexus sped away in the direction of downtown, Alex speed-dialed Charlie.

"Ruthlier just beelined it out of here. It looks like Quizzy was right again: Drago must have called Big Daddy." He looked at Quizzy, and she offered a weak smile. Alex said to Charlie, "We're going in!"

Alex started his truck and drove out of the apartment complex, down the street, and into the church's rear parking lot behind the shopping center. He pulled up next to the loading ramp and shut off the engine.

"Are you ready, Quizzy?"

She nodded her head in determination. "I am, but this is crazy!"

He reached for her hand and squeezed it; then they exited the truck into the night. Alex led the way to the metal junction boxes at the back of the building where the utility lines converged, and he located the phone cable. They both pulled on thin gloves, and Alex popped open the box where the phone cable terminated. Using his flashlight, he searched for labels to the terminal lugs inside.

"Nothing is marked. People just don't take pride in their work anymore. I'm going to have to cut them all to make sure I get the alarm circuit." He set a small paper bag of Radio Shack capacitors on top of the metal box. He withdrew one, and with a pair of needle-nose pliers wrapped one wire of the capacitor around a lug of the first telephone line, and then wrapped the other wire around the other lug. He repeated this procedure until all six of the incoming phone lines were bridged with a capacitor. Alex proceeded to snip each of the lines behind the lugs with a stubby pair of wire cutters.

"That should do it!"

"Should?" Quizzy asked.

He smiled and said, "All we can do is our best."

They moved over to the heavy gray metal door next to the loading ramp. Quizzy selected a thin, hardened-steel tool from her kit and inserted it into the slot on the stain-less-steel industrial doorknob.

Alex's phone buzzed.

"Ruthlier just showed up at the Continental Club," Charlie said. "He came walking down the sidewalk, and he's talking with Drago now. He must have parked on one of the side streets—I don't see his car. Wait ... they're crossing the street now ... heading to the Hotel San Jose. They just went inside."

"I can't spring the lock, Alex!" Quizzy said with a strained edge to her voice.

"What did she say?" asked Charlie.

"Quizzy's having trouble with the lock on the back door. I've got to go. Keep an eye on that hotel and call me if either one of those bastards leaves."

"Got it," said Charlie.

Alex turned his attention to Quizzy and the doorknob.

"It won't release!" she said.

"Time for more technology, then." Alex went to his truck and removed a yellow DeWALT cordless drill from behind the front seat. He slipped in a carbide bit, tightened it down, and walked back to the metal door. Placing the bit on the key slot of the knob, he squeezed the trigger and leaned into the job. The drill ate up the key cylinder, and the whole mechanism fell onto the concrete when Alex withdrew the bit. With a gentle push, Quizzy swung the door open, and they entered the dark building.

***

"Turn your jacket collar up," Ruthlier told Drago. "I want to ask the desk clerk some questions. That damned tattoo isn't going to help in getting any answers."

Sulking, Drago took a chair in the lobby. Then, to deepen the wound: "I'd even pay to have that thing removed," the elder Ruthlier said.

Turning to the young woman at the check-in desk, the

313

preacher said in a silky voice, "I'm supposed to meet someone here in the lobby. Would you mind ringing her room so I can let her know I'm here? Her name is Irena Davidoff Ruthlier."

The clerk checked her computer and said, "We don't have anyone by either of those names registered here."

"Hmm.... I thought she said she was staying here. She must be lodging elsewhere and just wanted to meet me here. This place has such a nice atmosphere, I can see why."

"Oh, yes. Everyone loves it here," the clerk said, beaming.

"If you don't mind, we'll wait in the courtyard. We are early, so we might as well have a drink and enjoy the night air."

Ruthlier walked out to the courtyard, with the rattled Drago close behind him. They took a table near an overhead propane-fired space heater and ordered drinks.

"This whole thing stinks," Ruthlier said to his son with a frown. "Tell me again what happened at the club across the street." Drago recounted the story. "Now it stinks even more," his father repeated. "I think we're being played."

He swallowed the last of his vodka tonic and clanked the glass on the table. "I'm not going to just sit here and wait."

He looked at Drago and said in a clear, slow voice, "Listen carefully. I'm going back to the church. I think someone should be there. You wait here until ten forty-five. If your mother or any other woman shows up, see what she has to say. Then call me. If no one shows up, come home. Drago, if that woman shows herself, don't believe anything she tells you. Especially if it's a story about Kansas or Romania. Your mother was always a notorious liar! You've got to believe me on this."

Drago nodded with renewed energy. "Yes, Father! I believe you!" he barked with puppy trust.

"And for God's sake, no matter what she says or does, don't kill her!"

Another nod.

Ruthlier arose, and when he was out of earshot said to himself, "At least not in public." He started for the lobby and then changed direction. "I'm going to find a back door," he said to Drago as he passed by.

***

In an Austin hill country suburb, Captain Steiner was lying in bed with his wife watching the local news on KWIB TV when the phone rang. "Damn," he groaned. He rarely got a call after ten p.m. that wasn't bad news. He reached over to the nightstand for the phone and answered.

"Captain Steiner, this is Professor Sorensen. I'm sorry to bother you at so late an hour, but there is something I've worried about all day. You said to call no matter what time."

"Yes, yes, thank you. What is it, Professor?"

"Charlie Colvin came to my office yesterday and asked me to give him a small amount of the bioluminescent liquid

I have been developing. I asked what he was going to do with it, but he said the less I knew, the better off I'd be. He said that it was urgent and of the utmost importance. I relented and gave him two ounces. Now I wish I hadn't. I have the feeling that he and his cousin are going to get into big trouble with it. Maybe even tonight."

"What do you think they're going to do?"

"I have no idea. I just thought I should let you know."

"I appreciate the call, Professor, but I'm not sure I can do anything. No one has broken any laws, and there's no compelling reason to think they will. Even if there were, I still wouldn't know what to do."

"I understand, Captain," Sorensen said in a tone of resignation.

"You did the right thing. Good night, Professor."

Steiner's wife found his hand under the covers.

"Trouble?" she asked.

"Hard to say. Maybe. There's not much I can do, though."

He thought for a moment and then dialed Alex Colvin's home. After the machine answered he kissed his wife and turned off the television and the light and closed his eyes. Five minutes later he turned the light back on.

"Going out?" his wife asked.

"I need to check on something."

"Why am I not surprised, Greg?" she said.

Steiner changed into his Ranger uniform, started his patrol cruiser, and set out for the Church of the God Particle.

***

Flashlight beams reflected off the polished concrete floor of the dark loading area. Contorted shadows danced along the walls as Alex and Quizzy moved through the building. They made their way to the main chamber, with its rows of folding chairs fading into darkness. Twin black steel staircases at either end of the elevated walkway led upward to the closed metal doors of the Ruthliers' apartments. They climbed the stairway.

Quizzy tried the closest door. Locked. They proceeded across the walkway to the second door. Also locked.

"Which is Ruthlier's?" Alex asked.

"Flip a coin?"

"We're here, so let's try this door. We've got a fifty-fifty chance. See if you can unlock it."

"Why are we whispering?" asked Quizzy. "We're the only ones in this place."

Alex laughed with nervous tension. "I don't know about you, but the quieter the better, as far as I'm concerned."

Quizzy jimmied the doorknob with a thin, straight pick. When it clicked, she turned the knob and they entered. They swept the interior with their flashlights.

"Whose place are we in? Drago's or Ruthlier's?"

"I think it's Ruthlier's," she said. "It has too much class for Drago."

"I never thought of Ruthlier as particularly classy."

"Relative to Drago."

The flashlights revealed a leather couch, matching chairs, oak end tables, expensive-looking floor lamps, and an entertainment console with an aquarium next to it.

"Yeah, we must be in Ruthlier's," Alex said. "I envision Drago's place as ... colder. Like a dungeon. This place has paintings on the walls. Look, there's even an antique golf putter in the corner. It has to be Ruthlier's."

Quizzy pointed her light at the coffee table.

"Well, the fireball isn't there, obviously."

"I guess we just start looking through things. You take the kitchen, and I'll start here in the living room."

Alex looked under the couch and chairs, inside the doors of the end tables. In his peripheral vision he could see Quizzy digging through the kitchen cabinets. Light flared as she opened the refrigerator.

He worked his way over to the entertainment center and looked behind the television and audio system components. He flicked on the aquarium light and peered through the glass. Nice angel fish, he thought.

Frustrated, he set his flashlight on a shelf next to the television, the beam shining through the open front door. Wondering where to search next, he picked up the antique golf putter in his gloved hands. He wiggled the club, testing its weight and balance.

The doorway exploded in a white flash. Another flash and detonation. Alex twisted to see Ruthlier's face illuminated in a smoky haze by the flashlight on the shelf.

Stunned by the twin revolver blasts, Alex took a wild swing with the golf club. Ruthlier fired again at the flashlight on the shelf that was shining at him. The preacher waved his revolver from side to side, squinting to pick out a human target.

Alex swung the putter down across Ruthlier's extended forearm, snapping the wooden shaft across his wrist. The preacher cried out, and the revolver clattered to the floor.

"Alex!" Quizzy shouted. Her flashlight beam revealed the gun on the floor.

Alex dived for the weapon. He heard a grunt, and Ruthlier's full weight came down on his leg. He felt powerful arms wrapping him.

Alex wormed toward the revolver and kicked the preacher in the face with his free leg.

Ruthlier held on, but the kick was enough to propel Alex to the gun. He wrapped his fingers around the grip and swung the weapon around. He jammed it against Ruthlier's forehead.

"Let go of me!" he screamed.

Ruthlier relaxed his grip on Alex's leg, but roared at him, "You're going to ruin everything!"

"Get the hell off me!" Alex yelled, coughing from the acrid smoke of burned gunpowder. Quizzy held her flashlight on the preacher. Alex slowly got up, keeping the bigger man's chest in the gunsights.

"Get up." Alex followed Ruthlier with the revolver as he got off the floor. "Sit on the couch. Put your hands on the coffee table." He glanced at Quizzy. "Are you okay?"

She squawked, "Yes!"

"Turn on the lights."

She ran to the door and flipped the wall switch, and the room came into focus through the hanging smoke. Alex pointed the gun at Ruthlier's head. "You're an asshole, Ruthlier. Shoot first and ask questions later." Alex aimed the revolver above Ruthlier's head and pulled the trigger.

The explosion rocked the preacher back against the couch. Smoke swirled into his face.

"Where's Drago?" Alex said. If the elder Ruthlier had slipped out of the hotel unnoticed by Charlie, maybe Drago had, too.

Ruthlier worked his jaw side to side as if to pop his ears and said, "He's waiting for his mother, as you well know. That was a sick ploy."

"Oh, please. Spare me. It's nowhere as sick as murder." Alex felt his anger rising again. "Your crazy obsession with that meteorite is the reason you have a gun stuck in your face. I just wanted to get on with my life. You and your stalking lunatic son are done hounding me." Alex took a deep breath. "I want that meteorite. I'll give you one chance, Ruthlier. That's one more chance than you gave us on the zip line."

"I only found out about that after the fact. Perhaps Drago may have been a little overzealous."

"Overzealous? You say that like he was just rude! I'll show you overzealous!" Alex cocked the hammer and aimed at Ruthlier's forehead. "This is your last chance. Where is the meteorite?"

Alex could see that the preacher was shaken, but Ruthlier still forced out a laugh. "I don't think you'll shoot me. They'd give you the needle for home invasion and murder."

From the corner of his eye Alex saw a stricken expression cross Quizzy's face.

He fired another shot to the right of Ruthlier that shook the couch. "The next shot will be into your fat head. I'll put your gun in your dead hand and tell the police that you came in here and went berserk. You shot up the place and then killed yourself. I'll get away with it, too. The police will want to believe me. And I have a witness." The terrified Quizzy nodded rapidly. "The cops hate you and they like me. They know you and your crazy son have already killed three people. Not to mention the botched attempt on my zip line. You almost killed a kid. You're a real piece of shit."

"I have cause greater than all of you!" Ruthlier said, then corrected himself. "All of us."

Alex leaned over the coffee table, stuck the revolver in Ruthlier's face, and cocked the hammer again.

"My only cause is to end your cause. Where's that meteorite?"

Ruthlier blinked, swallowed, and said, "You're standing on it. It's under the floor. There are two short planks that lift out."

"Quizzy," Alex said, "can you check that?" Quizzy knelt beside him and ran her fingers over the floor near his feet.

"I think I found them. The boards are loose." Alex heard her set a board on the floor, followed by another. "There's a metal box."

"Set it in front of me on the coffee table."

Quizzy lifted the ammunition box out of the hole in the floor and set it in front of Alex.

Carefully watching Ruthlier, Alex pulled open the lid.

He inserted his gloved hand into a fold of bubble wrap and touched the hard, uneven exterior of its contents. Slipping his thumb and forefinger into holes in its surface, he pulled out the heavy object and raised it.

"Jesus!" he shrieked as he turned his head away in disgust. He held up Trina's head, encapsulated in a thick layer of clear acrylic plastic. His forefinger pushed against her opened eye, and his thumb hooked her mouth. Alex's gun hand dropped a few inches.

Ruthlier exploded off the couch. He heaved the coffee table forward. It knocked Alex and Quizzy backward, and he went for Alex, pawing for the revolver.

Alex felt the preacher's arm around his neck. Ruthlier's breath huffed against his face as they grappled for the gun. Quizzy jumped on the preacher's back. Ruthlier's head jerked back and Alex heard bone crunch. Quizzy sloughed off the preacher's back and fell to the floor, blood running out of both nostrils.

Ruthlier got a hand on the revolver. It discharged, shattering the overhead light. Alex fought for control of the weapon in the eerie greenish light of the aquarium. Ruthlier's strength was too much. He wrestled the gun away, and then broke free of Alex.

The gun came up to Alex's eye level. He jerked sideways and the muzzle flashed. The explosion snapped his head backward, and he staggered. He heard the sound of breaking glass and felt water flowing over his face. Or was it blood? Darkness enveloped him and he saw angel fish.

***

Ruthlier turned on one of the floor lamps, its dim reading bulb illuminating the devastation.

Quizzy sat on the wet floor, bleeding out of her nose, and screamed at Ruthlier, "You shot him! Over a stinking rock! Oh, God!"

Alex lay motionless in the gravel of the aquarium. Sobbing, she scooted across the floor to him and touched the side of his head. He lay unmoving on his back, blood pooling in the socket where his right eye had been. Beside him on the floor, the Lavender Fireball lay in the water and gravel from the aquarium in which it had been buried.

"You should have just left us alone!" Ruthlier shouted. "You had to go poking your goddamned nose where it didn't belong. I have a calling—a duty to God. You couldn't possibly understand. There is nothing more important for me—or for the human race. You have forced my hand!"

"Bullshit! Pure bullshit! You're a fraud!"

Ruthlier raised the revolver and pointed it at Quizzy. A curl of smoke wafted from the end of the barrel. She shrank backward, the destructive power of the weapon evident from the man in her arms. Her mind scrambled for options. She looked at the ripped-out knee of her jeans. The wire Alex had so carefully placed was hanging free.

"My duty is paramount," Ruthlier said, "and infinitely more important than you." He cocked the gun.

He's a religious fanatic. Use it. Buy some time....

"Wait!" Quizzy shouted. She knelt on one knee as if she were praying.

Ruthlier hesitated.

Keep talking, Quizzy told herself. "I can't believe the Elemental One would condone this killing," she said. "This meteorite isn't worth it!" The gun barrel wavered.

She placed her hand on the fireball.

"It's just a rock!" she shouted at him.

A glow emerged from between her fingers. Brilliant lavender light shot out from the flesh of her hand. The dark bones and joints were visible through her translucent skin, as if her hand were being X-rayed. Slowly, the incendiary emanation rose to her forearm, then her biceps, and into her shoulder.

Quizzy yanked her hand away from the meteorite, but the glow progressed.

"What's happening to me?" she cried out. She felt an intense energy moving through her body, and she knew it had nothing to do with Sorensen's bioluminescent goo. She saw Ruthlier, mouth agape, transfixed by the lavender light consuming her. It traveled through her chest, lighting her from the inside, and then it began to move downward. When the shimmering light reached her midsection it intensified and stayed.

"There's something inside of me!" Quizzy screamed. "I

can feel it!" All thoughts vanished in the face of this unnatural intrusion. The light from within her was so bright that it overpowered the glow of the floor lamp.

Ruthlier stood motionless, gun hanging at his side. Through her panic, Quizzy could see he was crying. Gradually, the light in her body faded and then was extinguished.

"What happened? I don't understand! What *was* that?" she cried out. Slowly she got to her feet and looked around the room, then at Alex on the floor. She turned and stared at Ruthlier. He still held the revolver at his side, but he somehow seemed impotent. Her panic faded. She felt in command, empowered with newfound strength.

"That, Ms. Shatterling, was the arrival of the Elemental One," Ruthlier said. The preacher set the gun on the coffee table. He sat on the couch, and for the first time Quizzy saw him smiling with genuine emotion.

She picked up the revolver as if it were a stick of dynamite and threw it out the open front door. She went to Alex and tried to stanch the bloody wound on the side of his head. She stroked his hair with her other hand.

Ruthlier said in a calm voice, "It's over for me. My work is finished, and yours has just begun. Do whatever you need to do. I only ask that you take care of yourself."

Quizzy sat cross-legged next to Alex and cradled his head. He moaned softly. She took her cell phone out of her jeans pocket and dialed 911.

***

Steiner's car squealed through the quiet front parking lot and then around to the back of the building. Backup officers and ambulances were en route. He screeched to a stop next to Alex's truck and Ruthlier's Lexus, both parked near the wide-open, lockless back door. Drawing his Glock from its holster, he turned on his Maglite and entered the building.

Steiner strained to separate the sounds inside from the approaching wail of the sirens. He hurried through the loading area and then up the metal stairway. He studied the open door of Ruthlier's apartment. Pistol ready, he stepped into the carnage.

***

Drago sat on his Honda in the parking lot of the apartment complex where an hour earlier Alex and Quizzy had observed the rear of his father's church building. He watched across the trash-strewn vacant lot as the aftermath of the shooting unfolded. A fireworks of red, blue, and white emergency lights blazed against the back of the church as police secured the area. EMS technicians rushed equipment inside.

The rancher was the first to be hustled out to an ambulance. Flanking his gurney were two men in blue pants and shirts, each holding aloft a clear plastic container with a descending tube. Twenty minutes after the ambulance departed, police escorted out Drago's father and the bitch reporter, both handcuffed behind their backs. Captain Steiner, the persistent and unpleasant Texas Ranger, watched as they were shoehorned into the backseats of patrol cars and driven away. Drago paid particular attention as officers in latex gloves carried out cardboard boxes. He knew one of those boxes contained the Lavender Fireball.

Drago had seen enough. He started the Honda, drove to Interstate 35, and hunkered down on his machine for the long ride south.

36

I N SPITE OF Alex's twisted interpretation of the Texas burglary statute, he and Quizzy were charged with the crime. In addition, they, Charlie, Anita Loya, and Jimmy Razure were also charged with conspiracy. Lucas Ruthlier was charged by the Travis County district attorney with accessory to murder.

An all-points bulletin was issued for Drago Ruthlier, now the focus of an intense south Texas manhunt. U.S. Border Patrol had discovered his motorcycle in the Rio Grande River near Laredo. He had run it into the brown water, but the river was too shallow to submerge one mirror. It had caught the sunlight—and the eye of a fisherman. The Mexican authorities were alerted, but their energies were consumed by the murderous turf wars of drug cartels. No one expected Drago's apprehension unless he ventured into the more stable interior of the country. Captain Steiner told the press that Drago's identifying throat tattoo would be a severe liability. Alex was hoping that he would just turn up dead anywhere in Mexico.

Lucas Ruthlier was not charged with shooting Alex Colvin. "A man has the right to defend his home," was the predominant public sentiment, and the district attorney agreed. However, Ruthlier had far weightier legal problems, starting with his identity. After his arrest he was fingerprinted. His prints matched those of Fred Zimmerman, who was supposed to be deceased. Zimmerman's records were in the FBI database because he had a security clearance when he worked at Fermilab in Chicago. The FBI descended and unraveled Ruthlier's Romanian story. He now faced charges of espionage and treason.

Despite the gravity of his predicament, Ruthlier refused to implicate Alex and Quizzy in the church shootout. He insisted to the district attorney that "they sought comfort in the sanctuary of the Church of the God Particle, and I mistook them for burglars. The shooting was wholly a misunderstanding on my part." Faithful to his mission, Ruthlier believed that he could still ease the earthly arrival for whomever or whatever he thought was developing in Quizzy Shatterling. The skeptical district attorney wasn't as magnanimous, and the burglary charges remained.

Anita Loya had posted bail for everyone but Ruthlier, saying that she hoped he would fry. Her refusal was a moot point, though, because the judge had denied him bond. He cited the gravity of the charges and the accused's propensity to change identities and flee to less hostile environs.

Anita Loya was also paying the legal expenses for those

she had bailed out of jail. Because of the recalcitrance of Lucas Ruthlier, her legal team predicted that the burglary and conspiracy charges would eventually be dropped, notwithstanding the far more serious charges against the Ruthliers.

The *Austin Chronicle* fired Quizzy, stating that she had used poor judgment and maligned their reputation by violating journalistic standards. She had crossed the line from news reporter to newsmaker, employing illegal methods to root out her sensational story. Nevertheless, the alternative newspaper was trying to rationalize a way to run the story to which she had devoted so much of her time. Lawyers had been summoned.

The Lavender Fireball and Trina Colvin's acrylic-dipped head were locked away in the Austin Police Department's downtown evidence room. Because of its stability within the plastic encapsulation, the head remained in the possession of the police, despite the protests of Alex and her family. The DA assured them that both the head and the meteorite would be returned to their rightful owners after the legal proceedings were concluded. Alex made sure the DA understood that Trina was the rightful owner of her head, and it needed to be reburied. Submissions of "request-to-examine" paperwork for the items were incessant. Just as when the meteorite had first fallen on the Twisted Tree Ranch, morbid curiosity seekers still gravitated to it and its aftereffects.

The Church of the God Particle was in disarray. Services were canceled as its parishioners scrambled to find someone else to guide them. A city council member authorized herself to lead a minister-selection committee, but the congregation soon realized its existential fears when not one particle-physicist preacher answered their multicity Craigslist ad. The parishioners were holding together out of sheer, binding faith—for the time being. But without a charismatic leader steeped in the knowledge of subatomic structures, the congregation was headed toward dissolution.

Quizzy's black eyes had disappeared in the weeks since the church invasion, although Alex couldn't see them because his right eye was bandaged shut and his left one was gone. The doctors said his good eye needed to remain motionless while the severed muscles of his missing left eye healed.

A shady breeze cooled his face. The quiet canyon was a respite from the stress in Austin over the shooting. He could smell Quizzy's faint scent; she was fresh out of the shower. She sat next to him, and he extended his left hand to touch her wet hair, pinned back on one side. He longed to see her dark curls.

Alex's doctors were optimistic. The bullet had struck his right eye at an oblique angle and then exited through the outside of his orbital socket. His eye was gone, but the bullet had missed his brain. The reconstruction surgeon wouldn't yet speculate on the extent of his facial disfigurement, but he was hopeful. Alex faced several surgeries, including having a stainless-steel plate implanted in his head, but the doctors said he should resume a normal life in a year or so. *If I avoid prison*, he thought.

Charlie had built a ramp for Alex's wheelchair so he could get onto the front porch and over the threshold. One of the upcoming surgeries would repair the vestibular canals in Alex's right ear that had been ruptured from the shock of the passing bullet. Until then, his balance was precarious. Even a sudden movement of his head or tipping it to the side caused a nauseating vertigo. He was too unstable to even stand.

He thought about Seven. Trina's parents were caring for her in San Antonio. They had brought her to see Alex in the hospital, once when Quizzy was visiting. For now, Quizzy was assuming the role of a close friend, but the inquisitive glances from Seven's grandparents were a harbinger of a sensitive conversation he would soon have to have with them.

Alex reached down beside the wheel of his chair and scratched the top of Jessie's head. Her convalescence was far ahead of his. The vet said that in three weeks the aluminum leg cast could come off. In the meantime, the dog limped around the ranch, dragging the attachment that looped over the top of her hip. *We're quite a pathetic pair,* Alex thought. He would do well to emulate the bull terrier's no-problem attitude. While he was in the hospital, Quizzy had said Jessie was eager as ever to play, just unable.

"I'm done digging out the grunge around the edge of this lens," Quizzy said. Alex heard Quizzy snap the lens cover back on her camera and faintly click her Swiss army knife shut before she put it in her pocket.

"I'm going to take the test," she said.

Alex breathed deeply, and very slowly turned his head toward her. "Is there anything I can do?"

"No, just sit tight." He felt her hand brush his cheek. "I'll be back in a minute."

He listened as she went into the house. A child with Quizzy.... Deep within him the thought resonated. He wanted *everything* with Quizzy. But the timing was awful.

"Well?" Alex said after she returned and sat back down.

"Too early to tell. I'm holding a white plastic stick about the size of a straw. I just peed on it. It takes a couple of minutes."

"Christ, what were we thinking—or not thinking? We were like a couple of teenagers in heat."

"I can see letters appearing on the stick. Oh, shit, Alex. I'm pregnant!"

"Oh, man." He reached for her hand. They sat in silence for a long minute. "What now?"

"I don't know. We'll work through it. Things could be worse—a *lot* worse. At least our baby will have a father. You're alive." Alex felt her arms gently wrapping his shoulders as Quizzy leaned over, and they held each other.

Finally, Quizzy said, "I need a little space right now. I'm going to take a walk up the trail while I get my head around this. Will you and Jessie be okay for a little while?"

"Yeah, sure. We'll be fine. Are you okay?"

"Yes. I'll be back soon." The sound of Quizzy's footsteps receded in the pebbly soil and crunchy dry grass.

A mockingbird sang through its considerable reper-
toire. After a few cycles from the songbird, Alex propped
up his head as best he could with a pillow from the side
pocket of the wheelchair.

Images swirled as he drifted off. He swam in synchro-
nization with a school of angel fish. They turned away from
the side of the tank, and the nearest fish brushed up
against him. As he tried to swim away, one of them shouted his name. Again, and in panic.

"Alex! It's Drago! He's here!"

Alex awakened with a jolt.

"Quizzy!" Alex strained to listen as his stomach twisted.
"Where? Where is he?"

"On the trail, asshole!" Drago's familiar voice yelled at
him. "I'm going to run down your sweetheart bitch so she
doesn't escape over the hill. Sit tight!

"Quizzy!"Alex shouted again. There was no answer.

Alex tore at the bandages on his head and he felt himself swirling with dizziness. He gasped, but worked his fingers under the edges of the bindings and lifted them off.
Even with his eye closed the light overpowered him. He
forced a blink, then another, and then opened his eye a tiny
slit. Searing pain knifed through his skull as the image of
his front yard materialized in a blurry dance. Gradually his
vision sharpened.

Drago was running along the path, ascending the side
of the canyon toward Quizzy, who was two hundred yards
ahead of him. Alex could see the glint of a knife in his right
hand. Jessie was dragging her aluminum cast as she strug-

gled toward the start of the trail. She had no chance of catching up.

Alex jammed his hands down on the arms of the chair and forced himself to stand up. The earth beneath him swept sideways, and he fell to his hands and knees. Fighting back nausea and pain, he grasped the chair and pulled himself back into it. He looked again at Drago and Quizzy running up the trail.

He turned his chair toward the front door and then wheeled himself up the ramp. He flung open the door and thrust the chair into the house. Banging into furniture and walls, he rolled into his bedroom and stopped in front of the nightstand. From his pocket Alex yanked out his key ring and unlocked the top drawer. He grabbed Sweet Pea with its ten rounds and set the gun in his lap. The box of shells on the top shelf of the closet would take forever to retrieve. He careened back outside.

Alex chambered a shell into the Taurus and located Drago halfway to the big tree at the top of the ridge. He had shaved off fifty yards on Quizzy and was closing.

It was an impossible shot. Alex extended the gun with his right hand and attempted to sight his target through his left eye. He fired two shots and watched the dust plumes kick up twenty feet behind Drago moments later. He adjusted his aim and fired two more shots. Closer.

Drago slowed at the clearing where Alex had cut back a stand of cedar, and he grabbed the ax from underneath the rock shelf. He ran up the trail grasping the ax just behind the head, as if it were a rigid snake. Alex fired two more shots.

Drago was receding from Alex and closing fast on Quizzy, who had reached the tree at the top of the ridge. Alex fired again, trying to judge the drop in trajectory over such a long distance.

Drago stumbled! A hit? He and Quizzy were minuscule figures so far away. He had as much chance now of hitting Quizzy as he did Drago.

"Take the zip line!" Alex screamed, but he knew Quizzy couldn't hear him. He grabbed Quizzy's camera and flicked off the cover of its telephoto lens. He sighted through the viewfinder, found the big tree, and then located Quizzy and the approaching Drago. She was kneeling at one of the padlocks that secured the two roller assemblies.

"Smash it! Alex screamed.

Quizzy reached to her head with one hand and crouched over the locks.

She's picking them! Alex remembered running his hand through her wet, pinned-up hair when they had embraced. *Open, open, open, dammit!* Quizzy jumped to her feet. She'd done it!

Drago limped toward Quizzy with the ax in one hand and the knife in the other. Quizzy grabbed the freed roller assembly on the steel cable above her head and ran toward the cliff. Drago swung the ax at her midsection as she went off the precipice.

Alex didn't think it was possible, but he heard her scream.

Drago dropped his knife into the breast pocket of his

shirt and with both hands buried the ax into the chain of the unopened lock. He clasped his fingers over the remaining roller assembly and followed Quizzy off the cliff.

As she hurtled across the canyon rim, Alex pumped his wheelchair in the direction of the terminating tree on the other side of the spring. There were two shots left in the Taurus. Maybe he could get a better angle as Drago passed in front of him on the zip line.

Out of time. Alex stopped the chair. The swirling world seemed to accelerate. He pointed at Drago's torso and fired. The figure didn't fall. He fired his last shot.

"Shit!"

Alex bore down on the chair again, but there was no way to beat Quizzy and Drago to the bottom tree. He thought about the stop at the end of the zip line. It was sudden and disorienting. Quizzy would go through it first. Maybe she could recover and then attack Drago with her knife or a rock while he was vulnerable.

Alex could barely see the plastic block of the bungee brake near the end of the line as Quizzy rushed toward it. He watched as she instinctively bent her knees, preparing for a crushing impact with the tree. Instead, her rollers struck the brake block. The elastic cord stretched to its limit, and she hung on with what had to be her last shred of strength. She stopped two feet in front of the tree. Her grip gave out, and she collapsed on firm earth.

Sitting on the ground looking stunned, she turned toward Drago coming in hard down the line. Quizzy reached into her pocket and opened the Swiss army knife.

Kill the bastard as soon as he stops, Quizzy! Don't let him recover!

Alex frantically pumped the wheelchair toward her, and she looked at him. He knew it would all end in a moment. Drago hurtled toward the bungee brake block.

Quizzy dived to the ground.

What is she doing? Alex watched helplessly as Quizzy's arm gyrated strangely.

She was sawing the bungee cord.

Quizzy held up the severed end of the cord.

Drago flew past her and the useless brake. He slammed into the unforgiving trunk of the oak tree. Alex heard the impact and then a primal groan as Drago crumpled to the ground.

Quizzy ran at Drago, her puny knife raised. He rolled onto his back, writhing. She stopped and stood over him and then stepped back. She sat down on the ground and waited until Alex wheeled up to her.

Blood spurted from a jagged gash in the side of Drago's neck. The knife he had dropped in his shirt pocket was sticking out of the mortal wound. He had hit the tree feet-first and crunched down onto the blade.

Drago died at the same time Jessie arrived. The bull terrier was panting and limping in pain. The aluminum cast had rubbed a raw spot on the skin of her hip. She sniffed Drago's bloody body and then started to tear off his right arm.

Quizzy somehow found the strength to separate Jessie

from Drago. She picked the dog up in leaden arms and placed her in Alex's lap. Then she pushed them both home, grateful for the cool breeze that ruffled Alex's sandy hair and the touch of his hand on hers as he reached over his shoulder.

Epilogue

Adjusting my helmet, I step off the edge of the cliff. I never tire of the ride and the rush of wind across my black leather eye patch. Charlie designed a brake lever on the roller assembly that pinches the steel cable, so I can go halfway across the canyon and then stop in midair. I sit out there in my harness, sometimes for more than an hour if the sun's not too hot.

When the black vultures appear, I reach into my side pack, but instead of Sweet Pea, I pull out a small Baggie filled with raw hamburger. I stick a dab of meat on top of the cable, release the brake and roll a few more feet, then place another dab of hamburger on the line. And so forth, until I've left eight or ten treats. Then I roll another fifty feet and wait for the majestic soaring birds to circle downward and try to land on the line.

Like feathered clowns on a banana peel, they teeter back and forth as they pick the meat off the cable, wings half flapping to maintain their balance. As close as I am, I still watch them through binoculars sometimes. I love to tell my daughters about the intricacy of the downy feathers on the wrinkly skin of their dark heads. I observe things few other people could ever see. When they finish eating, the great birds fly away. Like Pavlov's dogs, the vultures have learned to watch for me from their roosts. Knowing food is on the way, they take flight when they see me walking up the ridge trail.

I relax in my harness, perched on the zip line, looking up the valley toward Charlie and Flora's house. The views are endless in the ever-changing light, and my landscape paintings capture them with a unique one-eyed perspective. Beneath me is the natural spring with its red-handled spigot. I look toward our house and the shin oak tree we planted when we buried Jessie across from the garden.

I wave to my younger daughter in the front yard. She lifts her hands from the tablet she is using to read my work and waves back. I know she is almost finished, and I'm eager to hear what she thinks.

"Hey, Lavender!" I yell. "Do me a favor and send me back to the top, will you?"

She shouts back to me, "Okay, Dad. Hang on!"

I release the brake on the harness and begin to roll down the line. She's told me a hundred times how she does it, but I'm still amazed. She says that she focuses inward until her body no longer feels the pull of gravity. Then she just imagines me traveling in the opposite direction. As simple as that.

My speed decreases, and soon I stop rolling. Slowly I begin to move up the line, back toward the top of the ridge. "Thank you!" I shout from farther away. She waves and then releases me. I reset the pinch-brake at the higher van-

tage point.

Lavender's mother is up on the ridge talking to the general contractor for the new church. Pale limestone walls with tinted thermal windows support the sweeping metal roof. Quizzy likes to observe him and his crew as closely as I watch the vultures.

Lavender's half sister, Seven, is inside the house. She's in her sophomore year at UT and comes out to the ranch on weekends. She lives in a scholastic dorm, making good grades and new friends.

When Lucas Ruthlier shot me two decades ago and then went to prison for espionage, his congregation dissolved. The lease on the old Nations Home Hardware building expired, and the interior of the church was scraped out to make room for another big-box store.

Nevertheless, those original parishioners were forever bonded. They still stay in touch with one another, waiting. Some have moved on or died, but the true believers would come back together if they heard a credible call to reunite. Quizzy and I now understand this, and we have accepted Lavender's aspirations. We sheltered and educated her as she learned to control her power in those first years. We lost count of the broken windows from loose objects flying around the house.

Our family had the wisdom and discipline to keep her power a secret from all but a few we trusted. Even so, several trespassing hikers or hunters claimed they saw floating rocks or a child suspended in midair above the trees. Rumors started. But when the government men visited, they found nothing but an active zip line. By the time Lavender was old enough for public school, she had harnessed her abilities.

She has a power unheard-of in the twenty-first century—at least for now. But her abilities are inherent in all human beings. They are no more foreign than Charlie's visions, except that her abilities are far more developed. Lavender has the power Lucas Ruthlier sought his entire life. His theories were well developed in their own twisted way. What he failed to understand, though, was that for a human being to receive the energy of the Lavender Fireball, she had to have more than a quieted, receptive mind. She had to have an un-formed *mind*. When her mother placed her hand on the meteorite in Ruthlier's apartment, Lavender had been conceived only hours earlier.

From my vantage point on the cable, I gaze at the top of the ridge and the limestone cliff. Behind it rises the great twisted tree. Behind the tree, workmen are placing solar panels on the roof of the new church. Lavender's new church.

To avoid unwanted prejudice, she will not use "God particle" in the name of her church. But no matter; enough of the faithful from the old church will come. Soon one of them will be newly pregnant. Others will follow.

Anita Loya kept the fireball as a memorial to her husband. It rests quietly in her gallery. She and Lavender are compatriots, and they understand its importance. Anita will offer the Lavender Fireball to those future mothers. They, in turn, will bear the children of a newly evolved race.

The time has come for Lavender to gather her flock. She and I will use the myriad of twenty-first-century technolo-

gies to disseminate her message about the new abilities of man. Her story needs to be told, and the pages of this book are the beginning.

Acknowledgement

The effort and focus I invested in *Church of the God Particle* could never have been sustained without the care and support of many people. My editor, Tiffany Yates Martin with FoxPrint Editorial helped push divergent points of view into focus and insisted that I fully dig out characters' emotions. Brian Greenstone generously shared his Hill Country ranch and taught me how to build a zip line.

My neighbors and social touchstones, Mary Walker and Rae Vajgert, dragged me out of the house for innumerable stimulating dinner conversations. Tyler Levy, Kirk Scanlon, and my sister, Jane Mahoney, kept me out of the ditch on my alternative road. Michael Leonard, Philip Carpenter, Debra McNeil, and Florence were gas in the tank. I oil-painted the front cover, and Harry Cabluck, my friend and mentor of imagery, photographed it. Bruce Wiland laid out the design of the novel. Thank you, all.

David Piper
www.DavidPiperWriting.com